APRIL'S FOOLS

IVY ASHER

RAVEN KENNEDY

Edited by Robin Lee at Rainy Day Editing

Cover Design by Nichole Witholder at Rainy Day Artwork

To the soldiers, active and non-active, and their families.
We see you. We thank you. We owe you.

1

BRANT

The morning air has an edge of a chill to it that I'm still not used to, even after living here for a little over two months. I walk up to the front of the shop, digging into my pocket for the keys, while Puddles, my huge brindle English Mastiff, trots happily beside me, her tongue lolling out of the side of her mouth like she doesn't have a care in the world. Must be nice to be a dog.

I'm steps away from the front door of the gun range that I now help run when I catch movement in my peripheral and turn to find someone slinking around the corner. My hand automatically flies back to where my gun would usually be holstered, but of course, I'm not in the Army anymore, so I grip nothing but air. The intruder moves more into view, and just before they step out of the shadows, I tense, ready to attack. In the next instant, my gaze falls on a familiar face as the early morning sun brightens her features, and I blow out a relieved breath. But that relief is *very* short lived. I immediately jerk my head skyward, looking as far up as I can, just to be safe.

"Dharla," I grit out. "What the *hell* are you doing?"

The woman is in her late sixties, and she's known

around town for being eccentric as fuck. I mean, this is a small town, so *everyone* knows everyone, and all of the people here are a bit eccentric, but Dharla...well, she takes her notoriety to a whole other level. Case in point: She's standing in front of me, on this otherwise beautiful morning, where anyone can see her on Main Street, buck naked, and holding out a half-empty can of soup. She shakes the soup can at me, and I can hear liquid and loose change slapping around inside.

"Feed the poor," she says, before hacking a surprisingly robust cough and spitting a nice, thick wad of mucus onto the sidewalk.

Fucking great.

I keep my eyes up, because for fuck's sake, I do *not* want to see Dharla Cornburner's pale, flabby, and nude body first thing in the morning. Her tits are down to her belly button, and I'm quite certain there's a red mole on her thigh that needs to be looked at.

"Dharla, you're not poor," I remind her, as I try to keep my eyes on my shop sign so that I don't do further damage to my eyes or my brain. Puddles is big and scary looking enough to warn off any threats, but apparently she doesn't see anything wrong with this situation, and she trots off to sniff around the parking lot, abandoning me in my dire time of need. Traitor.

"I *am* poor," Dharla insists with an indignant sniff. "My Willy left me without a cent when he died!"

I sigh. I am not awake enough for this shit. "Dharla, your husband died ten years ago, and he didn't leave you anything in the will, because you're rich as fuck and you already had all of the money."

She completely ignores that and sloshes the can in front of my face again, making broth splash out onto my boots. Damn it all, I just fucking cleaned them. I take a step back and release a frustrated huff. I dig my phone out of my front pocket and hold it above me so that I can see the contacts without having to catch an eyeful of Dharla Cornburner's...cornburner. My first few dealings with Dharla were not of the nude variety, but her crazy is always in full-effect. I managed to get the number of her live-in nurse the last time I had a run-in with Dharla, and luckily, I had the foresight to save it.

Nurse June picks up after one ring. "She at the range again?" she asks me, no preamble or greeting as she gets right to the point.

"Yes, ma'am. And she doesn't have a speck of clothing on her, so you may want to bring something," I inform June, and the line goes dead with no response from the other end except for a long-suffering sigh. Now, if you weren't familiar with Endstone or with Dharla, you might think that kind of rude, but June is a fucking saint, and she doesn't waste precious seconds on pleasantries when she needs them to wrangle Dharla and all of her insanity.

A small, frail hand suddenly grabs my crotch and I jump back, startled, nearly dropping my phone on the sidewalk. "Dharla, that's not cool!" I chastise as I push her hand away.

"A blond-haired, blue-eyed boy with muscles to spare. You'll do just fine," she nods, eyeing me up and down lasciviously. "I usually like a beard, but clean-shaven will be alright."

"Glad I passed the test," I say dryly.

"Those glasses make you look smarter than you are," she says, which I'm pretty sure is her version of a compliment. "You need a haircut," she adds.

I run a hand over my short mohawk. "I'll get right on that."

She just cackles and reaches out to pinch my nipple

through my shirt. "There, I serviced you," she says. "Now pay up."

I dig into my pocket and toss every last scrap of cash and coin I have into her soup can, just so that she won't accost me again. She cackles delightedly, but then sits down right in front of my shop's door, her legs spread wide in front of her. I groan and run a hand over my face, praying that June gets here real quick.

Dharla starts sipping from her soup can and spits out a penny, showing it to me. "This year is a real nice mint," she says.

I blow out a breath. "Right."

I turn on my heel and head across the street to hide behind the hardware store owner's truck. Cowardly? Maybe. But with her legs spread-eagled like that, I'd like to keep some space between us. Unfortunately, as soon as she drinks the rest of her gross broth, she gets up and follows me over. June finally shows up, just in time to find me running in circles to keep away from the randy and very senile Dharla as she chases after me, her flabby bits flapping in the wind.

As soon as Dharla catches sight of June's car pulled up next to us, she stops like she knows the jig is up. It makes me question if Dharla is as crazy as everyone says, or if she's just old, bored, and likes to get a stir out of the citizens of Endstone. If it's the latter, I'd have to be grudgingly impressed. June gets Dharla wrapped up in a coat in no time, and I help wrangle her into the backseat of the car as June promises more soup for her at home. "Thanks, Brant," June tells me with a wave before getting into the car.

"See ya."

As if I haven't been traumatized enough this morning, Dharla rolls down her window and waves a saggy boob at me in a goodbye. It's an image I'll have to burn from my brain.

"Fucking Endstone," I say with a shake of my head. This town is crazy. The guys and I have only been here for ten weeks, but shit like this is already becoming commonplace.

I shoot a glare at Puddles, who finally decides to meander on over to my side again as I make my way across the parking lot to the front of my shop. There's a Dharla-shaped smudge on the door that will make Madix go crazy. I smirk, deciding it'll be a small consolation that I'll let him deal with. Puddles nudges my thigh as we walk, but I shake my head at her. "Some kind of psychiatric service animal you are," I tell her sternly. "You left me to fend for myself in a state of distress."

Puddles looks up at me, and I swear, if a dog could actually roll their eyes, that's what she'd be doing to me right now. I slip my key into the front door and twist it all the way to the left first, watching as the security shutters begin to roll up and expose the windows hidden beneath. When that's done, I fit in another key on the second deadbolt and turn it right at half a rotation, and hear the three locks in the heavy door release. The impatient beeping of the alarm greets me as I enter, so I disarm it and make sure Puddles is inside with me before shutting the door and locking it again from the inside. Dharla cut into my prep time, so I have to rush around to get the gun shop and range ready for the day before opening.

It's weird sometimes to think that this is my life now. The routine helps to fight off the shadows that stalk me, but I never thought I'd end up here. I hadn't even hit the five-year mark as a Ranger before the guys and I were medically discharged after one mission gone wrong. Now we're here in Podunk, Montana, running a gun range instead of executing missions and being part of the top tier of badasses. Funny how life fucks with you.

With Puddles on my heels, I go through the motions of getting the register and computer ready, and then double check that the gun displays are secure and that the glass counters are clean. I don't need to wipe them down, since Madix closed last night. He's the most anal dude I've ever met when it comes to cleaning. Maybe it was all the assignments out in the sand, or all the uniform checks that led to him not being able to handle anything out of place, or maybe he was just always like this. Either way, Theo and I never bitch about it, because when Madix cleans like a psycho, it means we don't have to. It's a solid win for us. Besides, I'm glad to have Theo and Madix at my back. We all have our "things," but we're closer than brothers, and we've learned to work and live together. We may not be in the Army anymore, but we're still a unit.

Once we were all free of the hospital visits and physical therapy, we didn't know how to acclimate back into society. But then Theo got a phone call. His crackpot, doomsday-loving uncle passed away, leaving him everything. And here the three of us are, in Endstone, Montana, running a gun store and shooting range, while trying to put ourselves back together and get to that "normal" setting that society demands of us.

Right alongside Dharla fucking Cornburner.

Yeah. Hindsight? Maybe this isn't the best place for us to lose our crazy, but it's too late now. Then again, maybe this town's kind of crazy is just what we need.

When I grab a cup of coffee from the back, Puddles looks up at me with a whine. She's been with me for four-teen months now. I don't know how I handled shit without her before. She always watches me with intelligent brown eyes as she gauges my mood. She's the best thing to come out of the VA. She helps with my PTSD, but she's also funny as shit when she slobbers all over Madix's pants and makes him freak out. I swear, she's so smart, she just does it to get a rise out of him. I grab her water bowl and walk over to the sink in our makeshift break room/office to dump out the old water and refill it for her.

I flip on the radio before heading back to the front, hearing the song fade out in the background as the local newscasters start droning on. "The government and CDC are keeping a close eye on recent outbreaks of a virus they're calling the Handshake Plague. The virus has been taking parts of the country by storm, and is suspected to originate in a small province of India. Officials are working hard to contain the spread of the virus, and they're advising the public to take proper precautions when dealing with anyone showing symptoms of infection. If you or someone you know has travelled in or around Bihar in the last six months, please report to your local hospital immediately."

I glance up at the clock over the door, realizing it's one minute to nine. Shit. Dharla really set me back. If I'm late opening, I'll never hear the end of it from Sheriff April and Zeke, who both like to come shooting every morning, right when we open, at nine on the dot. I hurry to the front and flip the switch that lights up the fluorescent *Open* sign and then disengage the locks, waving at the shop owner across the street who's doing the same thing.

When Theo first asked Madix and I if we wanted to move here with him to help run this place, I pictured an old, beat up shop that would probably need a ton of repairs, and a dusty old shooting range that would be in similar shape, but I was pleasantly surprised to find that this place was top-notch. And luckily, nearly everyone in town is gun owners who come shooting on a weekly basis, so business has been good.

Before I can walk back behind the counter, the front door whooshes open, and Sheriff April comes in. He's actually retired, but everyone around town still calls him Sheriff. He holds the door open for his buddy Zeke, and they both saunter over to the counter with rifle bags in hand. They're both in their late sixties, with round middles and scruffy salt and pepper jaws. Zeke lost the battle with his receding hairline and opted to go bald, while the sheriff prefers to comb his gray hair back and stuff a worn baseball cap over it.

"Morning, Brant. How are you, on what promises to be another balmy day?" Sheriff April asks me, as he tilts the bill of his cap down in greeting.

I chuckle. "Balmy? It's not even sixty outside, Sheriff. And even in the summertime, I bet this place has nothing on the Arizona dryness that I grew up with. Phoenix in the summertime is like visiting hell. Maybe you're just having hot flashes," I razz the retired sheriff. "You could trade in the slacks and button downs for a t-shirt and shorts," I suggest with a grin.

Zeke laughs. "I don't know what I'd do if I ever caught this man in a pair of shorts. Hell, he might as well be strutting around town in a bikini, for all the shock it would give people. We'd know for sure the end of days were upon us if that ever happened. His legs are probably whiter than the fucking snowcaps. Nobody needs to see that," Zeke says, chewing on a toothpick.

"Good point," I say with a shudder, making Zeke laugh again.

"Yeah, yeah. Laugh it up," Sheriff April says, fighting a grin.

I get them stocked up on ammo before they head to the range, chuckling and back-slapping as they begin to take bets on who will out-shoot who.

As far as I can tell, Sheriff April and Zeke have been

friends since forever. It seems that most of the people here in Endstone are born, raised, married, and buried without ever leaving this place. There's a saturated sense of camaraderie that I'm still not used to, but I have to admit, it's kind of nice.

Before long, I hear the faint but distinct sound of Zeke and the sheriff unloading their rifles in the indoor shooting range. Sometimes, it sets my teeth on edge, and I have to breathe through the panic that jumpstarts in me—fucking PTSD—but luckily, it doesn't phase me this morning. Looks like I may have just conquered that small trigger. I get into my groove, restocking the bathroom before checking our inventory.

An hour later, Sheriff April and Zeke come strolling out, busting each other's balls about who was the better shot for the day. They come over, slapping their paper targets down on the counter, and I sit back, sipping my coffee and hiding my smirk.

"Bullshit, Sheriff. I had the better shots, and you know it," Zeke argues.

Sheriff April rolls his eyes, but there's mirth in his blue gaze as he scratches the scruff on his chin. He has the telltale paunch in his belly that reveals how much he enjoys the beer and pie that he has every night at the diner. He's usually joined by a group of three other male widows, including Zeke, and all of them get doted on by the middle-aged diner owner, Jolene.

When we first moved here, Madix made the mistake of going into the diner on a Saturday morning, when nearly half the town was there. He got at least a dozen girls flashing him smiles and doe-eyes, most of them offering to bring him a casserole. Good thing he ordered our food to-go, or he might have ended up accidentally engaged. For some reason, the chicks dig his asshole ways. They think his broody quietness is interesting or some shit.

Theo draws attention too, but it's because he's the most outgoing and always seems to know how to make people like him. Madix has already been threatened by two shot-gun-toting fathers, and it's only a matter of time before another pissed off one shows up for Theo, too.

Sheriff and Zeke's long running argument is still background noise as I scroll through items on the supplier's website, but I look up when I hear the door open and see Mr. Stevens walking in. I offer him a friendly smile and take the small gun case he holds out. He owns the local butcher shop and normally comes in to shoot on Thursdays, which is my day off.

"Hey, Mr. Stevens. What can I help you with today?"

He steps up to the counter as I set the case down. "I bought this Smith & Wesson about a month back, but I'm having trouble with the magazine release sticking." Mr. Stevens begins to unzip the case, and all at once, a distinct smell hits me. Just like that, I'm not in the shop anymore. I'm trapped somewhere else. The last fucking place I ever want to be.

2

BRANT

It's quiet. *Too* quiet.

I can see, but it's blurry. I'm weightless right before I'm slammed to the ground. Dirt falls onto my face, but I can't hear a fucking thing, even as my head buzzes. The lack of sound is slowly replaced by a high-pitched ringing in my ears, and then I'm blinking past the flare of brightness. It's nighttime, but the flare nearly singes my eyeballs out of their sockets, and I feel heat at my back. The scent of smoke and dirt sticks to my nose and the back of my throat. I try to push against the ground to get up, but I stumble when I hear someone screaming. I look around, frantically trying to find who it is and why, but everything feels disjointed. My body isn't working the way it should.

"Brant, buddy, can you hear me? Brant!"

The voice is like an echo, but I can't latch onto it. All I can feel is pain and darkness and that god-awful feeling of being utterly stuck. It fills me with panic and dread. The screaming keeps going, and the smell of burnt flesh, smoke, and dirt throttles me.

"Move, so the dog can get to him," I hear from far away.

I start coughing from the dirt and smoke stuck in my mouth and nose, but I can't fucking breathe. Panicked, I try to clear my airways of the sand and soil, but my hands hit something soft instead of connecting with my face. I feel like I'm dying. Suffocating through the airless memory that I'm stuck in. I try again to wipe away the dirt and clear my nose, while I spit it out of my mouth over and over again, but something warm and wet against my face makes me freeze.

That's not right. There wasn't anything like that. It was just dirt and the smell of burning and screaming. Nothing warm against my face. Nothing soft at my fingertips. My brain stumbles over the memory as it tries to latch onto the present and pull me back to what's real.

"Brant, you're in Endstone, Montana. You're at work. You're not there, son. You're okay. Puddles is here. I'm here. Open your eyes and look at us, son."

I feel the lick of a dog's tongue on my cheek and neck, and then a furry head presses against my chest. I reach out and hang on to it, recognizing the necessary life-line. *Puddles*. It's my fucking dog, Puddles. My brain fires off, trying to connect, and I feel her lick me some more. I focus on the feel of her short fur under my hands. There are other voices talking to each other, but I just focus on bringing myself back to the here and now. Puddles wasn't there with the explosion. If she's here now, then the voice is right, I'm not there. The explosion already happened. Theo, Madix, and I were the only ones to survive.

I open my eyes, and the view of the explosion finally fades away, but I focus on petting Puddles some more, and I hear the music on the radio that competes with the ringing in my ears. The song is old, something I feel like my dad listened to when he was working in the garage, but it helps bring me more to the present. I pay attention to where I'm sitting and focus on the lifeline heavy in my lap as Puddles nuzzles further into me.

The music over the radio fades out, and a serious voice replaces the old song. "Death tolls continue to rise at an alarming rate, and a state of emergency has officially been declared. The president has advised citizens to seek out a vaccine that was introduced late last night on the east coast. Thousands of centers are being set up all over the country and Americans are being told to watch for an announcement that will indicate when it's their turn to receive the life-saving vaccination. We're being told that the announcements will be made in alphabetical order, and the center that should be attended will be specified at that time. We'll keep you updated as developments unfold..."

Puddles licks my hand this time, and my vision finally clears enough that I can see her sitting in my lap. Her brown eyes are locked on mine, and she pushes at my hand over and over again with her snout, forcing me to react and pet her, which I finally do. She rewards my reaction by licking my arm, knowing that she's grounded me back to reality again.

"There you are, son," I hear, and I feel Sheriff April pat me on the back. "I got you some water," he says, passing me a bottled water. "Can you turn your head and look at my ugly mug so I can get a look at you?" Sheriff April asks in a teasing but supportive tone. His voice drowns out the newscaster on the radio, and I feel a cold water bottle being pressed into my shaky hand. I take it and slowly bring the water up to my lips, emptying the bottle in a few long gulps. I finally have the ability to look up and focus on Sheriff April kneeling beside me. Zeke and Mr. Stevens are on the other side of the counter, looking down at me with worry.

The sheriff's mouth is in a grim line. "Do you know what triggered it?" he asks. "You don't have to tell me if you don't want to, but I'd like to correct whatever it was, if we can, so it doesn't send you back."

I swallow and try and focus on what was happening before my episode. "It smelled like smoke. Blood and dirt too, maybe. I don't know, but it was definitely a smell," I say, my voice embarrassingly croaky. I fucking hate when people see me like this. Usually, it's just Madix and Theo, but when this happens in public, it's a hundred times worse.

"I'm so sorry. I didn't know," Mr. Stevens tells me, and I immediately feel bad for making *him* feel bad.

"Not your fault," I mumble. "I don't always know what's going to trigger me."

Mr. Stevens nods, but I can tell that he still feels horrible. I give Puddles one last ear stroke and then push up off of the ground, hating how shaky I am. I give Mr. Stevens a wide smile, but it's strained. He takes a small step back, and I try to reassure him that it's okay, but I'm not fooling anyone. I grab the small gun case from the counter and finish unzipping it. I hate the way that they're watching me warily, and I hate that they just witnessed me be so weak and broken.

Trying to move on, I clear my throat and say, "Let's see what we can do about that magazine release, shall we?"

Mr. Stevens hesitates for a second, but when the sheriff nods at him, he comes closer so I can inspect the 9mm. I breathe through my mouth, just in case, but I don't miss the concerned looks that are being exchanged between Sheriff April and Zeke. I'd bet a million dollars that as soon as they walk out the door, they'll drive over to our place to tell Theo and Madix what happened. It's annoying, but I know they're just trying to look out for me. I wish for the millionth time that they wouldn't have to, but if wishes were fishes...or whatever the fuck that saying is.

I sort out the Smith & Wesson, and Mr. Stevens practically runs out of the shop when I'm done. Yup, he's going to stick to coming in on Thursdays from now on, and probably give me a wide berth forever. Sheriff April goes to the back to grab me another cup of coffee, and I take it gratefully. I take a fortifying sip and set it on the counter just before he pulls me in for a slap-on-the-back kind of hug. I try to get out of it because I'm still fucking embarrassed, but at the same time, I appreciate the gesture. He's a good dude, and since my old man is dead and buried, it's nice to have a father figure who's been kind enough to have taken the three of us under his wing.

"You okay, son?" he asks me.

"I'm good, Sheriff. Thanks."

He studies me for a moment before nodding. "I keep telling you boys, you need a woman."

I laugh, because he busts our balls about this every chance he gets. "Yeah, yeah."

"You know I'm right," he says with a shrug before turning back to Zeke. "I won the shoot-out, so you can buy breakfast."

Zeke curses, and they resume their shit talking before heading out. "You want the boys to come cover for you?" Sheriff April asks me as he opens the door.

I shake my head. "I'm good," I assure him.

He nods and they both leave, and I can hear them arguing all the way to their car.

Taking a deep breath, I pat Puddles, who's stuck to me like glue, and get back to work. By the time closing rolls around, I've had a dozen more people in and out of here to shoot, and I sold a gun along with some boxes of ammo.

Despite this morning's fiasco, today went pretty smoothly. When I hear the rumble of Madix's diesel truck, I look up at the clock, realizing it's already past five. Madix and I met when we were stationed in Fort Benning. Later, when we were deployed on our first assignment in Afghanistan, we met Theo Coleman, and we've been thick as thieves ever since.

When the shop door opens, Puddles immediately leaves my side to greet Madix, licking at his fingers as she sniffs him. I shake my head and laugh to myself at his outfit. Madix Ortega is a big dude. His mom was from Mexico, and from the pictures I've seen, he has her to thank for his good looks; dark eyes, dark hair, tan skin, and way too much of an asshole to be rocking skinny jeans. I don't care how "in style" he says they are.

Madix looks over at me knowingly. "How you doing?"

I roll my eyes. "Sheriff called you?"

"Yep," he says, scratching the short black beard across his jaw.

"I'm fine," I tell him. "Surprised you or Theo didn't come down here earlier."

"Almost did," he admits. "Sheriff told us to not to, and to get our sorry asses back to work on fixing up the roof."

I laugh, grateful that the sheriff filled them in but knew not to send them down here, since that would've just made me feel even more like a burden.

"You lock up in here while I secure the back?" I ask.

"Yep," Madix says, silencing the incessant buzz of the "Open" sign by turning it off. I head to the back to start locking everything up, and hear, "Why the fuck is there a person-sized smudge on the front door?"

I chuckle to myself as I finish securing the place, turning the alarms on before walking out and locking up. We walk to the parking lot, and I open up the passenger door of Madix's truck, letting Puddles hop in first.

"You guys finish up repairing the roof?"

Madix shakes his head. "Ran out of shingles. Gonna have to swing by the hardware store to pick some up when they open in the morning."

I nod and flip the radio on as Madix drives to the diner. None of us are even remotely capable of making edible food. Bachelorhood, base life, deployment, and military Meals-Ready-to-Eat—MRE's—pretty much doomed us, so the local diner is our salvation. It helps that it's damn good food.

I wait in the truck while he runs in to grab our dinner, and I see the girls inside perk up at his presence. I chuckle to myself as he strides right past them, oblivious. The news starts up and pulls my attention away from the preening women in the diner to the smooth voice of the local radio DJ.

"Over half a million cases of the Handshake Plague have been confirmed on the east coast, along with a high number of reported cases that continue to rise throughout the rest of the country. Everyone is being told to contact their nearest hospital for information on the mandatory vaccinations, and refer to local officials for travel restrictions. Medical masks have sold out, and citizens are starting to panic, despite the president's address that they are working hard to contain the rapid spread..."

"What the fuck?" I wonder aloud, just as a knock on the window startles me. Madix motions for me to roll it down. "Jolene says they're out of peach pie today. You want blueberry?" he asks.

I nod, and he turns and heads back inside. I tune back into the radio, but a twangy song has replaced the ominous news report. I pull out my phone and try to open a search engine so that I can figure out just what in the hell is going on in the rest of the country, but as usual, my internet is taking forever to connect. I have full bars, but service is spotty as fuck in this town.

The internet issue doesn't usually matter, since the three of us don't give a fuck about having any kind of social media presence. To be honest, we don't even use it much anymore. Living in this town is like living in the fifties, but we needed a break from all the bullshit, so we welcomed the lifestyle change. This town definitely doesn't boast any free wifi spots or Facebook Pages. Nope, they stick with their small local radio tower and a weekly newspaper that usually runs a story about whether or not a new stop sign should be installed. It's a quieter, slower way of living, but it serves as a good balance to the loud and messy bombardment from our own internal shit.

Madix opens the driver's side door and climbs back in the truck, placing the dinner bags in the back seat, and shoots Puddles a *don't you fucking dare* look. Puddles sits down with a huff, ending their stare-off, while Madix puts the truck into gear and starts to drive towards our house on the outskirts.

"You hear about the shit that's going down in the rest of the country?" I ask, unable to let the foreboding statistics that I just heard go.

"Yeah, we caught a couple reports on the radio earlier, but you know how the media likes to hype all this shit up. They get off on scaring people and then sell them something that will supposedly solve the problem."

I huff out a chuckle, unable to deny the legitimacy of that statement.

"Well, if shit does go down, we'll have to add *avoiding plagues* to the pros of living in a small, defensible town."

Madix cracks a smile. "In peace, prepare for war." he

sounds off, mimicking the tone and cadence of our old unit leader.

"Rangers lead the way," I respond automatically, and knock my knuckles against Madix's outstretched fist.

Puddles immediately sits up and lifts her paw to land against ours, and Madix lets out a snort. "I can't believe you trained her to do that."

I grin and scratch her behind the ear. "I didn't train her. She's just smart. She likes to be included."

"You're such a needy chick, Pud," Madix informs her playfully.

Puddles leans in and licks his neck, leaving a nice string of slobber on his collar. He grimaces and lifts his shoulder to his ear, trying not to run us off the single lane road that leads up to our place. "Fucking gross."

It takes a good twenty minutes of curvy back roads to get to our house. For a weird hermit fucker, Theo's uncle sure did have good taste in real estate. Ten acres to ourselves, a five bedroom spread with exposed wooden beams, and a brook in the back. It's a little touch of paradise I never knew I wanted until we were here, standing on the edge of the property and taking it all in.

Madix parks, and as soon as I open the door, Puddles jumps out with me, while I grab the food and head inside. Our entryway leads into an open floor plan so I can see the kitchen, which we just finished updating, and the living room, which we've turned into a makeshift gym. There's a treadmill, a weight machine, a bench press, and some more free weights lined up on the far wall. We tried to hang a punching bag too, but we learned the hard way that the ceiling wasn't equipped to handle the weight, which is why there's a plaster patch clearly visible.

Theo is working out, which is no surprise, since he's *always* working out these days. He pushes the bar up and away from his chest, a small grunt escaping him as his arms straighten and he sets the bar in its holder.

"You shouldn't be doing that without a spotter," Madix says with a frown.

"It's a light load. I can handle it," Theo replies, taking a breather.

His pants have ridden up his calves from his position on the bench press, and the metal of his prosthetic leg is just visible. Like he can feel my eyes on it, he quickly sits up and pulls the hem of his sweat pants down. Theo always says he's accepted it, but his actions just confirmed how self-conscious he still is. It's been almost two years, and he still doesn't like anyone to look at it.

I'm pretty sure his insecurity is the source of his obsession with working out. I mean, we've always trained, but Theo eats, sleeps, and breathes gym life now. Like he's trying to make the rest of him as perfect as it can be in order to overcompensate for the loss of his leg. He's always pushing himself, even though he probably pushes his body past its limits sometimes. Madix and I keep our judgement to ourselves, though, because there's no point in calling him on his shit when he'll just turn around and call us on ours. We're all just trying to cope and find a new normal. For now, that means we all keep our mouths shut and let each other try to deal.

Theo swipes an arm across his forehead and runs a hand through his sweaty brown hair. Theo is half-black and half-white. His tawny skin and piercing green eyes have women lining up to try and stake a claim, but since his injury, he's stopped taking advantage of the physical gifts he's been blessed with. He's not as big as Madix, but the guy is ripped. It's not surprising, since he works out all of the time.

He grabs the remote from the coffee table to turn down

the music pounding from the stereo, and then his steady, jade gaze returns to me. "You good, man?"

"I'm good," I say, walking to the table and pulling out our food from the bags while Madix grabs the beers.

Theo washes his hands in the kitchen sink and then dunks his entire sweaty head underneath, making water drip all over the floor and counter.

Madix glares at him. "Dude. What the fuck? I just cleaned the kitchen."

Theo rolls his eyes and then goes to grab the shirt that he'd left draped over the back of the couch. "You've *always* just cleaned the kitchen," he reminds him as he pulls his shirt on, his brown hair dripping water onto the shoulders.

Madix grumbles something about us being slobby fuck-heads, but then sits down at the table and digs into his dinner. The three of us eat in relative silence, aside from the music still playing and the sound of Puddles gnawing on her kibble. This is how it's been every night since we moved here. Just the three of us, shooting the shit and trying to acclimate back into some semblance of a life. It hasn't been easy, and we piss each other off sometimes, but we also understand each other.

One mission gone wrong. One explosion, and life as we knew it was over. Theo lost his left leg just below the knee. Madix's right eardrum was damaged, and he had to recover from burns on his back and legs. My brain took a good rattling, which caused it to swell and left me with some vision issues, and then there are the flashbacks I have to deal with. But even with our injuries, at least we made it out alive. Others hadn't been so lucky. We're bonded and broken in ways that only we can understand. It sucks, but at the same time, it connects us in a way we all need.

This, living together and running the gun range, it's been the only thing that we've been able to handle. It's peaceful here, but I always worry that we're all too fucked up to ever really move past what happened. It wouldn't surprise me if in fifty years, the three of us are still here, at this table, drinking beers and eating diner food. No wives, no kids, nobody to really miss us when we're gone. The thought is fucking depressing, but that's life these days.

3

MADIX

Someone pounds on my bedroom door, and I groan into the mattress and cover my head with a pillow. "Fuck off!"

The booming of a fist on the hollow door of my bedroom bombards me again, and I grab for my phone and curse at the time. It's only ten in the morning, which means I've only managed to get about three hours of sleep. The constant ringing in my ear was loud as shit last night, and I couldn't tune it out like I normally do in order to sleep. I shouldn't have to wake up today because it's not my day to open the shop, so whoever is banging on my door better have a good fucking excuse.

My door vibrates in the frame as one of the guys bangs on it again, and I throw off my blankets. "Alright, I'm coming! What the fuck?"

I swipe my pants off the floor and slip into them as I tear the door open. But one look at Theo's face sends adrenaline and worry spiking through me.

"We have a situation," he tells me and then pivots and walks away.

I follow him, tying the drawstring on my pants and

freeze when I make it out to the living room to find Brant. He should be at the shop right now. My muscles knot with tension as I take in Puddles sitting on Brant's feet, her body pressed against him and her full attention on his face. The way she's acting immediately raises a red flag. Puddles is Brant's service dog, so she helps him cope with his PTSD, and I can tell that she's definitely picking up on a shit ton of anxiety from him right now. His hands are shaking slightly, and when he catches me looking, he shoves them into Puddles's short fur.

"What's wrong?"

"Brant opened the shop today as usual, but what fucking *wasn't* usual, was that practically the whole town was there waiting for him so they could buy every gun and bullet we have in the shop."

My eyebrows shoot up in surprise but I stay quiet, knowing Theo will get to the point.

"Everyone was cleaning us out and going on about the Handshake Plague," Brant explains, taking off his glasses to rub a hand down his face.

"What is that? This influenza shit?" I ask.

Theo nods, making his brown hair fall partially into his eyes. "They just reported that the vaccines failed. The last report from the CDC says the mortality rate jumped to eighty-five percent."

I feel the blood drain from my face. "What?"

Theo casts a quick look at Brant before going on. "It's bad, dude. Cell towers are down," he says, indicating the phone on the coffee table. "Can't make any calls. We also can't get any national radio stations, only local, so who the fuck knows what that means? Either the powers that be are trying to stifle panic and information from spreading, or somehow, shit's worse than we thought, and everything is shutting down because of what's going on."

24

"Fuck." I scratch at my short beard and try not to shake my head in disbelief. "This shit moves that fast?"

Theo nods grimly. "That's why they're calling it the Handshake Plague. They think it spreads from skin-to-skin contact. People start coughing and vomiting their fucking guts out, and then they're dead, less than a week later."

I run a hand through my black hair and pull at the roots as if it will somehow tether me to a different reality. "This is fucking insane."

"New York, L.A., Houston, Chicago...it hit all the major cities the worst," Theo says. "Luckily, we're isolated out here, and most of these people have never left the state, let alone the country, so the likelihood that anyone in town is sick is low. But the mayor is calling for a town meeting in a couple of hours. We should get down there early. See if we can find out anything else."

Brant clears his throat, trying to look unaffected, but Puddles gives off a small whine and pushes into him even more. "They were putting up fliers at the shop and around town. Anyone with any symptoms is to be immediately quarantined," he digs into his pocket and pulls out a folded piece of red paper.

I take it, and quickly read through a list of what symptoms to watch out for, how to best prepare, and a safety order not to leave town.

"The town lines are already blockaded," Theo says, drawing my attention back to him.

Holy shit.

Everything about this feels completely surreal, and I have no idea how to even begin to process this. I was ten when 9/11 happened. I remember going home and just staring at the TV with my parents, convinced that somehow it couldn't be real. Stuff like that didn't happen in America. I was wrong then, and what's happening now has me feeling exactly like I felt that day in September. I've seen enough fucked up shit now to know that anything is possible, and life as you know it can change for the worse in just a matter of seconds.

Theo shakes his head. I can see he's trying real fucking hard not to lose his shit for Brant's sake. I knew people were getting sick and dying, but I never expected it to become...this. If this shit started somewhere in India, then we aren't the only country that's fucked two ways from Sunday. An *eighty-five* percent mortality rate? Just what the fuck would be left standing when this shit killed most of the world?

* * *

We get onto Main Street, and the first thing I notice is the mob of people filling up the entire square. The normally lazy street looks jam-packed with half the town. "Damn, I've never seen this many people in one place except during that chili cook-off last month," Theo says.

There's absolutely no place to park. The street is full of double and triple parking all the way down the block, and townspeople are teeming everywhere. I manage to pull up onto the asphalt curb and park the truck in front of the dumpster behind the grocery. As soon as I turn off the engine, I can hear the crowd yelling. I exchange a look with the guys, and the three of us get out.

"Stay here, girl," Brant orders Puddles.

We make our way to the street, pushing past people, noticing that everyone is congregating around in the middle of the square. We're no doubt the bulkiest guys in the town, since the population is mostly made up of retirees, so we have no trouble making our way past people. When we get to the front, an elderly lady next to me is in her slippers and robe, screaming something about hand sanitizer. Since my eardrum was damaged, her shrill voice instantly makes my ear start to ring painfully, and I flinch away from her.

"What's going on?" Brant asks the people around us. I recognize the guy who runs the fish and tackle shop beside him.

"Handshake Plague. People have to be quarantined," he tells us, and our heads whip back to the front, where there's a line of local police officers standing sentry and talking to a group of people I don't recognize.

"They're sick?" Theo asks with a frown.

From what I can see past the gazebo, the current sheriff is talking to a guy, probably mid-fifties, and a woman around the same age. The woman next to me pipes in. "Says they aren't sick, but they just got back into town this morning, before the barricades could be put up. Walked into town like nothin,'" she says with a distasteful shake of her head. "Who knows if they've been exposed. It ain't safe for them to be walkin' around, spreadin' their germs to the rest of us."

Somehow, the crowd seems to take on a one-track-mind mentality, and everyone starts yelling "quarantine" at the couple. Some folks get so worked up, that the police officers have to start holding them back. All of a sudden, guns are drawn, and the people start demanding that the couple get put away in isolation.

"What the fuck?" Theo curses when the guy next to him draws a gun. Theo reaches out and clamps his hand around the shotgun barrel. "Lower your weapon, or I'll do it for you," he growls.

The man shakes his head so hard that his jowls shake from side to side. "You wanna get sick, boy?" the man asks. He points at the arguing couple with his gun. "Those people could be infected. We have to protect the town. If the virus spreads here, we could all be dead come next week. This town is clean right now, but if we aren't careful, that could change real fast. Endstone is the priority. We gotta play every scenario smart, for the good of all."

"For the good of all," another guy next to him echoes with a nod.

"So you're just gonna shoot them?" I demand.

The man shrugs. "If it comes down to it. Two lives versus hundreds. What's the lesser evil?"

"Put your guns away!" the cops shout.

The guy grumbles, but finally lowers his shotgun, and Theo lets go.

Brant, Theo, and I are coiled tight with tension as we watch this madness go down, seeing the crowd grow more and more frenzied. I've heard the death tolls and mortality rates, but in this moment, the virus and its ramifications really hit home, and it all becomes brutally real. Fear and worry spike through me like icy needles, and I shudder at the realization that life as we know it has just changed, and nothing about it is going to be for the better.

"Enders! Listen up!"

Everyone turns to the sound of Sheriff April's voice. He might not be the active sheriff anymore, but the entire town loves and respects him, which is obvious by the way the crowd actually stops screaming and quiets down enough to listen to him. We've only lived here for ten weeks, so I don't know all the ins and outs, but I know enough that I doubt the younger sheriff could demand that kind of courtesy.

Sheriff April stands front and center with a megaphone, his belly hanging over the belt of his pants as he sets a steady glare around the crowd. "Now, I know everyone is scared, but violence is not the answer. We've heard your votes and concerns. Sheriff Dunn here is going to quarantine Mr. and Mrs. Wilks in case they show signs of symptoms."

As if on cue, Sheriff Dunn and a few deputies start leading the couple away to a cop car, all of them wearing masks and gloves. The couple looks completely distraught, the woman just about ready to burst into tears.

"In the meantime, the mayor has called a town meeting. Every one of you best get your butts over to the high school gymnasium," Sheriff April orders loud and clear, lifting a finger in rebuke. "And no speeding or parking like chumps. I might not drive a cop car anymore, but I have no problem doing a citizen's arrest. We're Enders. We're family. We take care of each other. Y'all hear me?"

To my surprise, the crowd grumbles its assent and begins to clear. The three of us stand there, watching as everyone begins to disperse and the other, younger cops look at Sheriff April like he's a god.

Brant whistles under his breath beside me. "Damn. Didn't know the old man had it like that."

"Good thing he does," I reply. "Or this could've gotten ugly fast."

They nod in agreement, still watching the crowd on alert, just in case someone's fear makes them do something stupid. "Let's get to the gym."

* * *

We park in the high school parking lot, none of us saying a word as we climb out of my truck and make our way toward the gym of the school. We're one small group amongst many others, and we're surrounded by anxious faces and the sounds of shoes scuffing and squeaking on the floor of the basketball court as we're herded to the packed bleachers.

Theo veers off to the left and picks a spot to lean against the painted white cinderblock wall. Madix and I follow without question, keeping our backs to the wall and the gathering in view. Muffled conversations buzz around the room as all of us wait for the mayor to appear and address questions and concerns.

Right on time, the mayor walks in front of the a single-file line that heads toward the table in the middle of the basketball court. I expect the people in the bleachers to start firing off questions in a panic as soon as someone in authority appears, but everyone remains calm, looking patiently to the leaders of their community for answers. Zeke and Sheriff April have a seat at the table alongside the mayor, and the current sheriff and his two deputies have a seat on the mayor's other side.

The mayor turns on the microphone and taps it a couple of times to check that it's on and working. "Thank you all for being here. We don't have a ton of information at this point, but we're working to get answers and as soon as we have them, you will too. A state of Martial Law has been called for across the country. Our priority right now is to keep you and your families safe and to eliminate the risk of exposure. There have been no cases reported in town and no one is showing any signs of infection. We need to keep it that way. We suggest that citizens of Endstone move into the main part of town and we propose to build a defensible barrier in an effort to protect the citizens within. We'll need volunteers for the build and to start patrolling."

The mayor's suggestion makes sense, even though it feels extreme. The fact that I think that, probably shows just how much I'm still not wrapping my mind around what's happening. People start raising their hands to volunteer, and it's weird how calm and organized all of this is. Maybe it's because the community is so tight-knit, but I expected more chaos from this meeting, more demands for answers, given the circumstances.

They talk about food distribution and rationing, making sure to keep our water wells clean and clear, and then the local doctor's office brings out boxes of rubber gloves and paper masks for people to wear when in public.

"This is fucking insane," Brant says as he takes a box of gloves from the volunteer passing them out.

"Do we know how many casualties there have been?" someone in the crowd asks.

Mayor Jeffries shakes his head. "As of now, we don't have those kinds of numbers. Communication has gone down, which is why we need to be safe here and take every precaution. Endstone is an extended family. I have every faith that this town can pull together and take care of one another," he says, looking grimly at all of us. "After all, that's what Enders do. We handle everything as it comes, and we do it together."

The crowd looks considerably chastised, obviously feeling rebuked for their behavior in the town square.

The mayor scans them all with his disappointed gaze for added effect. "I know this is a frightening thing to go through, but as long as we stay calm and vigilant, we can increase everyone's chances to survive this. Luckily, Endstone has always been prepared for disasters. It's one of our mission statements. Which is why this is the perfect place to hole up in and stay safe. I just checked with the rest of our Town Council, and our food reserves can sustain us for a couple of years, worst case scenario. We also have our crops and our livestock, plus most of you folks are diligent about your own gardens. Everyone needs to be smart, and your families will be okay."

I recognise the hardware store owner as he rises from his seat in the bleachers and clears his throat. "What about those of us that have family up the mountain? Are we allowed to go get them and bring them here? Most of them won't know what's going on."

Mumbled arguments ripple through the gym and the mayor covers the microphone and leans back to discuss the question with the men around him. After a couple of moments, he uncovers the microphone and leans into it.

"If you have family up the mountain, you have every right to go and get them or stay with them if you so choose, as isolation is a recommended defense per the CDC. We will implement a mandatory week-long quarantine for anyone who decides to risk leaving and comes back. You'll have to check in at the town border and wait for someone to escort you to a designated place. The abandoned farm house on Grove Street is looking like our best option for housing those who need to be secluded. It's well away from the rest of the population of Endstone, and right on the main road into town, so it's the safest place for it. No exceptions on being quarantined. Is that clear?"

The crowd whispers among themselves, but no other arguments are raised.

"Rest assured, Endstone is the best place to be for this," he goes on. "And not just because we have food and doctors. Hell, lots of cities have that. But because we have each other. We are a close-knit community, and we are ready for any kind of disaster," he says, driving his point home with a raised fist. The crowd cheers and claps, probably relieved to be able to feel anything other than fear. The mayor is good, I'll give him that. Where Sheriff April was able to scare the crowd into calming down, the mayor is able to instill hope. It's exactly what everyone needs.

"Any other questions?" Mayor Jeffries asks, and a few more people raise their hands, asking about town check-ins and food rationing. The mayor wants everyone to do check-ins every couple of days, and if someone shows signs of symptoms, people are to put white fabric on their front door so people know not to enter.

As people continue to talk about food rationing, Theo shakes his head. "Well, I guess it's good we didn't throw away the crates of MRE's we found stacked in the shed."

I nod grimly, hating to think that we might have to live off those if the entire country collapses and food becomes scarce. I'm going into soldier survival mode, like muscle-memory, and I'm suddenly looking at my surroundings differently. Who appears to be the most susceptible to disease? Who might try to steal more food than they're allotted? Who has water wells on their property or farm animals in their pastures? Who's armed?—pretty much everyone—and would any of them use those firearms against their neighbors? These questions and crazy what-ifs start running through my mind.

I'm listening as the grocery store owner discusses a purchase maximum being implemented for each household to ensure that everyone will have enough food, when a man from the front row interrupts. "Is this really necessary?"

All eyes swing to him, and it's clear from the irritated huffs and eyerolls that pass over the faces in the crowd, that this guy is not popular.

The mayor gives him a hard look. "Harry, it's vital that this town reacts and prepares as best we can. If you disagree, you're free to walk out of here, but for everyone else, we work together. Preparedness and action. That's the Endstone way."

Harry grumbles under his breath but stays put and doesn't speak again.

The mayor pauses and asks for anymore questions, but when they don't come, he stands and declares the meeting is over. People swarm to the table to get extra masks, rubber gloves, and the printed papers. The fliers talk about which symptoms to watch for, how much food is allotted per household, other jobs to volunteer for, and a whole bunch of other shit. There's still no sign of the panic I keep thinking will show itself, but that doesn't help ease the knots of worry that have formed in my gut.

Brant joins the crowd and grabs more gloves and pamphlets. On his way back, Sheriff April ambles to catch up with him. The sheriff nods his goodbyes to other people as they swarm out of the gymnasium, and then motions us over to the far corner of the room. He hasn't shaved this morning, which is odd for him, and he has heavy bags under his eyes.

He looks like shit as he runs a hand over his face. "Boys, I have a favor to ask you, and I want you to know that I don't ask it lightly."

I exchange a look with Theo and notice Brant's hand come down to rest on Puddles's neck. Sheriff pulls out a paper from his back pocket and hands it to me. I unfold it and stare at it for a second before he explains.

"This is a map of the quickest and least populated roads that lead to Libal Bluff, Idaho," he tells us, tapping on the map to indicate the place he's talking about.

Theo crosses his arms over his chest and adopts a mission-prep demeanor, while I focus on where Sheriff is pointing.

"And what exactly are you wanting us to get in Libal Bluff, Idaho?" Brant asks.

Sheriff April looks up at him. "My kid."

I was expecting Sheriff April to say water, or some other type of vital supplies, so when he says *my kid*, I'm completely taken aback.

Sheriff must sense our shock, because he quickly explains. "Remington lives there and runs a big game

34

hunting outfit. As you know, the phones are down and I've no way of reaching out. I'd go myself, but I'm needed here in town, and let's be honest, you boys would be faster and way more efficient than my old bones any day," he looks at each of us, his tone and body language beseeching.

I shift my weight from one foot to the other, not sure what to say. My immediate reaction is to say I'm in, but it's not just me I need to think of.

"There's a travel restriction," Theo points out.

Sheriff April nods grimly. "There is. But...it's my kid, and we haven't spoken for a while," he says, and I can tell by his tone and the way his eyes dart downward that this is something that's hard for him to talk about.

I look over at Theo and Brant, and their expressions tell me all I need to know. We have the skills and the know how. We're a little broken, but sheriff is right, if anyone can bring his son home, it's us.

"I wouldn't ask you if...anyway, I understand if you say no. I've tried asking a few others..." he trails off, and my jaw clenches. I don't know which fuckers he's asked in this town, but I hate that they turned him down. I haven't known Sheriff April for long, but it's been long enough to know that he never asks for help lightly.

An electric hum starts up in my belly and quickly moves throughout my whole body. It's a familiar sensation, one that I always got whenever the higher-ups announced a mission to my Unit. I haven't felt this unique sensation in over two years, and its presence excites me in ways I didn't realize I missed until this exact moment.

Being needed—being the best option to execute a mission, fuck, it makes me feel whole again, and that equally scares and excites the shit out of me.

Brant leans in, studying the map that I'm still holding. He's quiet as his eyes roam over the path that Sheriff has drawn out for us. He taps the map twice and then steps back, and it tells Theo and I that this is in fact the best way to get where we need to go, and that he's willing to do this. Theo gives me an almost imperceptible tilt of his chin, and I turn to Sheriff April.

"We'll do it."

His eyes find mine, and a relieved breath escapes him. "I know you guys only have the truck, so Lewis Robisson has a new Explorer that we can have fitted and kitted in an hour. It should be big enough for all of you. I'll make sure there's enough gas in the trunk to get you there and back, and any other supplies we can think of that could come in handy. Meet at the church whenever you're ready, and we can make sure you have everything you need."

"We can be ready to go in thirty minutes. We'll grab food for Puddles, so we'll need room for kibble and weapons, too." I tell him.

"Of course," he replies, and then pauses. "Thank you, boys."

With that, Sheriff April turns and goes out the door, before any of us can so much as smile at him and throw out a *no problem*. I look to Theo and Brant, and see the same excited spark of ability and usefulness that I'm feeling in their expressions.

"Well, I guess let's mount up."

4

THEO

The car ride is silent as Madix hauls ass back to our house. As soon as we get there, we each grab our Army-issued duffles and start packing. We're ready in exactly eleven minutes, and we grab our guns, a box of MRE's and supplies for Puddles. Our cells have no service or internet, but I stuff mine in my pocket anyway, out of habit.

When we get to the church, Sheriff April and Lewis Robisson, the guy who runs the gas station, are just loading up the last of the gas cans. We hop out and haul all of our shit to join what they've already packed in the back of the Explorer.

Lewis passes Madix the keys, and Brant opens the back door for Puddles to jump in first.

"You've got a full tank of gas. Follow the map and drive safely, boys. This car here is new," Lewis tells us sternly, giving two slaps to the hood of the SUV before walking off where his wife is waiting in their other vehicle.

We watch Lewis leave, and then Sheriff April turns to us, his face grim, but his blue eyes hopeful. The hope that I see there makes me uneasy, and I'm not sure how to respond.

What if we can't get to his kid? The last thing I want is disappoint sheriff or bring him back bad news and see that ember hope turn to ash and crumble into nothing.

"You boys don't have to do this..." he begins.

Madix cuts him off. "Sheriff, you were the first person to welcome us here. We know this town isn't exactly used to outsiders, but you've always gone out of your way to make it feel like home to us. We'll do everything we can to get your kid."

A flash of gratefulness crosses his aged features. "I know it's a big ask."

I nod. "Yeah, but it's a direct route using back roads. As long as our supplies hold, we shouldn't need to cross into any high risk areas or come in contact with anyone. We'll be back here in a couple of days, so long as the weather is on our side."

He holds out his hand for us to shake, and when it's my turn to take it, I pull him in and clap him on the back to let him know we don't resent him for asking this of us. Sure, it's a big fucking deal and potentially dangerous, but I respect the shit out of him, and he's a good guy. "Here," he says, passing me an envelope from his back pocket. "Give that to my kid. With that, there won't be any confusion as to who sent you guys."

I nod and stuff the envelope addressed to Remington into my bag before tossing it in the car.

"We'd better head out so that we have plenty of daylight," Brant says, looking up at the somewhat cloudy sky.

Madix goes around to shut the trunk and Sheriff idles by the car nervously. "You boys are the best thing to happen to Endstone in years," he muses. "With your military training and survivalist experience, I have no doubt that Remington will be safe in your hands."

We nod and start getting in the car. I ride shotgun while Madix takes the driver seat and starts the engine, and Brant and Puddles settle into the back.

Just before we leave, Sheriff April taps hesitantly on my window. I roll it down expectantly, but he seems to stall for a moment, like he doesn't quite know how to say what he wants.

"Sheriff?" Madix prompts.

He rubs his scruff jaw and quickly looks at all three of us. "It's just...Remington can be a bit of a...handful. But I'm sure you'll be fine," he amends quickly with a shake of his head. He taps the hood and waves. "Good luck. And thank you."

We watch as he strides away, his last minute revelation floating around the car. Madix puts the SUV into gear and we pull out onto the highway.

"This is fucking crazy," Madix says as he grips the steering wheel, but the hint of a smile peeking out at the corners of his mouth gives away just how excited he really is for a dose of insanity and the adrenaline rush of a mission.

All Brant and I can do is nod and hold back our own smiles, because he's absolutely fucking right. This is crazy, and we fucking thrive on it.

* * *

My chin hits my chest hard and it jars me awake. I blink slowly as my eyes follow the winding road that we're on, and I try to process where I am. I look over to find Brant in the driver's seat while Madix breathes steadily in the back with Puddles's head resting in his lap. It's dark outside, so I can't tell how long I've been out. I tap the touch screen that's nestled on the center-front console of the car, and it lights up, showing nine-thirty-two.

"We're a couple hours out still," Brant tells me, his voice tired.

"You want to switch out?" I ask automatically, and I fight the irritation that bubbles up inside of me when Brant's eyes dart down to my legs. "I lost my left leg bro, I can still drive with my right."

I know he doesn't mean to be an ass, but I'm over being treated like I can't function. I lost my leg from just below the knee down. It's not like I had a fucking lobotomy. Sometimes I wonder if my injury is harder for me to adjust to, or harder for those around me to deal with.

"I know dude, you just haven't been interested in getting behind the wheel since... you know..." he tapers off.

"Well that's because Madix is an anal psycho about his truck and we live in bum-fuck-nowhere so I haven't needed to drive. This is different. You're obviously tired and I just took a really long rest, and had an awesome dream about River's hot twin sisters."

Brant chuckles. "Why do I feel like he's going to pop up out of nowhere and kick our asses for what you just said?" he asks with a shake of his head. "Shit, remember that beat down that Magoo got just for staring at River's family photo for too long?" We both crack up at the memory of Magoo getting the shit kicked out of him while he yelled that he was just looking at the Christmas tree in the background. To be fair, it was a fucking hot picture of the twins dressed up like like sexy Christmas elves.

"Nah, I bet River is jumping out of planes and kicking ass somewhere in the Middle East right now. You're safe to fantasize about them," I tease, and release a dreamy sigh. "How the fuck those gifts from God were related to River, I'll never know."

Brant laughs, and then we both grow quiet for a beat.

"Anyway, I can take over if you need a break for a bit," I tell him again.

"I was actually thinking we should pull over for the night."

I roll my eyes and open my mouth to argue. I can fucking handle driving for a couple of hours.

"Not because of you," he quickly cuts in. "Get over yourself, bro. But I mean, come on, what is this dude going to think if the three of us show up at his house in the middle of the night? There was a sign for a campground coming up, so maybe we should all sleep and then show up tomorrow morning. We might have a better chance of convincing this dude that he'd be better off coming back with us in the light of day, versus showing up like harbingers of death in the dark of the night."

"Makes sense to me," Madix rumbles from the backseat.

"Yeah, but should we really be stopping and leaving ourselves exposed more than we need to with all the shit that's going down?" I ask.

"I doubt anyone would actually be up here. It's still too cold for vacation campers, and we're out in the middle of nowhere," Brant offers, and the car grows silent as we all mull over the risk.

"Okay, but we need to take shifts," I concede.

Madix unbuckles himself and starts rooting around the supplies in the back of the car. Puddles gives an irritated huff when her pillow gets too squirmy to be comfortable, and she sits up with a yawn.

"There are sleeping bags and a small tent back here. It'll be closer quarters with you fucks, but it's cold at night, anyway."

I chuckle. " It can't be worse than that one mission..."

"Fuck that was cold," Brant agrees, and Madix grunts in agreement. "Talk about serious misunderstanding of the local terrain and weather. I felt like I'd never get warm again."

Madix starts to laugh. "Remember when Stiles started to sing all those Beach Boys songs and telling us we just had to imagine we were somewhere warmer?"

I snort at the memory. "God, he had a shit voice. He had to stop singing when he was shivering so hard he couldn't get his lips to form the words anymore."

Brant cracks up, and Madix and I join him. I mimic shivering and, through faux-chattering-teeth, sing as off-key as possible. "Bermuda, Bahama, come on pretty mama..."

I run a hand down my face as we all sigh, our laughter tapering off. I push back against the longing that tries to sit up inside of me, and don't acknowledge the flash of memories that start playing through my mind. Maybe it's the nature of what we're doing right now and the fact that it feels like an assignment, but it has me talking freely about the other squad members that we worked with before, and I know I have to stop. We always try to focus on the positive and the fun times, but that inevitably brings us to the not so good memories and the things we'd rather forget.

We turn off the road when the exit sign for Sagebrush Campsite pops up. The road is not very well kept, and we're all bouncing around while still trying to be as vigilant as possible as we drive further into the trees. After a few more minutes, we reach a decently-sized clearing which I assume is the official campsite, even though there's nothing else that would indicate that's where we are.

Brant swings the Explorer around and lights up a patch of land before putting the SUV in park. "Brant, you grab a gun and stand watch. Theo and I will unload and get things set up."

Brant nods his head and I offer a, "Sounds good." We all cautiously step out of the safety of the car, each of us taking a couple of seconds to listen around us for the telltale signs of other campers nearby. When the sounds of crickets and other forest life is the only thing that serenades us, I relax slightly.

Madix and I make quick work of setting up the campsite while Puddles marks every shrub and patch of grass in sight. We get a small fire going and dig into a couple cans of Dinty Moore Beef Stew and some baked beans that we heated up on a rock over the flames.

We're eating and listening to the night air when Brant breaks the silence. "Who knew Sheriff even had a kid?"

"I've never heard him mention a wife or anything," Madix replies.

"Anyone surprised that he named his kid after a gun?" I add, and the others chuckle.

"Nope, no fucking surprise there. His kid is probably lucky he didn't end up being called Glock, or Smith & Wesson," Brant jokes.

While we continue to shoot the shit, Puddles's head shoots up from where she's resting next to Brant, and she lets out a low growl. The three of us immediately go on alert and reach for our weapons. We don't miss a beat as we triangle off, our backs to each other, our weapons hot and ready as we scan the surrounding trees for whatever set Puddles off.

My entire body is tense, my muscles ready to move at a moment's notice. I don't know how long we stand like that, but nothing comes through the trees at us, and none of us pick up on anything else that would be worrying. Brant swings a flashlight around the dark woods, but there's nothing. After another minute or so, Puddles lays down at Brant's feet and then promptly falls asleep. A slight snore puffs out from her jowls as she snoozes without a care in the world.

One by one, each of us relaxes, and we sit back down.

"Fuck," Madix sighs as he runs a hand over his short black beard. "This damn virus has us scared of our own damn shadows."

"We have to be on alert," I say.

He doesn't argue, and the three of us start to inhale our makeshift dinner. With the crackle of the fire, we watch sparks rise against the night sky, our spoons scraping against the tin cans as we eat.

"We could've been dead," Brant suddenly says, breaking the silence.

Madix and I both look over at him, the flames occasionally dancing up and teasing my view. "What?" Madix asks, eyeing Puddles when she tries to sidle up to him to beg for whatever he has left in his can.

"We lived in the city," Brant tells us hollowly. "If we hadn't come here with Theo to live in his uncle's place, we could've been dead right now," he points out.

He's right, and it's a sobering thought that steals away the illusion of this impromptu camping trip, and it sets us right back in the middle of what we're really doing here.

"Let's not play the dead game," Madix tells him. "We could've been dead in Afghanistan hundreds of times. Or Iraq or Bahrain. We could have even gone like Stiles did, on a motorcycle on our way to see our family. Life isn't guaranteed. We should know that better than anyone."

Madix gives up on trying to nudge Puddles's big-ass body away from him, and instead sighs and gives her the can. She happily licks it clean, and then releases a sound from her rear-end that is immediately accompanied by the smell of shit and rotten eggs.

"Ugh, fuck, Pud. That's disgusting!" Madix laments, as he tries to scoot away from her.

We all wrinkle our noses and do our best not to inhale too deeply.

"She is sleeping outside tonight if that keeps up," Madix warns Brant, who looks so offended you would think Madix just asked him to kiss his boots.

"She sleeps with me," Brant says sternly.

I laugh and elbow Madix. "Swipe one of those old-ass gas masks they packed for us in the back. I call first watch!"

Madix glares at me and pushes Puddles away from him when she tries to crawl into his lap.

"Come here, baby," Brant calls to her. "That dick doesn't know how to treat a woman right."

Madix's eyebrows drop, and his nose scrunches up even more. "No woman I'm interested in rips ass the way she does."

Brant covers Puddles floppy ears like he's protecting her from Madix's words. "Everyone shits and farts, Madix."

"Yeah, but no chick of mine is gonna lick her asshole right after it happens," Madix replies, not missing a beat.

In that exact moment, Puddles turns to Brant and licks his cheek, leaving a nice streak of drool behind.

"Gross, man," Madix tells him, and he gets up and heads for the tent. "I'm going to sleep before I see and smell any more fucked up and traumatizing shit."

I laugh, but lean away from Puddles when she tries to slather me with a kiss next.

"I'm not that kind of boy. Puddles," I tease her. "Think you can just go around kissing whoever you want? I need exclusivity!"

Her little nub of a tail starts going a mile a minute, responding to my playful tone. Brant chuckles and stands up, dusting himself off. "Three or four hour shifts?" he asks.

"Four, I got a good long nap in the car."

He nods at me and then strides toward the tent. "Ready for me, sailor?" Brant calls out to Madix with a joking grin.

He whips his shirt over his head and sends me a smartass smile over his shoulder before unzipping the front of the tent and climbing in. Puddles follows him, and I crack up at the *umph* Madix gives. He probably just took a paw to the balls.

As they get settled in, I add more wood to the fire before perching on a stump that Brant dragged over. I rub at my leg, trying to fight the urge to take my prosthetic off and let the skin breathe. The last thing I want is to do that and have someone come stomping through the clearing—which would be my fucking luck—so I rub around where the stump of my leg fits into the socket of the prosthetic, trying to massage some of the pain away. That will have to do in the meantime. Now I just have to count down the minutes until we can get back on the road, grab this dude, and hightail it back to the safety and comfort of Endstone.

5

MADIX

T he sun peeks over the horizon on my left, and the sky is lit up with pinks and oranges. I turn off the road we're on, and Theo reads me the directions as we make our way to Remington's house. There's no need for us to trace a back road path at this point. We seem to be surrounded by nothing, which makes *every* path to Remington's house a back road. We've been lucky so far because we haven't seen another car during this whole drive, and other than waking up with Brant's morning wood against my back and a crick in my neck, last night's camping trip went down without a hitch.

I massage the side of my neck, paying careful attention to the knot I find there.

"You want me to rub one off for you?" Brant asks, and I turn to him confused, and replay what he just asked me. "Did...you...just proposition me?"

"Brant, for the love of all that is holy in the world, 'rub one off' is another term for jerking off. It's not a fucking massage term!" Theo laughs.

Brant frowns. "I'll have you know that I was told that by

47

an actual masseuse. So, you'll just have to excuse me when I trust a professional over you two horny assholes who think everything has to do with fucking or jerking off," Brant defends as Puddles gives a supportive huff.

"Oh, she was a professional alright, but not the way you were thinking she was," Theo grins, earning himself a solid punch in the shoulder from Brant.

I chuckle and shake my head. "Thanks for the offer, but it's a hard pass from me."

Theo reaches over and smacks Brant playfully. "Hear that? He said he's hard."

"Shut the fuck up," Brant says, the tips of his ears going red. "I meant I'd help with his fucked up neck," he grumbles. "I was being helpful and shit."

"Is that what your masseuse said too?" Theo teases.

Brant grabs a water bottle and chucks it at his head.

I laugh at the back and forth that goes on, but refocus on our surroundings. So far, things are going as well as they can, but with each mile that brings us closer to our destination, the tension in the car rises. None of us are sure what we're walking into. Sheriff April didn't mention anything about his son having a family, so we're all hoping that it's only the one guy we have to deal with. Then again, we did just find out that sheriff even had a kid, so he's not exactly big on dishing out the details.

"Should we talk about what to do in the event this guy doesn't want to go with us?" Theo asks out of nowhere.

Judging by his question, his thoughts aren't far off from where mine just were. None of us answer.

"I mean, the sheriff did say that he and his kid haven't talked in a long time. So there's a good chance this Remington guy might not want a reunion with dear ol' dad. Do you think the sheriff is expecting us to bring his son back whether he wants to come or not?" Brant adds, and again, the car falls silent.

"He'd have access to more supplies and aid in Endstone than he would be out here. That's for sure. But I don't know that we have the right to decide that for him," Theo finally offers.

"We can give him his options, but if he doesn't care and wants to stay out here, exposed and at risk, then he's a dumbass and good riddance," I tell them. "We'll leave him behind and let the sheriff know we tried."

Brant chuckles. "You always were a softy," he goads.

I smile and meet his blue eyes in the rearview mirror. "If he doesn't want to come, then I don't want to waste daylight trying to convince him. I know this feels dangerously close to a mission, but no government official is ordering us to bring this guy back. If his issue with his dad is big enough that he can't see past it to do what's the safest and what makes the most sense for survival, then that's on him. I'll march my happy ass back to the car and be on my way."

"Well, looks like we're about to find out. Turn right up here, and then according to the map, we snake around a tight curve and the house is a mile or so down from that," Theo announces.

Brant pulls our guns from the very back and hands Theo his. Theo checks it over, and I catch Brant doing the same. A part of me feels like showing up armed to some random guy's house is a recipe for disaster, but another part of me acknowledges that since we have no idea what we're walking into, it's better to be safe than sorry. Dust trails behind us as we wind around on the road, and I spot a good-sized house not far in the distance. It's two stories with a wraparound porch, and there's a modern log-cabin look to the whole thing.

It's about seven in the morning, and everything seems

quiet and sleepy. There's no movement of curtains or any other indication that anyone inside is awake and aware that we're here. There's a round driveway in front of the house, and I can picture people renting this place for hunting trips, pulling up to the front of the porch stairs to unload their luggage.

The brakes give the faintest squeak of protest as we come to a stop in front of the house. I quickly pass out the gloves and masks that sheriff packed for us, and we all pull them on. With practiced ease, Brant hands me my rifle, and then we all get out of the car. Brant and Theo watch the house as we approach it, while I watch their backs.

My M4 is raised and ready while I scan our surroundings. I stop at the base of the stairs and wait until Brant taps off to trade places with me. I swivel and follow Theo up the stairs, leaving Brant and Puddles to guard us from behind. Theo knocks on the door, and adrenaline rushes through me at the sound. I move off to the side of the door, and Theo steps back and out of reaching distance, in case anyone inside this house is sick. Worst case scenario, I'll be able to get a shot off before anyone can reach either of us.

There are no sounds of movement inside the house. Theo steps forward to knock harder on the solid wood door before stepping back again. We wait, and I'm just about to voice that it seems like no one is home, when the sound of a shotgun being cocked sets off all of my internal alarms, and then the icy bite of a metal barrel is pushed between my shoulder blades, making my blood run cold.

Theo and Brant whirl in my direction, both of them quickly masking their shock. I can't believe whoever this is just got the drop on us. Not even the dog fucking heard him. The sheriff better forgive me for decking his son...which I'll do just as soon as he pulls the gun out of my back.

"Is there something I can do for you G.I. Joes?" a rich, smooth, *feminine* voice asks.

Brant keeps his rifle trained on the girl, but Theo points his gun to the ground and seems to take a second to collect himself before he answers.

"We're here to speak with Remington April," he announces, his voice authoritative.

"And just what business do you have with Remi?" she asks, her tone silky with just a hint of *fuck-off* to it.

"I'm sure you're aware of what's going on in the country ma'am," Brant starts. "And, um...Remington's father asked us to come here and invite him back to Endstone where it might be safer, you know, given what's happening."

It grows quiet, and I try not to think about the tickle I feel as a bead of sweat traces down the back of my neck.

"Oh, I'll just bet he did," she grumbles, and relief floods me when the barrel of the shotgun pulls away from my spine, and I feel the woman take a step back from me.

I lower my weapon but don't move more than that. I'm not getting my head blown off by some trigger happy redneck just because my curiosity got the better of me.

"Cobra Commander, tell Snake Eyes over there to move his sights away from me. Guns in my direction make me twitchy," the silky voice instructs.

Brant aims his rifle just wide of the woman behind me, and the wood of the porch creaks as Theo shifts his weight.

"Can I turn around, or are you going to get twitchy and put a hole in my back?" I ask, the irritation clear in my voice.

"I promise no new holes...for now," she answers.

I turn around slowly, not at all amused by the joking lilt in her tone. She won't think it's so funny when she's staring down my...*holy shit.*

My thoughts completely seize up when I turn around and come face-to-face with the shotgun toting woman, because fucking hell, she's *gorgeous*. She's wearing a half-cocked smirk that tells me she feels in complete control of the current situation, and if it were anyone but us, she might be right. She may have snuck up on us, but there's no way she'd get the jump on us twice.

My gaze dips down her body and slowly rises back up. The girl is wearing ripped jeans and a tank top under what I'm pretty sure is a man's plaid. But it's the neon pink hiking boots that give me pause. Well, that and her tits. Those make me linger a bit, too, before I shove her curvy body out of my mind. By the time my brown eyes reconnect with her glacial blue ones, I've turned off my attraction and assessed the situation. I relax my stance and my hold on my weapon, using my body language to invite her to do the same.

"Is Remington here, ma'am? We were asked to speak with him, and as soon as we do that, we'll be on our way," I tell her.

"Promise?" she asks, a little too innocently.

I suddenly feel like I'm missing something, but I want to get out of here and get that fucking shotgun out of my face, so I don't focus too hard on what it could be.

"Scouts fucking honor," I drawl back like a smart-ass, adopting the same tone she just used.

The blonde snorts. "As if you could make it as a Scout," she counters, and I bristle, because what the fuck? I'm a damn Army Ranger. That sure as shit is a whole lot more impressive than a pansy ass Boy Scout.

Before I can say anything though, she interrupts me. "I'm Remington, my friends call me Remi, but you Joe's can call me *bye* and then walk right back to your car and leave. I'm not interested in going back to Endstone, no matter how much man-candy dear ol' Dad wants to wave in my face as a bribe."

Theo huffs out a surprised laugh, but I don't turn to give

him a judging look for breaking protocol. I'm too busy trying to make my brain get rid of the pot-bellied *man* I had been picturing as Remington April and replace that image with this woman. "*You're* Remington April?" I ask dubiously.

"Sure am," she chirps.

Her eyes move from me to Theo, and I immediately pounce on the mistake. I push the barrel of her gun away from me with one hand and move in to disarm her with the other. The gun comes away easily, and I quickly turn it in my hands and redirect the Remington 870 Tac-14 at the flaxen haired, blue-eyed, Remington April.

But I don't get to bask in the victory of getting the drop on her, because as soon as I refocus my sights and the barrel of the shotgun on her, I see why the gun came away so easily from her grip. She let go of it in order to grab the Glock 43 that's now pointing at my chest. Well fuck, I was not expecting that.

All previous traces of humor are gone from her face, and she now wears a distinct *you just pissed off the wrong bitch* look. It looks like things might have just gone from bad to worse, which is definitely not what you want when you're trying to convince someone to come with you.

Brant holds up his hands in a placating gesture. "Why don't we all just take a breath and relax," he says, trying to draw her attention to him as he steps closer.

In reply, she tilts her head slightly but doesn't redirect her Glock.

"That's not very polite," I tell her with a cocky grin, looking more relaxed than I really am. Then again, it's not like this is the first time I've had a gun pointed at me.

"You know what else isn't polite? Trespassing," she volleys.

I open my mouth to explain *again* that we were sent here by her father, but an ear-splitting chirping noise suddenly erupts in the air. All three of us tense and go for our weapons, but Remington is already launching herself over the porch railing and running toward the sound in the woods.

We barely have time to glance at each other before running after her. Puddles whines and tries to shove her big ass under the car with no success, so she covers her ears with her big legs instead. I want to do the same, and I'm half-deaf in one ear. The mission that fucked us all up left me with hearing loss due to the damage that was done to the bones in my middle ear. I now suffer from tinnitus in that ear, and loud noises like this can really set it off, but I can't just stay here with my thumb up my asshole, so I race after her.

I'm the closest, hot on Remington's pink-booted heels, and I end up running up beside her first. "What the fuck is that noise?" I holler over to her.

"My clinger dinger!" she shouts back, still running.

We breach the edge of the trees, and she starts darting through them like she knows these woods better than the backs of her hands. The trees are thick and healthy with underbrush, so I stay behind her as I feel Theo and Brant right behind me.

"Your what?" Theo calls forward, his prosthetic slowing him down somewhat.

"It's my clinger dinger!" she calls over her shoulder. "It's Jim Bob for sure. He's the only one that tries to stalk me from this direction."

And I have...no idea what to say to that.

Just when the obnoxious noise is closer and threatening to burst my good eardrum, Remington hops over a fucking trip wire that I only barely manage to step over in time. I shout a warning behind me, and Brant nearly runs his ankles right into it, but stops just in time for Theo to run into him from behind, sending them both toppling to the forest floor.

They both grunt and swear up a storm, but I reach down and haul Theo up to his feet before he can even think about getting pissed about needing my help.

I start to shout at them to ask if they're okay, but the chirping noise suddenly cuts off, making my now much-too-loud voice echo through the woods. I look over and find Remington with her hands on some device that's strapped to a tree, equipped with a small solar panel and a red laser light. "Don't be so loud!" she chastises me, her blonde brows furrowing.

I look at her incredulously before turning back to the guys. "Is she *fucking* kidding me? That alarm was just blaring through the whole damn forest, and she's telling *me* to be quiet?"

The guys look just as bewildered as me.

"Aha!" Remington declares, making our eyes whip back to see her...standing triumphantly over a pile of shit.

To my horror, she kneels down next to it and starts poking at it with a stick. "Yep. Definitely Jim Bob. He's a stage five clinger to me and my girls," she says seriously.

"I...I don't know what's happening," I hear Brant murmur behind me.

"What is she doing?" Theo asks as he discreetly tries to check his prosthetic through his pants leg.

They both turn to me like I somehow I have all the answers, just because she chose me to point her guns at. I throw my hands up. "I don't fucking speak crazy."

"I'm on to you, Jim Bob! Stay away from my girls!" Remington suddenly shouts at the woods as she circles around the pile of shit and glares off at nothing in the trees.

"I really hope she's talking about an animal and there isn't some dude named Jim Bob walking around shitting on her property and setting off weird ass alarms strapped to trees," Theo mumbles.

Brant's lip twitches, like he isn't sure whether he wants to laugh or ask what the fuck we've just walked into.

Remington checks various spots in the clearing, but at this point, I'm not really sure I want to know what she's looking for. And yeah, the blonde-haired, blue-eyed girl is fucking hot, but I'm pretty sure that fancy wrapping paper is just nature's way of trying to hide the batshit lunatic underneath.

"Alright, well, this was fun. We'll just go."

Her eyes swing to me, and she puts her hands on her hips like I've somehow irritated her. "Oh, *now* you want to go? Right when Jim Bob shows up? Typical."

My left eye twitches with the comings of a wicked headache that I'm pretty sure isn't from the alarm that irritated the fuck out of my damaged ear drum.

"Who the fuck is Jim Bob?" I ask, exasperated.

"My bear," she says with the roll of her eyes, like I'm an idiot for not already knowing that.

My eye twitches again. "You have a *bear?*"

"Jim Bob. Yes. Try to keep up, Sloppy Joe," she says completely serious, as she tucks her gun into her thigh holster and starts making her way back toward the house. The three of us fall in line behind her, and even though she clearly has a screw loose, I can't help but check out her ass. When I look over at Theo and Brant, I catch them doing the same thing, although Brant's the only one who looks away once he realizes he's been caught. Theo just grins.

She's talking under her breath as she goes, and I might be able to hear her if it weren't for my ear ringing like a bitch. That alarm really fucked me up.

When we breach the edge of the tree line and see the house, Puddles comes racing towards us and sidles right up to Brant, sniffing his fingers and nudging him. "It's alright, Pud," he tells her as he pats her head.

"Well, isn't she just the cutest!" Remington grins, immediately dropping down in front of Puddles. The dog perks up at the attention, her nub for a tail wagging and tongue coming out to promptly slather her with slobber.

"Puddles, no tongue," Brant reprimands.

Remington rolls her eyes. "Don't listen to him. Men always underestimate the importance of good tongue when kissing," Remington says in a lovey dovey tone to Puddles, making the tips of Brant's ears go bright red. She smirks at his expression and gives the dog another scratch just under the jowls before standing up and heading back towards the house.

"I have bacon and eggs. Take your boots off before walking into my house. And be careful with Coon. She bites."

Just like that, she sashays her perfect ass up the steps of her porch and disappears inside. Theo, Brant, and I exchange a look.

What the fuck did we just get ourselves into?

"Hey! Is anyone else inside? Anyone sick?" Theo shouts after her.

She pokes her head back out of the screen door. "Nope, just me, Michael Jackson, and I don't have the sniffles, so you can lose the mask. There's no autograph hounds out here to chase you around." She pulls her head back into the house, the screen door snapping loudly against the door frame.

"Uhh, she does know that Michael Jackson has been dead for a while, right?" Brant aks.

Theo rolls his eyes. "I don't even look like that weirdo, and who the fuck knows what's going on in that crazy chick's mind."

A high-pitched whistle comes from inside, and Puddles goes running straight through the screen on the door and into the house, leaving a massive hole behind and tracking mud inside the house. Brant just stares after his dog and the damage left in her wake.

This shit just gets messier and messier.

6

REMI

The slap of the screen door reverberates through the house, and then I hear the distinct sound of heavy-footed men tromping towards the kitchen. I shove the pan of bacon in the oven and start cracking eggs into a big bowl. They walk through the doorway hesitantly, their eyes bouncing off of everything, including my ass, before they decide to just stand there awkwardly.

"Feel free to take a load off," I offer casually over my shoulder. When they continue to stand there, I add, "Or not. Whatever stretches your briefs."

The blondie with the glasses and the dog at his heels makes an awkward coughing noise, and I smirk to myself. A shy guy? I haven't been around one of those for ages. Actually, I haven't really been around anyone for ages. This cabin is my retreat right before I head off to do my long excursions for work in the spring. But I do like to tally up the action when I can, and I'm not about to look this gift horse in the mouth. My sexual appetites have always been of *the more the merrier* variety, and playing with these three just ranked at number one on my fuck-it list. What can I say? I'm a sexual free spirit.

The guys pause for a moment longer, but then they finally shuffle toward the table and sit down. I don't miss the slight limp that Cobra Kai has before he sits heavily in the chair. They've removed their medical masks and latex gloves, and I have to fight to keep myself from asking why the hell they were wearing them in the first place. If these guys are friends with my dad, then who knows what kind of crazy they're up to.

The big, beautiful mastiff they brought with them trots back into the kitchen after taking a quick sniff around, and then sits at my feet with an elk antler proudly clamped in her mouth and mud caked to her paws.

Blondie glares at her like she's somehow betrayed him, and I study him from my spot at the stove. He has a short mohawk down the middle of his otherwise shaved head, a clean jaw, and his body is fit, with his biceps nicely toned. Actually, all of the guys are ridiculously ripped. I bet they'd be a fun distraction for the end of my retreat, and since this is my yearly vacation, why not?

I whistle-click at the dog, and she looks up at me expectantly. I nod in his direction and she gets up, elk antler in mouth, and goes to lay at his feet instead. He gapes at me, a mix of shock and a little irritation in his expression, but I ignore him as I whisk a little milk into the eggs and move to chop up the chives.

"So? What did Daddy Dearest want you to tell me?" I ask the trio of gorgeous, well muscled, mask-wearing weirdos. If Dad thinks he can flash these hot little pieces in front of me and I'll come drooling back to Endstone, well...he's smart, but he's got another thing coming. Although I would *love* to know where he found these guys. They don't fit the profile of the kinds of people who usually live in Endstone.

As I finish with the chives, a hiss comes from the direction of the cellar. The door beside the fridge is open, and I frown over at it. "Coon, you'd best not let those rats out, you hear me?" I holler at the cracked door.

I pull open the fridge and grab a block of cheddar cheese, setting it next to the chopped chives as I get the pan warmed up on the stove.

"Um, ma'am?" the tan, black-haired, brown-eyed one I almost shot earlier starts. Dude is huge and muscled. Like, his biceps are bigger than my head, and he has those sexy veins running down his forearms. I bet he has a V below his abs, too. My favorite letter of the alphabet.

"Remi," I correct him. "Only my dad calls me Remington, and only condescending pricks call me ma'am. If you're that type, good for you for owning it and feel free to ma'am away. Otherwise, Remi will do just fine."

"Uh, Remi..." Sloppy Joe starts again, and I give an approving nod as I add the eggs to the warm pan and sprinkle the chives over the top. "Are you aware of what's going on? You know, in the rest of the country?"

I open the oven and pull out the pan of bacon so I can flip them over. "No, but I'm sure you're about to fill me in," I tell him, as a loud thump sounds just above my head. I look up to the ceiling and shake my head. Those chickens better not be stuck up on the roof again. I've told them that goose can't be trusted.

The hot hispanic looking guy clears his throat, and I look over at him. "There was a virus or something that started spreading a couple weeks ago. Everyone's been calling it the Handshake Plague. They thought they had a hold of the spread, but the vaccines they were giving for it failed, and it's killing a lot of people. The phones are down, the radio is out, and people are being told to take serious precautions against exposure." He gestures to the masks and gloves that they took off and have piled on the table. "Endstone is working to keep its citizens safe, and you'd be safer there than out here on your own. Your dad asked us to come get you and make sure you get back safely."

I chuckle and look at him incredulously. "Cool story bro, but I'm good here. You can tell my dad nice try, but even if the world was coming to an end, I'm still not going back there."

He looks at me with confusion, but his lack of answers is not my problem. I move the scrambled eggs around in the pan so they don't burn and hum *Somebody's Gotta Be Country* as I sprinkle in more cheese.

I hear a huff of annoyance behind me. "What do you mean by *nice try*?" the man with the green eyes and tawny skin tone asks me.

"A bit rude to come into someone's house and talk about plagues without properly introducing yourselves, don't you think?" I volley over my shoulder.

I hear them muttering back and forth to each other, and I give the eggs one last stir before pulling out the bacon and piling it on a paper towel-covered plate, which I set on the table. I put out cups and orange juice on the table next, followed by the eggs and toast.

By the time I sit down, they're still muttering to each other, but I ignore them as I pick up my copy of this year's Farmer's Almanac and open it where I left off.

"Remi?"

I look up mid-bacon crunch. "Hmm?"

The glasses-wearing dog owner clears his throat. "Umm, my name is Brant. Brant Shaw."

I pop out my hand for him to shake. It has some bacon grease on it, but I'm pretty sure he doesn't mind, because he certainly doesn't rush to pull away.

"Madix Ortega," the hispanic hottie says next, but he doesn't offer his hand and instead keeps his arms crossed, which is just fine by me because it makes his drool-worthy pecs stand out even more. My eyes travel down the rest of him with appreciation. His shirt is straining just enough around his muscles to look really good, without it looking ridiculous or like he's trying too hard by wearing shit that's too small. I mentally forgive him for skipping the hand-shake. His muscles give him a pass.

My eyes swing over to the third guy with the brown hair. He has these intense green eyes that should be too pretty to be masculine, but his chiseled jaw evens it out. "Theo Cole-man. Nice to meet you, ma—Remi," he corrects himself.

He reaches across the table to shake, and I have to admit, I like the way his warm fingers close around mine. It's a lot of stimulating hotness to have at my breakfast table, which is good, because I ran out of coffee four days ago, and this is just the pick me up I needed.

"So," I say, pulling back my hand so I can devour another piece of bacon. "What are three strapping men like you doing in Endstone?"

The other two look at Theo. "My uncle passed away. Left me his place there. So we decided to move in together."

Dawning realization washes over me, and I feel myself deflate a little. "Oh. Damn. I should've known a trio of hotties like you would prefer snakes to beavers."

Brant, who had just taken a bite of eggs, starts cough-choking on them. Without breaking a sweat, Madix reaches over and claps him on the back, while Theo passes him a glass of orange juice. Neither of their eyes leave me as they do this. It's a bit weird.

Theo lets a teasing smile cross over his face. "We aren't gay."

I brighten at that. "Oh. Thank you for clearing that up," I say seriously.

Madix runs a hand down his face. He's the only one who hasn't started to eat. "Not hungry?" I prompt.

Before he can answer, Theo does for him. "Madix is a bit particular about, well...everything."

I cock a blonde brow as I shovel more eggs into my mouth. "Meaning?"

Madix gestures around my kitchen. "Meaning you have homemade jerky hanging from a towel rack over your stove, loose birdseed all over the counter, four bowls of questionable pet food beside the oven, and your refrigerator door is wonky. Also, your jam looks homemade," he adds as an afterthought, glaring at the jar of preserves like it's going to grow arms and punch him in his face.

"Of course it's homemade. What do you take me for?" I snort.

"This kitchen is unsanitary," he replies.

"I'll have you know, I scrubbed it with lemons yesterday," I tell him matter-of-factly.

He blinks at me with an incredulous look.

"You do all this yourself?" Brant asks, now that he's adequately recovered from choking.

I nod. "Yep. My dad raised me to be totally self sufficient. It's just about the only thing we agree on anymore. I live totally off the grid for two months out of the year before I go back to work in Alaska."

"What do you do in Alaska?" Brant asks curiously, watching as I pass a piece of bacon down to his dog.

I open my mouth to answer, but Madix cuts in. "Look, we aren't here for visiting hour. We're here to retrieve you and bring you back to Endstone."

I roll my eyes. Figures this guy is a douche. Guess he can't have that many muscles *and* a good personality. Oh, well. I bet I could wrangle Theo in for a good time. I let my eyes trail down his trim waist and strong arms. His green eyes light up and his mouth twitches with amusement, but I don't mind being caught checking him out. I flick my eyes over to Brant, and I could totally see him doing that sweet, loving kind of thing. He's probably awesome at making a girl feel precious.

But Madix? He's the kind of guy who can pick you up and slam you against the wall while he fucks you hard and angry. Three totally different styles, and I'm a fan of all of them. Excitement courses through me at the thought of getting these three delicious morsels to give their special attention all to one girl. That would just be sex heaven.

I decide in that moment that it's my new goal. I've been meaning to make some new ones anyway. When I hear something loud shatter in the cellar, I groan and get to my feet. "Coon! How many times do I have to tell you? Stay off of my meat rack!"

I hear one of them snort behind me. "Is that some weird euphemism?" I think Theo mutters as I rush down the wooden steps to the cellar.

"Based on the interior of her house, I'm pretty sure it's not," Madix intones.

I jump the last step of the stairs and land nimbly on my feet. I tug the chain cord hanging from the ceiling, and the space lights up.

I hear the guys trudging down the stairs behind me, but I ignore them as I put my hands on my hips and glare at Coon and the destruction she's wrought in my cellar. The rats are loose out of their cage, nibbling on the knocked over grains that Coon no doubt pushed off the shelf on purpose. The climbing tree I built her with loose branches and spare drapery is also toppled over. There are teeth marks all over the meat I had drying on the rack, and my crate of apples has been totally ransacked.

I hear one of the guys whistle behind me. Coon pops up her head from where she's lying on my shelf of preserves, partially rolled up in one of my scarves. She has a glass jar of orange marmalade clutched in her clawed little paws and she dips her entire snout into it, licking up the contents.

"Coon. You are *not* an awesome opossum right now," I tell her with an angry jab of my finger.

"You named your opossum...Coon? As in *raccoon?* That's just confusing," I hear Brant say.

I roll my eyes and look over at him as I gesture to Coon who's still wrapped up on the shelf. "Coon as in *cocoon.* She likes to be wrapped up. My scarf is a favorite," I explain to him, but honest to Betsy, it should be obvious.

If I thought Madix looked horrified by the kitchen, he's truly aghast down here. I've never even *seen* someone look aghast before. I thought it was more of an old-school thing. But nope. Aghast he is. He keeps picking up his booted feet and wrinkling his nose at Coon's litter box that's stuffed into the corner. When one of the rats races by him, he jumps back, causing a grin to spread across my face.

"A big, tough guy like you isn't scared of a little rodent, are you?"

He crosses his arms in front of him and scowls, but I don't miss how he flexes slightly, as if to try and make up for the non-tough guy move before. "I'm not scared," he says convincingly. I'm still not fooled.

I walk over to the shelf and pick up Coon. She immediately wraps her tail around my neck and perches herself on my shoulders. Her little white muzzle is covered in orange preserves, and she keeps licking her lips. "Aww, I just can't stay mad at you," I tell Coon, petting her fondly.

Theo looks over at Brant. "Why does she have an opossum as a pet?" he asks, as if this dude will have the answer just because he has a dog. A dog who...yep. Sounds like she's eating the rest of our breakfast upstairs. There's a lot of slurping going on. Another rat goes skittering across the floor, and this time, Madix lets out an involuntary squeak of objection. I smile and tap Coon on the shoulder.

"Go get your little ones before the big man-babies wet themselves."

She scampers down from my shoulder with a huff, and then goes about trying to get the two rats back in their cage by picking them up by the scruff of their necks and tossing them onto her back.

"Babies?" Madix asks confused.

"Yeah, she thinks they're her kids. That's why she keeps springing them from their enclosure. Well, that, and she likes sharing the jam." I shrug and start straightening out the mess they've made down here. The three GI Joes scan the basement like they're not sure what to make of any of it, and they can't decide where their eyes should land.

Brant opens his mouth to say something, but stops when Coon runs over his foot to corral the rats back towards the blanket nest in their cage. I quickly shut and lock the door and give Coon *the look* as she scrambles back up into her little home.

"Why the fuck do you have rats?" Madix demands, and I don't miss the shudder that passes over him as he asks the question. *What a weirdo*.

"Well, Coon decided she wanted to move under my porch not too long ago, which was just fine by me, but when it started to get cold, I convinced her that the cellar might be a better option."

Madix just looks at me, still waiting for the answer to the rat question.

"I don't know how her and the rats came to be, they seemed to be a package deal when Coon and I met. She wouldn't come in to get warm unless they came, too. So I made them all a little home. Who am I to judge what she loves and how? And let's be honest, women have been loving rats since time began," I say seriously, bumping Madix's shoulder as I walk by and head back up the stairs.

I step into the kitchen and sure enough, breakfast is gone. Every single plate is licked completely clean. There's a trail of slobber stuck to Theo's fork and the glasses of orange juice are knocked over and dripping onto the floor. I look over to the brindle mastiff who's sitting in the exact same spot as before, looking like the epitome of innocence. I'm not even mad. A girl's gotta take advantage where she can in this world.

I crouch down to the dog and scratch under her jaw. "Do the uptight soldiers not feed you enough?" I ask her as she starts panting her bacon breath in my face. "If it were up to that Madix guy, I bet he'd make you eat hypoallergenic food in bleached dog bowls," I say with a shudder. She grunts, in obvious agreement, and I nod. "Mmmhmm. That's what I thought.

"Puddles! Naughty girl," Brant rebukes his dog when he sees the mess she's made. Puddles just licks her lips and lays down for a nap.

Coon comes up the stairs right behind the guys, my white-knitted scarf wrapped securely around her.

"That thing is like a giant rat with freaky as fuck claws and razor teeth," Theo says, watching Coon warily.

I look down at Coon as she starts climbing up the fridge using the vertical handle. "I know, isn't she adorable?" I beam.

"It's not sanitary to keep her inside," Madix informs me.

"She's a pet," I defend. "And she happens to love bubble baths. Also, she's a marsupial, not a rodent," I explain. "Good grief, did you three even go to school?" I ask seriously.

Brant blinks at me blankly, Theo looks like he's amused

again, and Madix opens and shuts his mouth several times before just giving up completely.

The air suddenly cracks with thunder, and Brant flinches and reaches for the holstered M9 at his waist. Theo grabs hold of Brant's shoulder, squeezing it lightly, his gaze intense on his friend's face which has paled significantly.

"Just thunder," I hear Madix mutter to him.

Brant's throat works as he breathes in and nods slowly. "Right," he says, letting go of the gun with an unsteady hand.

The dog has sidled right up against him and starts pushing at his palm with her nose. When he stops shaking enough to pet her head, she licks him lightly and continues pushing against his legs and stepping on his feet. I'm in awe as I watch the breakfast thief press her weight into him like she's grounding him. My heart breaks a little at the sight, and I know I've just witnessed something private. Something secret that isn't meant for a stranger's wondering eyes. I pegged them for military the minute they stepped out of their SUV, but it's obvious that they've been through some serious shit.

Dad always taught me to be self-reliant and observant, and as much as we fight and disagree, my survival and observational skills are always something I've been thankful for. I haven't missed the way Theo limps, or the way Madix kept messing with his ear after Jim Bob's alarm went off. And by the looks of it, my guess is that Brant suffers from some serious PTSD and the brindle beauty at his side isn't just a pet, but a service animal that helps him cope with whatever his triggers are. I knew there was some kind of inexplicable bond there. I mean, there would have to be for you to move out to the middle of nowhere with your guy friends, when there's no hanky panky involved. But now it all comes together for me. Their kind of bond only solidifies when you've been through hell together and battled to pull each other from the depths of it.

Respectfully, I pretend not to notice their exchange, and cast my gaze out the kitchen window, watching as the dark gray clouds rush in with a harsh wind that seems to have come from nowhere. At the next clap of lightning, Coon squeals and goes running back down to the cellar.

"Hello, beautiful," I grin at the lightning strikes, and then I rush back down to the cellar to grab the long, metal pieces that I have stashed down there.

I hurry up to the main floor again with the metal poles in my hand, banging against the door frame as I rush through it. The guys step out of my way and stare open-mouthed after me as I run out the back door. The screen door barely claps behind me before I hear the guys rushing after me.

Lightning flashes off in the distance, and I count to four before the thunder growls its hello. The clouds above us give up their hold on the rain, and I'm pelted by it as I rush over to the plot of land I use as a garden. This storm is fast and furious. My favorite kind. I find the perfect isolated spot out back, and jam the base of the first metal piece into the somewhat damp ground, and then get to work constructing the rest of it.

"What the hell are you doing?" Theo shouts over the wind at me, his shirt already soaked from the rain.

I look over at him and the others and gesture to the very obvious metal tree I'm putting up. "Lightning!" I tell him, pointing to the sky. "Gotta get this conductor in the ground."

They stare at me, and Brant rubs his temples. When Theo tries to stop me from installing the next piece, I slap his hand away. "I'm in a hurry. Believe me, this conductor is tried and true. We do not want to be here when the lightning hits it."

Madix swears loudly and then *he's* slapping *my* hands away. He grabs the heavier pieces of the metal tree and starts snapping them into place using the hooks and built-in fasteners. He doesn't even have to jump up to do the last piece, because he's that tall. I rub the water away from my face and look on, adequately impressed as his soaking-wet shirt shows off every muscle that bulges and stiffens as he puts together one of my many masterpieces.

He snaps the last piece into place like he's been putting the metal contraption together his whole life, and fastens it on the top. All four of us look at the impressive metal tree, nicely pointed and isolated for the perfect lightning attraction. And speaking of attraction...wet GI Joes are just as appealing as dry ones, no doubt about that.

"Nicely done," I tell him with an approving nod as I turn back toward the house.

As soon as I step through the back door and out of the rain, I see Brant's dog standing at attention in the kitchen with a suspicious puddle on the hardwood floor directly underneath her.

"Puddles," Brant says with exasperation as he steps into the kitchen and spots the same thing. He winces and looks at me. "Sorry. She hates thunderstorms."

"Yep," Theo says, coming inside and running a hand through his brown hair, getting water all over the rug. I'm not the least bit bothered. The whole sopping wet and slicked back look is really working for him. "It's why he named her Puddles. As soon as she hears thunder, she freezes up and lets loose a piss storm."

Madix comes in last, unlacing his muddy boots and setting them by the door. Dude really is a neat freak. "What the fuck was that?" he asks.

His level of anger takes me aback. "What?"

He points out the window as he slams the door shut.

"*That.* Why the hell did you run out *toward* the storm to install a fucking metal conductor?"

Geez Louise, he's wound up tight. I'd like to unwind him. Using his penis. I wonder how many twists it would take...

"Well?" Madix's furious tone rips me from my dirty thoughts.

"Oh. Well, lightning is an amazing fertilizer. Obviously," I tell him as I start to strip off the soaked flannel that's suctioned to me.

"That was stupid and fucking dangerous," he growls. "Your father sending us out here to get you makes a hell of a lot more sense now," he goes on. It sounds like he's gearing up for a really long lecture, so I stay quiet and continue taking off the rest of my wet clothes. I don't want to track even more water into the house. "You can't be trusted to ride this virus out on your own. You're hazardous to your own safety," he says, and then he goes on about how I probably have an abnormally good immune system based on my living conditions, because a normal person would probably have died from salmonella or something by now.

I snort as I pop open the button of my jeans and yank off the wet denim down my hips and thighs. As soon as I kick them off, Madix stops speaking mid-word, like he's just now noticed that I'm undressing. I yank the shirt off over my head next and then stand there, perfectly happy for them to look their fill as I stand in my underwear. Brant quickly looks away, which is adorable. Theo peruses me unashamedly, while Madix's angry gaze turns aggressively hungry.

I'm not the sort of girl to be embarrassed by my body, or cower away from the gaze of a man, I find their different reactions to my current state of undress amusing. Madix looks like he's trying hard to hang onto his irritation so he can still be pissed at me, but he also wants to fuck me. He

72

has that hungry alpha asshole look down pat. Speaking of down... I look down at their crotches and see three hardening lengths tenting their black cargos. I nod with satisfaction. "Very impressive," I admit.

It takes several long seconds, but Brant finally clears his throat and moves to the pile of wood stacked next to my fireplace. The goosebumps on my skin confirm the drop in temperature in the house, and I watch for a minute as Brant stacks the logs and adds kindling before lighting it all up.

"I'm gonna shower. You boys feel free to join me," I tell them with a wink before walking my panty-clad ass down the hall. I think I hear one of them groan, and I smile as a clap of thunder rumbles through the house, drowning out the noise. My time on the mountain just got way more exciting.

7

BRANT

Theo slaps a hand over his face while Madix just stares after Remi, shaking his head. Well, she sure as hell isn't what any of us thought she was going to be. The *she* part was quite the surprise, plus the odd and quirky part that is proving to keep us on our toes, and then there's the hot as fuck part, which is the surprise we seem to be struggling with the most. No disrespect to Sheriff April, but his daughter is downright fuckable. If only she weren't so crazy.

The distinct sound of a shower turning on reaches us in the living room, but it soon blends in with the sound of the rain falling furiously outside. Theo and Madix turn to me and we all stare at one another, completely bewildered. Puddles sits down at my feet and gives a squeaky doggy yawn, like none of this is a big deal. I give her a look that lets her know I haven't forgotten about her traitorous ways.

"So, what the fuck do we do now?" Madix asks, always the one to need a solid plan he can then execute flawlessly.

From the looks of things so far, this Remi chick is going to do all she can to mess up any plans we may have for the simple recovery and return mission we thought this was going to be. Thunder pounds through the house, and my fingers twitch at my side. Puddles presses into me and I take deep breaths, reminding myself it's a storm—not bombs, not gunfire, not a threat.

"You think she'll actually go with us?" Theo asks. "Because that's not the impression I got. I don't know what went down with her and the sheriff, but she seems intent on staying out here, regardless of what's happening with the rest of the country."

"She might be fine out here. She's pretty isolated, already off the grid, and clearly self-sufficient," I offer, and Theo nods his agreement.

"So what, we just leave her here?" Madix asks, a touch of incredulity to his tone.

"What happened to, *if he wants to stay out here exposed and at risk, then he's a dumbass, and good riddance?*" I ask, repeating his earlier words in the car verbatim.

Madix gives me an unamused look. "Well for starters, he's a she, and yeah, she might be okay for now, but for the long-run, she's going to run into a ton of issues out here alone. Plus, she's downright foolish. I mean, who the fuck purposely plants conductors into their backyard so lightning will hit it?" he asks, tossing his hands up.

At that moment, Remi's voice fills the house and we all grow quiet. It takes me a couple of seconds to place it, but as soon as she starts to rap Jay-Z's verse, I recognize that she's singing and rapping *No Church in The Wild*. I let out a humorous snort, and Madix gestures in the direction she walked off in like her impromptu performance is further proof that she can't be left out here on her own.

Theo grins. "I like her."

Madix rolls his dark eyes. "You would."

Theo levels him with a look. "Like you don't? Don't even try to pretend otherwise. That would just be embarrassing."

Madix flips him off and then opens the front door. "I'll get our shit. We can't go anywhere with this storm, and I don't want to have to pay that guy for a new car because Pud peed all over this one," he says, his point punctuating when another crack of thunder shakes the walls. "We'll have to stay here until this clears up."

He hurries outside and runs to the truck, returning seconds later with our bags. He tosses our duffles at our feet, and all three of us quickly strip out of our soaking wet clothing, while Remi continues to serenade us from the shower. Madix is mumbling something about opossums while I yank on a pair of sweatpants and a dry shirt.

All three of us leave our wet clothes and boots to dry by the fire. "We'll convince her to leave as soon as the storm ends," Theo says confidently.

I nod, watching while Madix starts picking up the random items around the living room. The stack of paperbacks on the coffee table get put on the bookshelf, the dirty rug gets rolled up and brought to the kitchen sink to soak, and he snaps at me to clean up Puddles's...puddle of piss on the floor.

Theo walks over to the entertainment table where an old, massive television sits. "She has VHS. Not even a DVD player," he muses.

I finish cleaning up Puddles's thunderstorm gift, and by the time I'm done, Madix is already doing his OCD clean-up shit in the kitchen. I can see him scrubbing the sink with one hand while simultaneously wiping the birdseed piles on the counter into the trash can. He even found yellow rubber gloves to wear while he cleans. The wrists have purple flowers on them. They go nicely with his scowl. If I

76

ever wished my phone worked, it's right now. This would be the best picture ever.

I turn around and see Remi walking out from the hallway, wrapped in just a white towel. Scratch that. *This* would be the best picture ever.

The old-school values my mother taught me about chivalry and how to treat a woman rear up and demand I look away from Remi when she re-wraps her towel and walks toward what I assume is her bedroom. But her long legs and the strands of water-darkened blonde hair that are plastered to her naked shoulder are like a siren song to my sex-deprived mind. As if she can feel my eyes on her, Remi looks back, her gaze immediately locking onto mine. A satisfied smirk crawls over her face, and she nods her head in the direction of her room before disappearing through the doorway.

Does that mean what I think it meant? I stand for a second and replay the moment in my head, trying to interpret what else it could have meant. I take a step towards the door Remi just disappeared through, but another rumble of thunder and Madix's commanding voice keeps me from advancing any further.

"Dude, Puddles just made another puddle, " he announces all pissy, and my thoughts immediately switch from visions of a naked Remi underneath me on her bed, to my poor dog who's currently owning her namesake.

I grab some paper towels and whatever cleaner Madix hands me, and clean up Puddles's second mess while talking to her and trying to soothe her with my calm tone. I wipe up the second application of cleaner and look up just in time to see Remi decked out in what looks like the rubber overalls that fisherman wear. She reaches for a jacket and moves toward the front door.

"Where are you going?" I ask.

"I heard pecking on my roof, so I'm pretty sure my goose has led the chickens astray again. They need roof rescuing from this storm," she says with a frown. "Too bad it's *after* my shower. I was all warm and toasty."

Theo's eyebrows scrunch with confusion and I find my face is doing the same. "Wait...What?"

Remi rolls her eyes at both of us like we're the ones being dense. "I need to go up on the roof," she announces slowly, before moving to go outside.

Before I know it, I'm at her side and grabbing her hand away from the door. "You can't go up on the roof in a thunderstorm. Are you *trying* to get hit by lightning? I mean, maybe it's good for the soil and shit, but I'm pretty sure our bodies don't fare so well."

"Oh, I've been hit by lightning before," she tells me seriously. "It wasn't so bad."

I...honestly don't know what to say to that.

She yanks open the door, and I'm cursing as I pull on my wet boots and coat, before rushing out after her. The rain is coming down in sheets that feel more like ice slicing against my skin. Seriously, for March, the weather seems like it's still trying to hold onto winter instead of welcoming spring.

I have to shield my eyes with my hand in order to see where Remi went. It's raining so hard that it looks like it's coming from above as well as below. Good thing her foundation is raised a bit, because this land seems like a real flood hazard.

I curse when I catch her shadowed figure on the side of the house where she's placing a fucking *metal* ladder against the siding and climbing up.

"Is this chick fucking for real?" I mutter to myself.

I look back at the house and see Theo grinning at me from the window. Asshole waves to me as he sips on a cup of steaming coffee and stays nice and dry in his warm flannel. I want to punch him. I stuff my glasses in my pocket, since I won't be able to see a damn thing with them on in the rain. They're just for distance, anyway.

I flip off Theo and then rush to follow Remi up the ladder. It's slippery as hell, and of course, as soon as I start going up, a flash of lightning cracks down, making me nearly jump out of my skin. I swear to God, if I get hit by lightning because I'm chasing this crazy girl up a metal ladder during a thunderstorm to help her catch her chickens...I'm going to win an *Idiot of the Year award.*

When thunder booms, I practically launch myself up the last two rungs and land hard on the roof, where I can see Remi running around *way too fast*, trying to catch chickens who are drenched and doing their best not to get caught. Remi keeps slipping, despite her rubber rain boots, and my heart nearly stops when I think she's about to topple right off the edge of the roof. She barely catches herself with her feet planted against the rain gutter, and then she laughs. She *laughs!*

I hurry over to her and help her to her feet, and despite the craziness, I'm caught up for a moment in her bright smile. Even soaking wet, with raindrops stuck to her face and dripping into her mouth, she looks gorgeous. Her wide, white smile makes her entire face light up, competing with the gloomy storm.

It's like my body takes over, because even after I've helped her up, I can't seem to let her go for a moment. I even step closer than my mother would consider polite, keeping hold of her arms as I look down at her. Her blonde hair is plastered against her forehead, and I can't help myself—I brush it back, away from her face, catching sight of the piercings she has all the way from her helix to her lobe. It looks sexy as fuck.

79

When she licks the rain from her lips, I find my head dipping down, and her blue eyes grow hooded. I shouldn't kiss her. I really shouldn't. But I *really* fucking want to, and when her breath quickens and her eyes dart down to my lips, I know she's game.

I lean down, but don't completely close the distance, doing that whole sixty-forty thing that Will Smith taught dudes in Hitch. She moves in, following the Hitch rules perfectly, but just when I'm certain I'm about to feel her lips on mine, she stops and I hear, "Don't move. Mother Clucker is right behind you. I'll snatch her up, and you get Cluck Norris who is currently pecking my leg, 'kay?"

It takes *way* too long for me to grasp what she just said, but the lust starts to clear enough for me to realize what she just asked me to do. I nod like the sex-addled dope I am. I don't know that she sees my reply though, because she's already moving to snatch up two of the errant roof chickens.

I lean down and snag a plump little brown one and get the shit pecked out of my hand for my efforts. I can't remember what this one was called, but as far as I'm concerned, it's now going to be called fried chicken.

I grapple its neck so that it can't keep pecking me or trying to escape, holding it at arm's length. I turn to get directions from Remi about what the hell I should do with it now, and see her chuck a chicken over the side of the roof. For some reason, it makes me panic. I mean, the roof is pretty high up, and I don't even know if chickens can fly.

I catch myself snuggling the chicken against my chest and watch as Remi throws two more off the roof. When she's gotten them all, she turns to me, hands out for my chicken, but I hesitate, and her lips twitch in amusement. Suddenly, a gust of wind decides right then that we need more complications than we already have, and slams against us. Adrenaline spikes through me as Remi teeters on the edge.

Fuck. *Sorry chicken!*

I chuck the brown little pecker over the side and then grab hold of Remi, stealing her away from the edge with my arms wound tightly around her. I fall with my back against the roof, Remi still in my arms, and more wind tries to upend us. It takes a few seconds before I can get breath back into my lungs, but I can feel Remi's laughter vibrate against my chest, even though the wind and pelting rain carries the sound away from me.

She leans down, putting her mouth close to my ear. "You know, there are much better places to make your move," she laughs into my ear, and my brain freezes when she nips at my earlobe and then sucks at the spot where it connects to my neck.

Holy shit.

Is she doing sixty-forty? I don't know, and I can't do math right now, because she's wet and pressed against me and her mouth is still on my skin. Instead of being the polite boy my mother raised, I find my hands moving down to her ass and squeezing. The movement makes an obnoxious squeaking sound because of the rain and the fact that she's wearing damn rubber overalls that should in no way look hot, but somehow do.

Like she's rewarding me for groping her, her hot tongue darts out and she licks her way from my neck to my jawline. I go as hard and as erect as the damn metal lightning rod she put into the ground. She feels me grow beneath her, and the little minx shifts her pelvis and grinds against me, making me moan.

I'm not sure who moves their head first, but we're suddenly making out, right there on the very uncomfortable roof, where I'm fairly certain I'm lying on chicken shit, while rain pours on us and lightning threatens to fry us as much as I threatened to fry the chicken.

I've been in exactly two relationships, both of which never made it past the sixth month mark. But neither of those women ever kissed me the way Remi is kissing me now. Her tongue digs into my mouth like she's trying to find an orgasm inside. Unfortunately, I don't keep them in there, but I really wish I did.

I can't help myself when she grinds against me again, and I grab her hips and thrust against her roughly. She lets out a little pleased mewl, which makes my cock even harder.

"Hey asshole! Did you get struck by lightning and lose the girl?" I suddenly hear Theo's voice shouting.

Our mouths rip apart, and we stare at each other for a moment, both of us panting slightly with swollen lips and tingling tongues.

"Dude! Brant! Fucking answer me!"

"We're coming!" I holler back.

Remi gives an irritated snort. "Neither of us are coming yet," she corrects, making me laugh.

I want to tell her I'm perfectly happy to stay up here and spend as long as she wants to taste and touch, but I don't say anything as she pushes off of me and then offers me her hand. She helps me up, and it seems like as soon as I'm on my feet again, reality slams back into me. What am I doing? We're supposed to be bringing her back to her dad, a man I like and respect, because the world as we know it is going to shit and people are dying. I'm supposed to be helping her, not feeling her up or following her lead into another crazy-ass situation.

I pull my hand away from hers and wipe the rain from my face. I don't risk looking at her and getting sucked back into whatever that was that had us ready to fuck each other on the roof in the middle of a thunderstorm.

Avoiding her eyes, I walk over to the ledge and help her step down onto the ladder. I follow her down, luckily without falling, and I watch as the dumbass chickens run to a small wooden coop on the side of the house that I'd previously overlooked.

When we get inside, Madix scowls at us from the kitchen. He's still wearing the yellow gloves with the purple flower bracelets on them and I try not to smile. "I put a towel down," he says, gesturing to our feet, where, there is indeed a towel put down for us. "Don't trail water and mud all over the fucking place."

I look at Remi, wondering if she'll be offended that he's practically taking over her house and giving her rules, but she's grinning at him like she finds his annoying OCD ways charming. I untie my boots and take them off, leaving them by the door while Madix watches us like an anal-retentive hawk. Remi continues to smile at him as she shucks off her jacket and very slowly and methodically slips one strap of her rubber overalls off and then the other.

Her eyes never leave Madix's attentive stare as she pushes the overalls down her hips, letting them fall to the ground. Remi steps out of them, not a care in the world or a single blush that crosses her features, as she stands there in only her underwear and a very tight gray tank-top. Now we've seen her twice, and this time, I don't look away. Her nipples are hard and pointed, probably from the cold, but there's this little piece of me that wants to think it's because of what we were doing on the roof.

With that thought, I shove the lust back down, refusing to look at it, and head off toward the bathroom. I know I'm leaving drops of water in my path, but Madix can fuck off. I need a shower. A very, very cold shower that will hopefully help me get my shit together. Remi is just a woman. I can wrangle in the needs of my dick. My dick is not in charge.

At least, that's what I tell myself as I stomp into the bathroom and turn to shut the door, just in time to see Remi walk into her room and bend over to pick something up. I get a view of her perfect ass, and I bite back a groan as I slam the door shut. *Fuck*. I hope the shower water will reach subzero temperatures, because that's what it's going to take to combat this hard-on.

8

THEO

Brant stays in the shower for a ridiculously long time. He's probably jerking off. I keep having to think about off-the-wall trivia to keep my own dick from growing. I've known Remington April for exactly zero four hundred hours, and I've already seen her in her underwear. Twice. Not that I'm complaining.

She has a plump ass, hips you can grab, and a heavy set of tits over a flat stomach. I'd love to get my hands on her, but we're here for a reason, and it sure as shit isn't to seduce Sheriff April's daughter. I've had enough flak from fathers getting pissed when I pluck their daughters' daisies. The last thing I need is to piss off the sheriff. He's one of the only men besides Madix and Brant that I actually like and seems to not hate me. I prefer to keep it that way and not ruin it with a quick fuck. Besides, chicks always get weird when they see my missing leg, and I don't want to ruin the fantasy.

I'm drinking the rest of the instant coffee I brought in from the car and made, when Remi comes out of her bedroom. She's braided her wet hair and is wearing leggings and a rock band t-shirt with a pair of fuzzy purple socks that have peacocks all over them.

I bite my lip, trying not to smile at her outfit choice, and watch as she goes over to the VHS movies inside the cabinet. "Wanna watch something? Power might go out, since I run mostly on solar, but I have a back-up generator with plenty of juice in it."

I shake my head. "We should conserve as much energy as possible," I warn her. "I don't want to scare you, but who knows how long the power will stay on? Cell phones are already down."

She waves a dismissive hand. "Now you're just being dramatic."

I frown. "Remi, I'm afraid you're not understanding the severity of this situation. The world—"

"Okay, okay," she says, cutting me off. "While I'm in this getaway cabin, I don't complicate my life with the outside world. It's my number one rule. Why do you think I'm even out here?" she asks with exasperation. "I do it to get away from the world. That means no phone, no internet, no people, or distractions. Just me and my animals, getting centered and calm." Before I can argue and get her to understand exactly how serious shit is, she snaps her fingers with an idea. "Oh! I'll get my old laptop. I have a few old movies saved on that."

She disappears into her bedroom and I scrub a hand down my face. Madix comes in holding a toilet brush in one hand and a bucket of strong ass smelling cleaner in the other. He even has a cooking apron on. This time, I don't try to stave off the smile that wants to take over my face. "Dude. You look ridiculous," I tell him.

"Fuck off," he says as he stalks to the bathroom and pounds on the door. "Get the hell out!" he hollers to Brant. "I need to clean."

I don't hear Brant's reply, but a minute later, he comes out, rolling his eyes at Madix as he passes. Brant collapses onto one end of the overstuffed sofa and Puddles immediately moves from where she was snoozing on the rug to lay at his feet. I sit on the opposite end of the couch and finish off the rest of the weak coffee in my mug. I miss the shit we used to get on our tours in Iraq. That black gold could keep you up for days if you brewed it right.

Remi comes practically skipping out of her room with her laptop in hand, and I try to focus on that instead of her bouncing tits. Never thought I'd be the one hoping a chick would put her bra on.

Instead of sitting on the armchair like I thought she would, she plops down right between Brant and me. I try not to think about the soft skin of her arm as it brushes against mine. I really need to get laid if this is the kind of shit that I'm thinking. Clearly, my sex-starved state is now officially an issue, since I can't seem to focus on anything other than where I'd like to stick my dick.

"So you guys are Endstone transplants, but I'm sure you know the major players in town," she says.

I look at her with confusion, and she gives me a smile that has me spending way too much time thinking about how nice of a mouth she has. Brant definitely had the right idea by going to jack off in the shower.

"You know the mayor and all the guys that hang with my dad and Zeke at the diner every night?" When we nod, she opens her laptop screen with a smirk. "You probably think they're all respectable, but I've got all the dirt right here," she pats the laptop lovingly, and her sweet smile grows mischievous. "Allow me to introduce you to April's Fools," she announces dramatically, and then presses play on whatever she has queued up on her computer.

A video starts playing, and I immediately recognize a younger version of Zeke and Sheriff April. The image is slightly grainy as it zooms in, but I see Zeke and the sheriff coming out of the Zeke's house, which is easily discernible by the lawn gnomes he has all over his yard. Those damn gnomes are still there to this day, just more weathered looking.

The video moves as the men walk off the porch and head into the camera's direction, but I can see from the leaves around the lens that the person taking the video is hiding in Zeke's hedges. When Zeke gets to the driveway, he and the sheriff stop short, their mouths agape as they stare at what's in front of them. I hear Zeke's voice yell, "What...where is my truck? And where the hell did this horse come from?"

Giggling erupts from the video, and the camera is whipped around to show a younger Remington with her hand over her mouth as she laughs hysterically. "He tried to beat me at this year's April Fools pranks," she whispers into the camera. "He wrapped the entire exterior of my house with plastic wrap." She shakes her head in mock pity. "Such an amatuer. I did that trick when I was twelve."

She swings the camera back to face them. Zeke is cursing up a storm and then points at Sheriff April's face. "This is your fault. Your girl's running rampant again."

The sheriff looks like he's trying really hard not to laugh as he settles his hands over his hips. "You do it every year, too."

Zeke doesn't seem to have an argument against that, so he curses again all while glaring at the white and gray dappled horse standing in his driveway, munching on a barrel of hay. "You'll need to give me a lift to the range," he tells Sheriff April.

"I'd be happy to, but I'll need you to help me clear my car of ping pong balls first," he tells Zeke casually, like it's some kind of regular occurrence.

Zeke lets off another string of swear words and Sheriff

April just shrugs and starts walking in the direction of his house which is about a mile down the road. I guess even back in the day, he's always had his morning walk, shared coffee and donuts at Zeke's house, and then gone to the shooting range. These people sure do like their routines.

"April! Get back here and call your daughter! Make her bring me my car back!" Zeke demands.

"No can do," the sheriff calls over his shoulder. "She replaced my phone and my police radio with a toy walkie talkie and a talking banana. Can't help ya."

Zeke huffs out a frustrated breath. "How the hell am I supposed to get to the range then, April?"

This time, the sheriff can't hold back his laughter. "I guess you'd better hop on Hi-Ho Silver there and get to galloping."

Video Remi and the Remi sitting next to me snort in unison as Zeke approaches the horse warily, still cursing up a storm. I can only catch snippets of it here and there, but every time he swears at Remi, she giggles beside the camera.

Zeke manages to heft his beefy foot up into the stirrup and hoist himself up into the saddle, but Remi nearly loses it and gives herself away when he overshoots his mount and almost goes ass over head to the ground on the other side.

Brant leans closer to the screen. "Is there something painted on the horse's side?"

Remi snorts again. "Yep. It's says, 'Happy April's Fools Day, Neigh-bor.'"

All three of us bust up laughing.

"He didn't notice it was there until he was halfway to town and people kept honking and neighing at him. Or at least, that's how he tells it," she laughs, but there's a hint of melancholy to the sound of it.

"You seemed like you had a good childhood, so what happened?" I ask, not able to stave off my curiosity.

Sheriff said they hadn't talked in a while, and that seems out of character for the doting father and rambunctious daughter that I just saw in the video. You can tell that Remington hangs the moon in Sheriff April's eyes. Remi leans back and huffs out an exhale.

"That's a long, boring story. I just couldn't handle living in that town anymore, and my dad hated me for leaving it. To him, I should've stayed inside Endstone's borders and lived next door to him for the rest of his life. But that town…" she trails off, shaking her head. "I couldn't do it. I needed to live and experience life outside of Endstone."

Brant scratches Puddles's ears when she sets her big block head in his lap. Remi reaches over and rubs at her muzzle, and I don't miss the slight tension that creeps into Brant's shoulders. If I weren't so used to keeping an eye out for it, I probably wouldn't have noticed, but I cock a brow, immediately wondering what that's all about.

Brant clears his throat and drops his hand. "Before we moved there, I wasn't sure how we'd fit in, but we actually like Endstone and how they do things there. It's tight-knit and welcoming, which isn't a bad combo to have to adapt to," he confesses. "Sure, you don't have the anonymity like you would pretty much anywhere else, but it grows on you. Granted, we've only lived there for about ten weeks, but so far, so good."

Remi closes her laptop and leans back. "Of course you three would like it," she says with a slight roll of her eyes. Then she turns to study the two of us. "Anyway, let's talk about *you*. If you guys don't diddle each other's pickles— which I would be totally cool with by the way, especially if you let me watch—then how did you meet and decide to move to a small town like Endstone?"

"Madix and I met at Fort Benning and then were assigned to the same squad. We met Theo on our second deployment when he was reassigned after we lost our Radio Operator. We were buddies on our squad, and then on our last deployment, we were three of the seven that came back," Brant's voice trails off, and it grows quiet in the living room.

Remi doesn't press for information, but she also doesn't let us off the hook. She simply sits quietly, stroking Puddles's head and giving us time to decide what we want to share.

"We were too close to an IED when it went off. I sustained a head injury which affected my vision," Brant offers, and taps on his glasses. "I also have flashbacks and trouble knowing where I am sometimes, but that's what she helps me with." Brant pats Puddles's head again, and she moves to lick his hand.

I wait for the *I'm sorry,* or some other form of sympathy to tumble out from between Remi's lips, but she stays quiet. Silence wraps back around us, and we all seem to settle into it.

My heart thumps boldly in my chest. Brant opened things up, even admitting he has PTSD, but none of us like talking about what happened when we lost four of our squad members. Not even me. But it feels weird to just sit here and not say anything. I feel the pressure closing in on me, which is odd, since it's not like we even know this girl. I've never felt compelled to talk about my injury before this.

I find myself opening my mouth to talk about what happened to me, but before I can get a word out, a white ball of fabric falls into my lap from out of nowhere. I jump, startled, and then go still when two black, beady eyes stare back at me.

"Fuck," I exhale, looking at the opossum that's still wrapped in Remi's scarf and looking at me like she's trying to decide if she wants to bite my nose off or snuggle.

I freeze, my hands hovering over her in alarm.

"What...what do I do?" I ask, too afraid to look away from the animal in case it decides a side profile of my nose becomes too tempting.

Remi gives me a look. "What do you mean? You just pet her, silly," she says, reaching over to grab my hand. My eyes snap to the contact, and I watch with tunnel vision as Remi's smaller fingers wrap around mine. She pulls my hand down to her weird ass wild pet and helps me go through the motions of petting Cocoon through her...scarf cocoon.

Her beady black eyes continue to watch me as Remi guides my hand awkwardly down her side. But I'm not focused on the pink-nosed, triangle face of the opossum. Instead, I'm honed in on where Remi is touching me. I'm oddly content with the contact, even though I wouldn't admit it out loud. "See? Isn't that better?" she asks.

I nod, and she beams a smile at me before releasing my hand, much to my disappointment. When she gets up to put her laptop away in her room, I glance up and see Brant's cocked brow and sardonic expression. *Busted.*

I look away and focus on the damn opossum who is now trying to stuff her snout under my t-shirt. I tug it back down over and over, trying to push her away, but after the fifth time, I give up. She ends up crawling under my shirt and settling against my stomach, and her little claws are fucking sharp.

Brant snorts out a laugh. "Nice baby bump," he teases.

"Shut it," I tell him. "How was your cold shower?"

He shrugs. "Necessary. You held her hand. I made out with her on the roof with the damn chickens," he says quietly so that Remi doesn't overhear.

My mouth drops open. "You *kissed* her?"

Brant nods a bit guiltily. "She was sopping wet and so fucking cute. I couldn't help it."

I close my mouth, swallowing my lecture. "Can't argue with that."

"Can't argue with what?"

We both look behind us at Madix standing there, still holding a bucket and wearing the gloves.

"How's the OCD?" I ask like a jackass.

"Eat shit," Madix retorts. "Did you guys get her to agree to leave as soon as the storm passes?"

Brant and I exchange a guilty look. "We're working on it," I say.

Madix levels a look at me, unimpressed. "You haven't even tried yet, have you?"

"Nope."

"Get to fucking work. This is still a retrieval mission. I don't want to disappoint Sheriff April, but I'm also not going to stay here with this crazy chick. I want to get back to our place where all of our supplies are and ride this shit out."

"We know," Brant says, running a hand across his jaw. "But we can't go anywhere until this storm passes."

I nod in agreement. "The dirt road is like a river right now, dude."

"Then we leave as soon as it clears up," Madix says without missing a beat. He starts heading back to the hallway, where he passes Remi as she walks out of her bedroom. "Looks like we'll have to stay the night, so I'll get the sheets and blankets washed," he tells her. "Towels, too."

Remi blinks at his back as he continues to walk. "Wow. You're serious about this cleaning stuff."

"Yep," he replies as he continues forward and then disappears into her bedroom without invitation.

"Sorry," Brant says with embarrassment, while Remi just blinks at the spot where Madix was. "He can be...intense."

Remi turns to face us and walks into the kitchen, and we follow her in. We all stop in the doorway in surprise. The place is gleaming. Literally. I can see my reflection in the stovetop.

"Wow. He's hired," Remi announces, her head swiveling from side to side as she takes it all in. "What's his foreplay game like? Is he this attentive as a lover?" she asks seriously. I'm barely able to hold in my laugh when she turns her expectant eyes on me.

"Jesus, you just come right out with it, don't you?" Brant asks with a snort.

"Yeah, why wouldn't I?" she replies, looking at him like she really doesn't understand the question, but the innocent look morphs into a smirk. "Oh, I forgot, only men like sex and actively pursue orgasms. My bad."

I chuckle, not sure how to respond to that, but I'm turned on by it all the same. Brant seems to be feeling the same way, judging by the sheepish smile he's wearing. He rubs his short mohawk with one hand and discreetly adjusts himself with the other. This chick is trouble, in all the best ways, and I don't think the three of us have even seen the half of it.

9

MADIX

I aggressively attack the smudge on the mirror in the bedroom before I realize that it's a defect of the glass, and it's not coming off no matter how hard I scrub at it. That would irritate me to no end. If I lived here, I'd have to replace the damn thing.

I put my back to the mirror and run my gaze over the bedroom, double checking that I tackled everything in here and it's now up to a standard I can live with. I exhale a sigh of relief, able to relax just a little for the first time since we chased crazy in the shape of the hot blonde through the front door. All in all, the place wasn't as bad my first glance convinced me it was, but now everything is gleaming and sanitized, and I can move around without getting the fucking heebie jeebies. She lets way too many fucking animals inside her house.

My stomach grumbles, and I grab all of my supplies and head back into the kitchen, finally relenting to my hunger pains and conceding that I need food. When I walk into the room, I see Brant and Theo sitting at the table and Remington moving around the kitchen making sandwiches. I put the cleaning supplies away and snap off the rubber gloves. I wash and then dry my hands on the clean towel I just pulled from the dryer an hour ago. I shoot Brant a questioning look, and the answering shrug of his shoulders tells me that they still haven't explained to this chick that we need to leave as soon as the roads are passable.

Of course they haven't taken the bull by the horns, or in this case the hot weird girl by the pink combat boots. Despite what we're here to do, they keep getting distracted, although maybe I'm not one to judge, since I've just spent most of the day cleaning her house.

I clear my throat, knowing that I'll have to do this myself. "Remington, we need to talk about the plan after the storm ends," I announce.

She gives me a passing glance and then goes back to sandwich making.

I soldier on. "You're pretty secluded out here, which is good, but it doesn't change what's happening out there in the rest of the country. People will start leaving the cities and flocking out to less populated areas in an effort to limit their exposure. Who knows how long it will be before a group stumbles on this place," I tell her.

"The same could be true of Endstone," she answers with a shrug.

"Except we have strength in numbers there that you don't have here," I respond.

Remi turns around and stares at me for a beat, her eyes calculating as she takes my measure. "Consider this, soldier —even if everything you say is actually true, things may not get that bad. They could find a vaccine that works and get control over this *Handshake Plague,*" she puts air quotes around the name of the pandemic that's shut down this country, obviously not taking it seriously.

I bite back a growl of frustration and take the sandwich-laden plate she hands me. I follow her to the table as she passes Brant and Theo their massive sandwiches next. I ignore the call of her nice ass when she bends over slightly to pass out the plates before grabbing her own and plopping down in a chair.

"What makes you so certain that the Handshake Plague won't touch you here?" I challenge, placing the same insulting air quotes around the name that she just did.

"What makes you so certain that it will?" she fires back. "How do you know it's not some hoaky bullshit thing that will blow over just like Y2K, the bird flu, and a dozen other things people were convinced would be the end of the world as we know it?"

"None of those things moved this fast, or shut down cell and radio towers practically overnight."

"Well, that seems extreme," she mumbles, before taking a huge bite of her food.

"Fucking hell, what is your deal? We heard the news and the warnings. This is not something you want to mess with or be unprepared for. I heard you say you come up here to live off the grid, so I know this seems far-fetched, but it *is* happening," I say, my jaw ticking. It's all I can do not to shout this at her, but her casual dismissal of reality is fucking annoying.

She bristles slightly at my tone. "There's nothing that can be done right now. This area floods, and until it stops raining, you're stuck here. Now, you three are welcome to stay, but don't be trying to bully me into following wherever you want to lead me. It won't work."

"Remi," Brant says gently, drawing her attention. "We don't mean to be pushy, but what he's saying is true, and this is urgent. Your father doesn't want you out here alone. He's worried about you, and he misses you. He wants you to come back."

At that, Remi looks down at her lap, taking a big bite of

sandwich so she won't have to answer. The three of us watch her as she thinks and chews, waiting for what she'll say. I really don't want to leave her out here, but I meant what I said before. If she refuses to come, we should get the hell out of here and go back home, where we can settle in and ride the plague out for as long as possible.

Based on the town meeting we went to, Endstone seems to have their shit together. I wouldn't be surprised if by the time we get back, a good portion of the town is already barricaded and fortified. They seem to have a solid emergency disaster plan, plus a stock of supplies and doctors needed for other shit. It's smarter to go there, and this chick needs to come to terms with that fact.

After a few long minutes, Remi finally swallows her bite and takes a long drink of water. She wipes the corners of her mouth and looks up at Brant with a sigh. "I'll think about it, okay? That's the best you're going to get out of me at this point."

I take an angry bite of my stacked sandwich, and ignore the burst of flavor that explodes in my mouth. But I don't care if she can make a kickass grinder, this chick isn't just fucking with her own safety. She's putting us at risk too by not taking things seriously, and that doesn't sit well with me.

The sky through the window lights up with purples and pinks as the sun starts to sink out of sight behind the storm clouds. Where some might find it beautiful, all I see is more evidence that we've spent way too much time here. My only comfort is that hopefully the same shitty weather that's keeping us here will also keep anyone else from moving out this way, but we'll still take shifts tonight to make sure.

We all lapse into contemplative silence as we eat, and I know that my presence has fucked with the friendly vibe that Theo and Brant seemed to have already built with this girl, but I don't think that's a bad thing. Maybe we've been out of the Army for too long, but there's too much dick-thinking going on around here and not enough tactical planning. They obviously need me to rein them back in and remind them about what's important.

"So, I asked these ones earlier, but they weren't very forthcoming," Remi says, surprising me when I find her attention fully on me. "Are you as thorough with a pussy as you were with cleaning my house? Because I have to say, I like your attention to detail."

I choke on the bite of food in my mouth and cough as I hit my chest with a closed fist. I don't miss the grin on Brant's face or the way Theo starts laughing. I get my airway clear and chug my glass of water, trying to get the coughing fit under control.

"What?" I croak out.

She motions a hand around the impeccably clean kitchen. "This. You're very good with your hands. You obviously pay attention to every nook and cranny. So, Mr. Ortega, are you that observant with a woman?"

For fuck's sake. Is she for real?

The corner of her lips are tilted up just enough to hint at a smirk, and her blue eyes are sparkling enough that I know this is a challenge. This girl probably pulls this shit all the time on people, seeing whether or not they'll back down. She seems like the type of person to thrive on saying and doing things that are completely off the wall and unexpected.

So instead of snapping at her or shutting the conversation down like a normal person would probably do, I lean back and look at her steadily. "I know how to take care of a woman, Remington April, and it's not the same way I take care of cleaning a fucking sink," I tell her evenly.

Her lip twitches up before she full on beams at me. "Hmm," she purrs, letting her eyes trail down my body.

I've never been so overtly objectified before. Is this how chicks feel when guys do this to them? I try not to fidget under her uncomfortable perusal of my body, refusing to show that she's getting to me. It'll take more than that to crack this nut. The more I don't react to what she's doing, the more excited she seems to be that I'm just going along with this. There's a glimmer in her eyes that makes me think maybe I didn't have the upper hand in this round after all.

Her gaze moves to Brant and Theo, and she openly assesses them next, just like she assessed me. Brazenly, she leans forward on the table to give herself a better view of Theo's lower half.

Puddles saunters into the kitchen, and I blanch when I see that the fucking opossum is riding on top of her. Brant does a double take, his mouth opening in surprise. "Umm…"

Remington sees our expression and turns around in her seat. "Oh!" she exclaims, hopping to her feet. "Isn't that just the cutest thing you've ever seen?" she croons.

She dashes out of the room and comes back in eight seconds flat, carrying an old ass Polaroid camera. She snaps a photo and then goes through the motions of pulling the photo out and fanning it back and forth.

"I didn't know anyone used those things anymore," Theo muses.

Remington shrugs as she continues to shake the film, waiting for the photo to develop. "This old thing was my mom's. I've always held on to it."

She looks at the photo and beams. "See?" she asks, flipping it around to show us. "That's a keeper."

She walks over to the fridge and uses a magnet that looks like a shotgun casing to hang it up. "Perfect," she says proudly.

I notice she has several other photos hung up there as

well, most of which are animals, but I spot one with her and Sheriff April standing side by side, his arm around her shoulders and her beaming at the camera.

I don't know what the deal is between them, and even though I'm curious, I keep my mouth shut. I have shit I don't like to talk about, and the last thing I'm going to do is force someone to air theirs.

Remi moves to a calendar that's hanging up on the fridge and taps it with a slender finger. A frown takes over her face and her eyebrows scrunch down with concern. "My delivery should've been here yesterday," she says, more to herself than to us. "It always comes. Rain or shine, that delivery has never been late," she adds, tilting her head slightly to the left like somehow the new angle she's using to look at things will suddenly provide all of the answers.

I exchange a knowing look with Brant and Theo. "The world is ending, remember?" Theo says sardonically. Brant gives him an exasperated look, but he just shrugs. "What? It is."

Remington rolls her eyes. "Right. There is that."

I shove my plate away and stand up. "Remington, I know it all sounds far-fetched, but I assure you, this is happening. If it takes your delivery person not showing up to convince you, then so be it."

She waves me off dismissively, which instantly irritates me. "There are a million logical explanations for a late delivery. Just because it's never happened before doesn't mean it couldn't happen. It doesn't mean the world is ending."

When she starts to walk away, I stand up suddenly, my arm shooting out to keep her from leaving. Her stomach bounces off my forearm and I cage her in against the edge of the countertop as I lean forward and place my arms on either side of her. She stiffens, but instead of leaning away from me, she does the opposite, and presses into me instead.

"Okay, Remington April, it's time for you to listen up," I begin sternly. "Your father sent us here to retrieve you because there's a virus that's burning through this country like fire, and we're all just kindling. People are dying, and people are scared. That is not a combination you want to run into alone, and I don't care how off the grid you are, someone will eventually find this place. The best thing for all of us to do is to hole up with people we can trust to watch our backs, stock up on supplies, and try to make it through this. Endstone is our best option."

Her full lips part slightly, and I can tell she's preparing to argue. "I don't know what the fuck happened between you and your dad, and honestly, I don't care. Whatever issue you have with Endstone, you need to get over it. People care about each other there and are willing to help each other out, and we know that because we're a part of the community now. As soon as this weather clears, we're getting the hell out of here. We came all this way to get you, because your dad wants you to come back. So are you coming or not?"

Our eyes stay locked on each other, but when her tongue peeks out to lick her lips, my gaze moves down to track the movement. I'm suddenly very aware of her body as it presses into mine. This is probably not the right moment to observe that this wild, outdoorsy girl looks like a fucking wet dream, but I do.

Way too many screws loose, I remind myself. Gorgeous, yes, but her shade of crazy is a bit too bright and outside the lines for someone like me. I'm more of a color-by-numbers kind of guy.

Her eyes dart down my body, and I barely keep myself from leaning into her even more when her glacier-blue eyes settle on my crotch. My dick responds, clearly missing the memo that sleeping with her would be a bad idea.

I study her face more astutely now that I'm so close, and notice she has a grouping of very faint freckles that look like the little dipper on her cheek. I clear my throat a little, the sound helping me to rein in my scattered thoughts. I take a step back and fold my arms over my chest in an effort to re-tap into my talent for intimidation. "Well? Are you coming?"

She shocks the hell out of me when she reaches around me, grabs my ass with a smirk, and says, "With you three? God, I hope so."

She drops her hands from my ass and rubs past me, strutting out of the kitchen before I can pick my fucking jaw up off the floor. She definitely wasn't talking about coming back to Endstone.

All three of us stare after her as she shakes her ass down the hallway, disappearing from view and singing some weird ass song about licking frosting off someone.

"Goddamn," Brant whistles.

I clench my fists, trying to force my blood to collect anywhere other than my dick. "She's going to be a problem," I finally say, turning around to face them.

Theo chuckles and runs a hand down his face. "You think?" he snarks, one eyebrow raised in a look that says, *no shit, Sherlock.*

Fuck. I hate when he's right.

10

BRANT

I pull back the curtains just enough for me to see outside but not enough to give myself away. Crickets sing their nightsong, and I run my eyes over every inch of the surrounding landscape, looking for anything that might be out of place or different from the last time I did this half an hour ago.

It's just past three in the morning, and the only sounds are the occasional noises a house makes as it hunkers down for the night. I hear insects chattering, the walls settling, and Madix's heavy breathing coming from the direction of the couch. Theo took the guest room despite Remi's offer to double up in her bed. The fucker probably would have taken her up on her offer if Madix and I hadn't shut that down right away, and I'm not sure just what the fuck to think about any of that.

Remi and I kissed up on the roof, and it wasn't your average, *Hmm wonder what this would be like* kind of kiss. It was hot as fuck, filled with need and pent-up sexual aggression, and felt right in ways I don't want to examine.

Especially not after we came back in the house and she acted like it never happened. Or at least, she seems to be fine with kissing me but is also game to do the same with my two best friends. I'm not sure what to make of her blatant advances on the three of us. Sometimes it feels like no big deal, simply because that's how she looks at flirting with all of us. Other times, I'm like, *what the fuck?* I licked her first and call dibs.

I shake my head to clear my thoughts and refocus on securing the perimeter. It stopped raining sometime when I was asleep and Madix was on watch, but there's a residual dampness hanging in the air like a threat promising more rain to come.

I walk quietly to the back of the house and peek through the window above the sink in the kitchen. I freeze when I spot a faint orange glow pretty far back in the trees, but not far enough to go undetected. That sure as fuck wasn't there last time I checked. My heart starts to race, pumping adrenaline through my whole system like an alarm that screams, *you better fucking get ready because shit is about to go down.*

I stare at the orange glow, daring it to do something, but it doesn't get any closer or move further away. I risk taking my eyes off of it to go wake the others. I waste no time kicking Madix's feet until he starts sputtering curses and sits up. One look at my face silences him, and he starts pulling on clothes and strapping on weapons while I move to alert Theo.

Theo's prosthetic is leaning in the corner of the guest room, and I almost knock it over in my effort to wake him up. He's awake after my third nudge, and once again, I don't have to say shit. He notices my expression, and he's up and getting ready for action. I know he'll take longer to get mobile, so I signal to him what the issue is and where, and then leave him to it, knowing he'll meet Madix and I at the back of the house as soon as he straps into his leg.

We fall right back into the *ready for action* mindset we've honed over our time in the Rangers, as if the injuries and trauma were just a bad dream that we're waking up from, and we're still active duty and in the middle of a mission. It feels oddly reassuring, but there's a slight feeling of emptiness now that I'm not sure I'll ever get rid of.

I walk quietly back to the kitchen, avoiding the three floorboards that squeak when you walk on them. Madix is there, looking through the parted curtains on the back door, already honed into the orange glow that's exactly where I left it.

"What do you think? Fire, maybe?" he asks, never taking his eyes from the potential threat.

"Yeah, that's what it looks like to me," I confirm, just as Theo walks in to join us.

He takes one look out the window and swears quietly. "I thought Remi said no one comes out here?"

Madix gives an incredulous snort. "Maybe not normally, but the country is fucking dying. It's probably chaos out there. There's nothing *normal* about anything anymore. I'm tempted to wake her up just to say I told you so."

I turn to Theo. "We should wake her up anyway, if there's a threat. Maybe she knows whoever is out there?"

"That chick is more likely to cause a problem than solve one. Let's check it out first. We'll assess the situation before we go inviting more trouble by waking up the hot love child of Ace Ventura and the Tasmanian Devil," Theo says. "Let her sleep, and we'll appraise the situation."

I chuckle lightly, but quickly expel the amusement and replace it with tactical seriousness as Madix says, "Theo and I will cover the front. You cover our back and keep an eye out on the house as we check things out."

Theo and I nod, and then we're pouring out the door and advancing on the distant glow in no time. We're all on high alert, and we walk quickly and quietly through the

106

mud toward the treeline. We slow down a bit once we hit the foliage, picking our way through it carefully in order to stay as silent as possible so we can maintain the element of surprise.

As we slink closer, Madix suddenly stops and gives us the hand motions to split up and surround whoever is out here. Theo and I both nod our understanding, and each of us takes a different path toward what is now confirmed as a campfire.

There's no noise giving away how many people might be leeching warmth from the decent sized fire, and I don't have a clear vantage point yet from my spot in the woods. The rifle in my hands feels more like an extension of my arms, and I weave through the trees until the fire comes into view.

My eyes dart around, but I don't see any tents or even people-filled sleeping bags surrounding the orange and yellow flickering blaze. The smoke is curling into the humid air, and through the smoke, I see a hint of a shadow from someone who's sitting on the other side of the fire. I can't make out their details, but there's a makeshift spit that's triangled above the flames and cooking pungent fish.

I start to move so that I can get a clearer view of the person, when a booming, angry voice shatters the silence, and I respond to it without consciously making the decision to do so. I run towards the fire, weapon-ready, at the same time Madix comes into view from my left.

"Are you fucking kidding me?" he shouts, stomping forward. "What the hell are you doing out here?" Madix demands, rage bleeding out of each word.

Theo and I flank him, and my eyes widen when I can finally make out the shadowed shape and see that it's none other than Remi. No wonder Madix is spitting mad. But how the hell did she sneak out of the house? I never heard or saw a damn thing.

Remi stands and puts her hands on her hips. "What does it look like I'm doing? I'm smoking fish," she replies, pointing to the fish on the spit like Madix is the daft one in this situation, even though it's four in the morning and she's out in the middle of the wet, cold woods wearing nothing but cutoff jean shorts, bright yellow rain boots, and a *Wonder Years* sweatshirt.

Anger gets the better of Madix as he sputters incoherent swear words, punctuated by infuriated hand motions in Remi's direction. There have been a couple of times since coming here that I've thought that Madix's approach to Remi was too intense and overbearing, but now is not one of those times.

What the fuck was she thinking? What if someone else had found her, or one of us got trigger happy when we were checking things out? This shit is not a fucking joke. We've told her what is going on out there multiple times, and we've explained what that means for all of us. Clearly, none of that is sinking in if she's pulling stunts like this. It's reckless and fucking stupid. Even Theo looks pissed off, and he's the most laid back guy I know.

"How the hell did you even get out here?" I ask incredulously.

"Keep pointing yours at me, and I'll point mine at you," she says testily, waving a hand at the shotgun that's leaning against the stump she was sitting on.

All three of us realize that we are indeed still holding our weapons up, and we immediately lower them. "Remington, what are you doing out here?" Madix grits through his teeth.

She huffs and gestures at the fire again. "I told you, I'm—"

Madix cuts her off. "*Why* are you smoking fish at four in

the goddamn morning, without telling us you were coming out here first?" he demands. "It's dangerous."

Instead of bristling like I expect her to do, she rolls her eyes and starts to remove the spit from the fire to balance it against a rock. "I come out here every morning around this time to feed Jim Bob. He likes it when they have a smoky flavor," she explains, nodding toward the fish on the rock. "It's not dangerous, and last time I checked, I don't need your permission to walk around my own property."

"This is different, and you know it," Theo says, completely skating over the fact that she's smoking fish for a fucking wild *bear,* who at this point, could be imaginary for all we know.

"Does nothing we say register? We could have hurt you! We thought you might be someone fleeing the plague," I explain to her.

She throws up her hands in frustration. "I know you guys think the world as we know it is coming to an end, but I don't! You show up out of nowhere from Endstone of all places, which quite frankly, screws up any credibility you might have had."

"What the fuck does that even mean?" Madix snaps back. "Is your phone working? Your radio? Have you been able to reach anyone outside of this little hidey hole of yours?"

Madix doesn't give Remington a chance to answer as he hammers her with one question after another. He steps closer to her with each point he makes, getting closer with every fact that he spews in her direction. Remi is breathing hard and her cheeks flush with anger, but she doesn't step back or concede even a centimeter as Madix's chest presses against hers, invading her personal space and ramping up the tension.

"I won't allow your denial and your stupid fucking antics

to put me and them in harm's—" Madix's rant cuts off abruptly when out of nowhere, she lifts up on her tiptoes and kisses him. It's so outlandish and such a completely ridiculous response to what was going on, that we all seem to fall into stunned inaction. Well, everyone except Remi, that is.

Her mouth moves against Madix's frozen, unmoving frown, and I watch as her tongue snakes out and flicks at his top lip. Remi presses into him, her movement sensual, the exact opposite of his aggressive advance, and I feel the ghost of her breasts when they had pushed against my chest on the roof when I was the one tasting her.

Just as suddenly as this random kiss started, it stops. Madix seems to come to his senses and pushes Remi away from him. He looks pissed and confused, but there is no mistaking the heat he's trying to hide under the annoyed mask he just pulled into place.

"What the fuck are you doing?" Madix demands again, but there's a quiver to his voice now.

I know how he feels. Remi has a talent for leaving a person unsettled in the best, yet worst, possible way. I expect Remi to look hurt or have some kind of reaction to being pushed away and rejected by Madix, but she just wears a half-tilted smirk. There's a mischievous gleam in her eyes that I'm starting to realize is a signature look she gets when she's dancing outside the circle of normal.

I don't know what to think about any of this. It's clear we're all attracted to her, regardless of the off-the-wall shit she pulls. I'm sure if asked right now, Madix would refute it, but there's no denying the tent in his cargo pants, no matter what words fly out of his mouth.

True to form, Madix points in her face, his expression full of fury that burns hotter than the flames at my back. "Get your ass back to the cabin."

"Oooh, are you giving me an order, soldier?" Remi quips, suddenly standing at mock attention.

Madix's eyes narrow at her in a dangerous way that I know not to fuck with. Theo tenses beside them, clearly in the same *what the fuck do I do* boat that I'm paddling around in uselessly.

"Yeah, I am," Madix tells her, not backing down.

"I should tell you," she says, her voice barely audible over the crackling flames. "I only follow orders when I'm naked."

I swallow hard at her response, all of us affected by the visual that her words create. I find myself moving closer, like my cock is a leash that's pulling me along. I'm half-wishing she'll turn to me and kiss me next, just so I can taste her again, and half-wishing that she'll start up again with Madix or Theo, just so I can have the perfect view of her sexy body getting all worked up.

I shake away that lusty thought, not sure how to analyze it. We've never shared a girl before, and that odd desire would've never found purchase in my mind before this, so just what the fuck is happening now? It's like she's this weird magnet and we're all helpless pieces of iron, unable to stop ourselves from drawing closer to her. I don't miss the way Madix's breath gets faster, or the fact that he stays quiet, like he can't form a coherent response.

Suddenly, an odd huff of sound I can't immediately identify fills the trees around us, and a prickle of awareness flashes through me. I'm not left guessing for long what the source of the sound is, because a very large, very wild black bear comes sauntering toward us from the trees.

"Holy shit," Theo breathes.

The bear ambles into the small clearing that we're standing in, not at all bothered by the fire that I'd have guessed would be a deterrent for a wild animal. I feel like a dumbass when Remi turns to give the animal a wide smile, and the pieces fall into place for me.

"Morning, Jim Bob," she coos, and the rest of us freeze, not sure just what the fuck to do.

I consider playing a solid game of *if I can't see you, you can't see me,* but decide taking my eyes off the wild creature may not be smart either. I do a quick run through of anything and everything I might have ever heard about what to do in the event of a bear attack, which doesn't take long, because I realize I know fuck-all.

Are you supposed to play dead, not play dead, punch 'em in the nose? Run in a zigzag motion? No, that last one is for running away from a gunman, but maybe it could be used for a bear, too?

Yup, I'm fucked.

The bear makes quick work of the cooling fish on the rock, and then goes right for a small pile of them stacked in a wicker basket next to where Remi was sitting. The bear eats that stash a little slower, and Madix, Theo, and I watch, each of us stiff with tension and not sure what to do. When it has devoured all of the fish in that pile too, the bear gives another huff, swinging its huge head in our direction, and Remi raises her hands in response.

"I know, these guys interrupted me, so I didn't get them seasoned the way that you like, but I don't appreciate that tone," she says, her hands dropping to her hips, as she chastises a fucking bear.

As if this situation isn't piss-pants-terrifying enough, the bear gives a weird kind of roar, making even Madix jump, and then proceeds to stand up on its hind legs. Theo takes a step towards Remi, but she holds up a hand and gives him a look that demands he doesn't take one more step.

To our horror, Remi casually walks over to the disgruntled bear and then she...fucking *bear hugs it.* Her tiny arms dig into its espresso-colored fur, as her body and cheek press up against its belly. I swear to God, the bear looks over at me with a smug look on its furry fucking face.

Each of us hold our breath, trying to figure out what the hell we can do if this wild animal suddenly decides to take out all of us. Can we shoot it with Remi still in its grasp? I don't dare raise my gun, just in case it feels threatened by the movement and hurts her.

Remi's arm tightens for a quick second, and then she lets go and steps back a few feet. The bear drops back down to all fours, and I feel the vibration of it when its mass connects with the ground. It licks its fishy chops and sniffs around, making sure it got all the fish.

"Don't be greedy," Remi chuckles. "That's all you get."

Without a fucking care in the world, or any acknowledgement of the trauma it just inflicted, the bear turns and saunters back into the trees and just like that, disappears into the star-cloaked early morning.

Remi smiles contentedly, her eyes following the bear until it's swallowed up by the dark, and I suddenly realize I can hear my fucking pulse throbbing throughout my whole body. I'm swimming in adrenaline, and I run a shaky hand down my face in an effort to show my brain that we're okay and it can stop pumping me full of *fight or flight* response.

"What the fuck?" Theo pants out, his eyes still locked on the spot where the bear just disappeared.

"Jim Bob," she shrugs, as if somehow that explains it all. She seems to just now recognize the looks of shock that we're all wearing. "Don't worry guys, he seemed to like you. Even though you *did* fuck with his breakfast, which even Jim Bob knows is the most important meal of the day."

I release a mortifying snort, which normally, I would spend a moment being self-conscious about, but her explanation is just so fucking insane, that I have no choice but to laugh. A frantic, slap-happy, girly giggle that I have no control over pours out of me, and the next thing I know, I'm bent over at the waist, laughing my ass off. Whatever kind of mental breakdown I'm having must be fucking contagious, because it doesn't seem to take long for Madix and Theo to drop into hysterics too.

"You guys are so weird," Remi admonishes perfectly seriously. It just makes us laugh harder.

Every time we start to wind down and get a grip, one of us simply says, *bear hug,* and we're right back to square one, laughing our guts up and trying to figure out how the hell we ended up out in the middle of nowhere, as the country goes to shit, with the craziest person any of us has ever met.

11

THEO

I pull my shoes off at the back door and stomp into the house, Puddles greets me as I walk into the kitchen. Remi and the guys are behind me, and each of them takes off their shoes and follows me into the house. None of us have said more than a handful of words since the bear incident and the subsequent crack up, but the silence isn't laced with tension or unease like it was before. Oddly enough, I feel light—lighter than I can remember feeling in years. Which makes no sense, given what's happening around us with the Handshake Plague.

We're losing things in life that none of us ever thought we'd have to live without, but maybe this group was made to handle exactly that. Each of us have lost pieces of ourselves, figuratively and literally, over the past years. Maybe this change in the world and our environment doesn't seem so impossible to manage given what we've already been juggling.

I rub at my thigh, even though the ache I want to rub from my leg is further down. The IED, that robbed us each of something, cost me my left leg from just below the knee all the way down. My prosthetic is top of the line and fits perfectly, but I've been pushing things to the extreme, and my residual limb is crying out for a break. I sit heavily on the kitchen chair and immediately want to pull my prosthetic off to let my leg breathe and take a break, but I don't, because I don't want to bring attention to it.

With everything that's been going on and how we've handled it like the team we are, I've been feeling like I'm getting pieces of the old me back, but I convince myself that it can all disappear if I show weakness. The others join me at the table, and Puddles shoves her blocky head into Brant's lap as soon as he sits, demanding some love.

I watch him as the weight of the impending conversation starts to press in on the content silence that currently surrounds us. He's been handling his anxiety like a fucking champ, but I know some of this shit has got to be triggering for him. Not that I'd say that aloud, because he'd shut down as soon as the words started to come out of my mouth. I don't like to talk about the pain in my half-missing leg, and Brant doesn't like to talk about his PTSD.

"As soon as it's light outside and we're showered and packed up, we're going to leave and head back to Endstone. You've heard what we've had to say. Now it's time to decide what you're going to do."

I'm surprised that it's Brant who delivers the *shit or get off the pot* speech, and not Madix like I assumed it would be. I run my gaze over to Madix and find that he's watching Remi like he's trying to figure her out. I don't blame him. She thoroughly fucked up what he was sure he knew about the situation when she shoved her tongue into his mouth.

The image of the globes of her ass peeking out from her cutoff shorts, and of her tongue teasing Madix's lips is burned into the forefront of my mind. I bite at the inside of my cheek and shake away the look of her hard nipples pushing for attention through her sweatshirt when Madix moved her away from him like an idiot. If it had been me, I would have grabbed that delicious ass and lifted her up to straddle me, while I explored that naughty little mouth of hers. But it wasn't me she was kissing, and I was surprised by the pang of disappointment that shot through me as I watched her try to coax Madix into a response. I'm trying not to read into it too much, but she kissed Brant too, so maybe at some point, I'll get my turn.

I frown at the thought of *my turn.* I'm not sure why I'm okay with her messing around with the others as long as I'm not excluded. This end of the world shit is clearly fucking with my normally good sense. Remi leans back in her chair and looks at each of us in turn.

"I know you three are eager to hightail it out of here, but..." she pauses, and I can practically feel the mental eyeroll that Madix is giving her at whatever excuse she's about to make, even though he watches her with quiet intensity. "If you can give me the day, I can get my animals sorted for a while and pack up the ones I need to take with me."

None of us respond, shocked silent that she's actually agreeing to come with us. I expected her to argue that we're wrong, or that she'll be fine out here on her own, but she doesn't.

"What's with the change of heart?" I ask curiously.

She turns her attention on me. For once, her blue eyes are shaded with sadness, and it makes my throat tighten. "I haven't seen my dad in years. We had a really bad argument and...well, it's stubbornness more than anything. I told him I wouldn't go back to Endstone unless it was the last place on earth." She gives an incredulous snort and shakes her head as she messes with the frayed threads of her jean shorts. "I guess it's time to face the music and try to reconcile. The fact that he sent you three Joe's up here to get me just shows how serious he is."

I frown. "What do you mean?"

She stands, moving to start getting her house ready. "He knows I'm a sucker for soldiers," she says, her flirtatiousness sneaking through once again as she smirks over at us.

Madix continues to watch her, like he has no idea what to do with her. "So you'll come? Just like that?" he asks, his tone laced with doubt.

Her smirk morphs into a grin. "Well, not *just like that*. Every woman needs some warming up, Mady."

"Don't call me that."

She shrugs, unconcerned. At this point, I'm fairly certain that she does everything just to see what kind of reaction she'll get from him, or any of us for that matter. If our situation weren't so stressful, it would be downright hilarious.

"Will your chickens be okay?" Brant asks, trying to redirect her attention away from Madix to give the poor guy a break.

"Oh, yeah, they'll be fine. They're not actually my chickens," she answers as she grabs a cooler from the cabinet and starts piling food in.

Brant and I exchange a look. "If they're not your chickens, why the hell are they here?"

"They came with the place," she says matter-of-factly. "But they're pretty wild. They mostly roost in bushes and trees, even after I built them the hen house. I keep them fed when I'm here, and I always think they'll be wiped out when I get back every year, but the damn things just multiply," she explains. "But Jim Bob keeps trying to get to them. I thought we had a solid smoked fish instead of terrified poultry agreement, but he likes to test the boundaries...literally. It's why I set up the clinger dinger alarm. When he starts stalking too close to them, I have to remind him to back off. That bear is just crazy."

"Pot. Kettle," Madix mumbles.

Remi pretends not to hear him. "I'm going to shower, then you boys can have at it. The water heater is small, so you'll have to be quick. I'm all for energy conservation, so once again, feel free to join me," she says with a wink before walking out of the kitchen and into the bathroom. "We can share a towel, too!"

"That's not sanitary," Madix calls after her.

She just laughs. "Everyone needs to get a little dirty every now and then, Mady!"

He shakes his head and runs a hand over his trimmed black beard. When he drops it back into his lap, he looks over at me. "I'll make something quick for us to eat, and then let's start helping to move her along. The sooner we can get out of here, the better," he says, looking out the window at the dawning sun. "I want to make it back to Endstone as soon as possible."

I rub my leg again through the fabric of my pants as the guys start moving around. Brant looks over his shoulder at me. "You okay, bro?"

"Fine," I say, dropping my hand with a grimace.

"We can pack up if you—"

"I said I'm fine," I snap, before standing.

Brant holds up his hands in surrender and moves to the living room to start packing our shit. I hear the water turn off from the shower. She wasn't kidding. She does take a damn quick shower. I don't know why, but I'm oddly turned on by that. She's not one of those chicks who takes three hours to get ready, and she's still fucking gorgeous.

After Remi is finished in the bathroom, Brant, Madix, and I shower consecutively. Madix gets in last, which means the hot water runs out on him. He was already in an off-mood since his kiss with Remi, so he turns downright pissy after that.

We've had missions in countries whose temperatures would give hell a run for its money, and we were there bogged down by tons of gear and always on the move. We would have killed for a cold shower then, and I remind Madix of this when he snaps at me about how I stored our extra ammo too close to a fireplace that isn't in use. He's still wearing his angry eyes, but at least he's brooding silently now. Maybe I should encourage Remi to give him a roll in the hay. He clearly needs to let the poison out.

Remi is outside putting enough birdseed down to feed an entire aviary when I hear it.

A motor.

Alarm slices through me at the faint but distinct sound, and I rush out onto the porch, passing Madix on the way. "What's wrong?"

His hearing was damaged in our last mission, so I quickly fill him in as I scan for the source. "Vehicle approaching."

His head whips around to the road where I'm looking. It's a long, windy drive, and there are too many thick copses of trees to see anything, but the noise is definitely getting louder. Remi's house sits on higher land than the winding passes that lead up to it, and it has a good view of anything that might be approaching.

"Remington!" Madix shouts, getting her attention from where she's standing by the chicken coop. "Come over here."

She cocks her head and opens her mouth to say something, but then her head turns to the road. "Huh. Sounds

120

like someone is coming," she says thoughtfully, and not at all worried.

"Remington!" Madix snaps again.

When she doesn't immediately do as he asks, he launches himself over the railing, stalks over to her, grabs her by the arm, and starts yanking her toward the house. She actually looks pretty excited to be manhandled by him, judging by the smug smile on her face. "Aww, are you gonna protect me, soldier?"

"Get inside," he orders.

The smile leaves her face, and her eyebrows raise. "You're really worried, aren't you?" she asks, as if this surprises her.

"We have no idea who that is," I point out. "In case you've forgotten, there's a virus that's killing eighty-five percent of the people who catch it. We can't run the risk of being exposed in order to be a friendly fucking neighbor. We have no idea who will be in that car or what they might bring with them."

Brant must have been listening, because he comes stomping outside with four masks in hand and passes them around. The three of us immediately pull them over our mouths and noses, but when Remi just frowns at it, Brant steps forward and puts it on for her, tucking the straps around her ears gently. She mutters something too low for me to hear, and then Madix disappears inside before returning with our weapons. He also hands one to Remi, which seems to surprise her.

"Is this really necess—"

"Yes," all three of us cut her off.

Madix rubs at his ear and shakes his head with frustration. "I can't get a lock on it," he admits. "My fucking ear is ringing too goddamn much."

"I'll check it out."

Brant makes a hand motion to Puddles, ordering her to stay where she is, and she obeys as he follows me. We quickly make our way across the yard and to the road. As soon as we get around the bend, we spot it. An older SUV with at least two people inside that we can see. The motor is revving, but the wheels are stuck in the sludgy mud.

"Shit," Brant breathes as we stay hidden behind a pair of trees.

"Remi said there wasn't anything up this way other than her house, right?" he asks.

"No, but they could be lost. No one knows where the fuck to go anymore since we usually let technology do all the navigating for us," I say.

"I don't want to wait around to see if they get out or if they decide to ditch the car and walk. If they walk, they'll find the house for sure," Brant tells me, as he re-positions his hands around the gun.

I nod my head in agreement, but stop to observe the driver as he gets out of the car to stare at his back two wheels that are thoroughly caked in mud and not going anywhere anytime soon. Then the man pulls a handkerchief from his back pocket and proceeds to blow his nose. That one seemingly innocent gesture has my blood running cold. *Are they fucking sick?* Brant swears next to me and points his rifle in the direction of the stuck car, and I know he has the death threats in his sights.

"Do we shoot them?" I ask, the threat feeling way too real right now.

I'm struggling to picture this seemingly innocuous man as the enemy. I don't want to go near these people, but I don't want to kill them either. This right or wrong debate isn't a first for me. I've killed as part of my job to keep myself and my squad brothers safe, and because I was ordered to.

But that didn't stop me from lying awake at night, wondering about the people who died. What were their families like? How did they get pulled into the never-ending conflict? Did they wonder about the lives of the people they killed too? When I looked at my hands, I saw them stained red with blood. I shouldn't have to get more blood on them now that we're out of service. I won't take another life unless I absolutely have to.

"Don't shoot them, Brant. We'll save that for when we really don't have a choice. We're leaving anyway. We'll just move up the time table to *now*."

Brant nods his agreement, and we both back away from our vantage point. We sprint back to the house to find a tense Madix still standing where we left him, and Remi scanning the surroundings with a fucking spyglass that looks like a prop from *Pirates of the Caribbean*.

Why am I surprised?

Madix sees us sprinting back towards him, and he grabs Remi by the shoulders and turns her toward the house to herd her inside. By the time Brant and I make our way up the steps and into the house, we can hear Madix and Remi arguing. It's obvious that Madix has already come to the same conclusion that Brant and I just did, because he has his arms full of our bags and hers.

"We're leaving. Now," he barks at a very angry looking Remi.

"I'm not ready yet!" she argues at his back.

He turns on his heel, his face a hard mask. "You have three minutes. Then, you're getting in that fucking car whether you walk or I have to carry you."

In a move so smooth, I could watch it on replay forever and still not figure out how she did it so fast, Remi's Glock 19 is out from wherever she was carrying it, and has it pointed at Madix's chest. She's not wearing her thigh holster, and even though shit is about to go down, I can't help but run my eyes over her to try to figure out where she was keeping that damn gun.

"Try it," she challenges Madix, her face deadly serious.

Shit goes from bad to worse when the rage in Madix's face disappears, and his features go blank. Our squad called this his Jiminy Cricket look. Except we didn't mean it was the arrival of his conscious, but the death of it. When he gets this look on his face, we know that he took that plucky little cricket right off his shoulder and stomped the shit out of it. Brant and I exchange a look because we know what's about to happen isn't going to be pretty.

Madix goes full Ranger-mode. No more holding back because she's Sheriff April's daughter or because she's a chick. His stance changes, and then before Remi can blink, he has overtaken her gun and shoved her chest against the wall. He tosses the gun to Brant, who catches it. Then Madix spins Remi around and tosses her over his shoulder. The air escapes her with an "oomph," but as soon as she gets a breath back, she's screaming and cursing up a storm.

"You son of a bitch! Put me down right now!" she yells, as she struggles to get out of his hold and does her best to punch his kidneys right out of his back.

Madix doesn't wait for us. He barges out of the house, letting the screen door smack closed behind us as he stomps toward the car, Remi's shouting and threats getting quieter as he moves further away from the house. Brant and I stare at each other in shock for a moment before we snap out of it and kick ourselves into high gear. We do a quick sweep of the house, but I don't know what the fuck she'd want to take, and I don't even attempt to guess. I grab her duffel from the floor that looks half packed, and I start pulling open drawers and shoving stuff into it.

I don't see any makeup or anything else that might be

needed on this trip—or kidnapping I should say, thanks to Madix's temper. Brant runs down into the basement, which confuses me until he walks upstairs with a cat carrier that's now housing a couple of rats. "I can't find Coon," he tells me, running a distressed hand over his mohawk.

Fuck! I look around frantically, not wanting to leave Remi's pet behind, but there's a possible infected guy by the car who could be heading our way as we speak, so we don't have the luxury of time.

"Let's go." I tell Brant, and he grabs Remi's bag from my hand so I can grab the guns and lock up.

I grab Remi's coat that's hanging by the door before shutting and locking it, and then hurry after Brant. He's loading stuff into the back of the SUV, and I'm surprised when I don't hear Remi's shouts ringing out of the open back door. I hand off two guns, and Brant puts Madix's rifle in its case in the back before he closes the door and moves to get in the front of the car. I pull open the door to the back seat and freeze when I see why Remi is suddenly so quiet.

She turns and glares at me, and I warily eye the red bandanna that's tied over her mouth. Her hands are secured to the *oh shit* handle above the window, and I definitely shouldn't notice this, but the position makes her tits look fucking fantastic. Her legs are fastened to something under the seat, and I wonder for a second how Madix did this so fast. The promise of pain and retribution stares back at me from Remi's ice-blue eyes, making my stomach clench, and not in a good way. It's probably safe to say that she won't be inviting any of us into her shower again anytime soon.

"What the fuck, Madix? She's not an unlawful combatant," I snap at him, watching as Remi gives her restraints another tug.

Puddles gives a whine, her head resting in Remi's lap in an effort to offer some comfort in what is obviously a fucked up situation. I can't stand this. This isn't us. We don't just abduct people. I get that he's worried about being infected, but surely there has to be a compromise. I want to fix this and erase the look of betrayal that's showing all over Remi's features. I get into the back seat and automatically reach over so that I can pull the gag from her mouth.

"Don't, Theo," Madix says harshly. "We need to get out of here as soon as possible, which won't happen if we wreck because she's having a fit and can't accept reality. She's pissed, and I get that, but we need to go, and we can't do it safely if she's going to attack me while I'm driving, or threatening to jump out of the car."

I shoot him an incredulous look and start to untie the gag anyway. "Fine, she can stay tied up until we're out of the area, but I'm not going to fucking gag her. We can just listen to the abuse until she's tired of dishing it out," I say. "We deserve it anyway," I finish with a mumble.

"Shit," I hear Brant mutter as he hops in the front seat and slams the door shut. Puddles moves to try to get closer to him. I navigate around the big ass dog and pull the bandana all the way off Remi's face. I'm ready for her to start laying into all of us, but when I pull the cloth away, she's quiet, which feels more unnerving than if she would just read us all the riot act.

Madix pulls away from the house, wasting no time getting us the fuck out of here. Mud flies up behind us as he punches the gas, and I bite down on the, *"slow down"* comment that wants to crawl out of my mouth. He's worried that Remi's tantrum will cause an accident, but I'm worried that *his* tantrum could get us stuck in the mud just like that other car.

I fidget under the weight of the tension oozing around the car, not liking the chasm that's opening up and separating us right in front of my eyes.

"We grabbed your rats, but we couldn't find Coon," I blurt, unable to take the silent treatment any longer. "When things quiet down and it's safe to venture out again we can come back for her," I offer, but Remi doesn't acknowledge me at all.

"Jesus, Remi," I plead. "We just want to make sure you stay safe. Those people could be sick."

"I am not some child you can order around and toss over your shoulder like a damn sack of potatoes!" she spits, turning her fury on me.

"You already agreed to go with us, we just had to move up the timetable," Brant defends, making her burning gaze move onto him.

"So you think your ridiculous need to '*up the timetable*' trumps everything I say?"

Madix's shoulders tense, and his voice comes out like a growl. "It fucking does when your location is compromised. It does when *you're* dicking around to smoke fish for a fucking wild bear that's perfectly capable of fishing for itself. It does when we have been more than patient, trying to get you to see reason. And it sure as fuck does when your actions could get you or us killed! Do you not get that? Your dad asked us to come get you. We are risking our fucking lives to do that. This isn't a fucking joke, and your fetish for animals doesn't trump our need to stay the fuck alive!"

Madix's knuckles grow white on the steering wheel, and his breathing is hurried as a result of his rage-filled yelling. I don't know if Remi recognizes that he's completely lost it, or if she just doesn't have anything else to say, but she stays quiet. I doubt her silence is because she's mulling over the points Madix just made, because for whatever reason, she's been resistant to anything we've had to say from the minute we stood on her porch.

I think about it as we make our way further and further

from Remi's house, but I can't decide if her outlook is a good or bad thing. Is she sticking her head in the sand and refusing to deal with reality, or is she just not stressed about the fucked up virus situation because there's nothing that can be done about it?

I watch her as she stares out the window, her face blank, her hands still tied up. I don't like to see her restrained, and even though I can tell Madix didn't make it too tight, I can see her skin has turned red from where the rope has rubbed against her. Frowning, I reach around Puddles and start undoing the knots around her wrists. This just feels wrong, and I can't sit here like a creeper, okay with her being tied up and taken against her will.

"Theo…" Madix warns, but I ignore him as I work to release her.

"It's not fucking right, Madix. I'm not going to sit back here and just be okay with this."

I turn to find his brown eyes glaring at me in the rearview mirror, but before I can say anything else, a fist lands in my throat and I'm suddenly choking for air. I grab my neck and turn wide eyes towards Remi, just in time to see another fist flying right for my face. I bring up my hand to grab it before she can hit me again.

"What the fuck?" I wheeze, but I have to block an elbow coming for my forearm.

Remi lunges for me, but her feet are still tied up, so it's more of an aggressive lean and doesn't pack the punch that she clearly wants it to. I twist and maneuver myself on top of her, wrestling to pin her arms down onto the seat and keep her from taking any more cheap shots.

"I was trying to help you, what the hell was that for?"

"You stood by and let *cro magnon man* over there do this to me in the first place!" she huffs.

I stare down at her, our heaving breaths mingling as we

just lay like that for a second, with her pinned between me and the seat. She starts to squirm against me, and I try hard to ignore how she feels underneath me, but her body presses against mine in all the sweet spots, and I can't stop my dick from getting hard at the contact. Puddles whines again from her place on the floor against the car door.

"Let me untie your legs before you hurt yourself," I grunt out as I take an elbow to the ribs.

"Stellar idea T," Madix snarks from the front. "Yeah, go ahead and untie her legs so that she can hit *and* kick at the same time."

Without moving my gaze away from Remi, I reply, "Fuck off, Madix. Just pull over so she can get out and go home if she wants to. I'm not going to force someone to do something they don't want to do."

"I can't fucking pull over. We could get stuck in the mud and never get out!"

"Jesus fucking Christ," Brant interjects with a sigh. "If we just let her run home, then what was the point of us coming out here? What's sheriff going to say when we show up sans daughter?"

"We'll just tell him that his daughter was too fucking dense to understand she was safer with us," Madix grumps.

"Stop talking about me like I'm not here, you assholes!" Remi finally cuts in, her voice like a whip across the car. She glares up at me. "I know I'm all irresistible and shit, but get off of me," she demands. I can't help it when my lips twitch upward. I know she's raving mad, and has every right to be, but she's fucking cute as hell.

Instead of being chastised, I try to make light of the situation in the hopes that I can turn this around and lessen her anger. "I'm surprised, Remi. I thought you'd be into this with all of the invites for sex that you've been throwing around. Being tied up isn't your thing?"

Remi rolls her eyes at me and maneuvers her hand that's trapped between our chests to pinch my nipple.

"Owww!" I yelp, pulling her hand away and twining my fingers with hers to keep her from trying to rip my nipple off. "Stop taking your aggression out on me, and I'll get off."

"I don't need the announcement of you getting off," she quips.

"I didn't...I'll get off *of you,*" I clarify.

Remi tsks, her body now completely limp underneath me. "So you don't *want* to get me off? Is that what you're saying? You're a taker but not a giver? That's not good," she says seriously, and my mind spins with the direction that my one simple statement took her. I don't even know what to address first.

My frown deepens. "What...no, that's not what I—"

"Stop falling for it, dude," Brant says with a shake of his head.

I narrow my eyes on Remi who is doing her best to look innocent. I might not have known her long, but I'm a damn good people-watcher. I watch their expressions, look for their tells, and usually find it easy to gain a general sense of how they act. It was a good skill to have when I was in the service. Especially when there was a language barrier in hostile territory.

So even though Remi isn't the enemy, I've still gauged her, and right now, that innocent look is full of shit. But what's not full of shit is the way her breath is still coming in fast, and the way her nipples have pebbles through the thin material of her bra and shirt. She's deflecting the conversation to gain the upperhand, since we overpowered her physically. And she's turned on from being pinned beneath me, but she wants to deflect away from that too, by mocking me. Too bad I'm not gonna let her get away with it.

"I *am* a taker," I confess as I stare into her eyes, and I

adjust my hand that's holding hers hostage. She scoffs and opens her mouth to retort something, but before she can, I lean in, take her bottom lip between my teeth, and bite down.

She squeaks in surprise and maybe a little bit of pain, but before she can do anything else, I suck her tender lip into my mouth, and then run my tongue down the rise of her plump lip, over her jaw, and nibble at the spot just below her ear. I nip and tease her there until I hear a soft sigh that barely suppresses a moan. With a grin, I pull back and speak low against her ear. "But just because I like to take, doesn't mean I don't give back. I do. Gladly. Over and over and over again."

I pull back completely, releasing her hands and intending to sit up, but before I can, she uses her free hands to grip the collar of my shirt and yanks me back down.

My lips crash against hers in a frenzied mess, and her hands are suddenly all over me. I feel her fingers dance over my biceps before they delve under my shirt to run over my abs, and then her palms are gripping my ass and giving it a squeeze.

As soon as she does that, I can't help myself from taking things further, because her bold touches are driving me fucking insane. I grind into her pelvis and grip her hair so I can angle her head just where I want it as I fuck her mouth with my tongue. She makes the tiniest noise of satisfaction, and I feel her hand slowly moving from my ass to trail around my thigh. My dick jumps when it realizes her trajectory, but just before she's about to brush against it, a splash of cold water is suddenly dumped over my head.

I jerk up in surprise and Remi squeals again, this time because of the water that splashed onto her head and chest.

"What the fuck?" I snap, sitting up.

Remi pushes up into a sitting position as well, her hair

messy and her lips swollen. But I'm too busy glaring at Madix, who's driving one-handed and holding a half-empty water bottle in his other hand. "Whoops," he says sardonically.

Fucking dick.

12

REMI

I wipe water from my face and move to sit up, which forces Theo to lean away from me. I'm pretty sure he mumbles something about how he didn't fuck up Madix's turn, but I have no idea what that means. My impromptu makeout session with Theo just now has left me wet and unsatisfied. Either Stockholm's is making quick work, or I'm not as pissed off by what happened as I should be. I did say I was going to go with them, and even though I don't really know shit about any of these guys, strangely enough, I do feel like I can trust them.

I shake my head to clear away those thoughts. What the fuck am I thinking? These assholes just tied me up in a car, in spite of my feelings on the matter, which again, if I'm being honest, are kind of conflicted. If I had a nickel for every pussy clench that occurred as Madix tied me up, well, let's just say I'd have a lot of nickels. Does that mean that I'm not going to knee him in the balls the first chance I get? Nope, it does not. I've always been very forward when it comes to satiating my needs, but am I so cock-hypnotized that I'm treating a legit kidnapping like a really fun role-play? Yes, yes I am.

I decide to give myself a break though, because I've been alone up on this mountain for nearly two and a half months. That means that it's just been me, some smutty books, and my trusty vibrator to handle things. And my dating life even when I'm around society isn't much to brag about. Guys always boast about how they want someone sexually outgoing and adventurous, but every time I've shown them exactly what I'm up for, things always got weird. They'd either become intimidated, or have some fucked up sense of jealousy. A lot of guys want some shrinking virgin violet, but that's just not me. I know what I want, and I like keeping things exciting. Like three soldiers kind of exciting.

Theo leans back, and my eyes zone right in on the ample bulge in his pants. He fixes the front of his pants, either for my benefit, or more likely for his own comfort. I lick my lips as his hand grips his dick through the fabric. When I look up, I see that he's watching me, both of us clearly feeling the effects of intense sexual attraction. His eyes wander down my body languidly, before sweeping back up to meet mine. There's so much promise in that green gaze that I clench all over in anticipation.

Again, I shake myself back into reality, ignoring the overwhelming drive of my overactive hormones for a cold dose of truth. What do I do now? Do I trek back home on principle, go along with this, or fight the rest of the way there? I smirk to myself. That could be fun.

"I didn't get a chance to reset my clinger dinger," I tell all three of the guys. "There could be any old animal sauntering up to the chickens and tormenting the poor girls."

"They're chickens. They're not as important as your life," Madix tells me evenly.

"What if those people were friendly?" I volley back.

He tosses an exasperated look over his shoulder at me. "Who the fuck cares if they're friendly? They could be sick."

"Or they could be perfectly healthy and not a part of your fucking delusion," I retort. When I see that little vein across his forehead start to pulse, I have to swallow down my triumph. I love setting this big guy off. He's so easily riled, and when he gets riled, I get riled. But in a hot kind of way. I would love to strip him bare and ride his grumpy face until his frown drips right off.

I turn my head to Theo. "Was it a man? Was he cute?" I ask.

A frown appears on his face. "What?"

"The man we're running from whose car is stuck in the mud. Was he hot?" I clarify. I get immense satisfaction when Theo's frown deepens so much that I could fit a dime in the crease between his brows. All three of the guys shoot me a look.

"What?" I ask with mock innocence.

"You kissed me, then Madix, and you *just* had your tongue down Theo's throat not even two minutes ago, and you're asking about another fucking guy?" Brant asks.

My eyes narrow at his tone. Suddenly, what was supposed to be me teasing them, has now morphed into them judging me. I fucking knew it. I shouldn't even be surprised. It was only going to be a matter of time. "You know what really irks me?" I ask. "Guys are all about fucking more than one girl at a time, and that shit is celebrated. But if a girl wants multiple guys, she's suddenly a whore or a selfish bitch. There's nothing wrong with being attracted to more than a single person for your entire life. Consensual sex is beautiful. It should be celebrated, not shamed. Just because I have a pussy, doesn't mean I can't have a healthy sexual appetite," I say, crossing my arms. "I happen to *like* liking guys. And let's be honest, men would be much better equipped to please a woman in *every* aspect, if you guys banded together and learned to share."

Madix gives an incredulous snort at the same time Brant asks, "What do you mean?"

His tone surprises me, because usually when I talk about this, the guys always get defensive and pissed. "I mean, we women are complicated creatures. At least, I know I am. It's why I've always struggled to settle down with just one guy. Sometimes I want the nice guy, you know? With sweet romance and lovemaking," I admit. Then I flick my eyes to Madix, catching his gaze in the rearview mirror. "And other times, I want to be spanked and fucked and bossed around," I say, and I see his nostrils flare slightly.

Yep. I wasn't wrong in the woods when I kissed him. He wants me just as much as I want him. When I peer at the other guys, my surprise goes up a level when I see the hungry expressions that they're wearing. I instantly sit up, intrigued. I've never had people react this way. It usually turns to some form of disgust or disbelief.

"Then there are the times where I need a little bit of both, a happy medium of naughty and nice. There's too much out there to decide on just one person. The thing about me is, I always seem to need more than what a single person can give me. I guess you could say I'm a handful."

Snorts and chuckles sound off around the car, and I roll my eyes.

"You sound like you've thought about this a lot," Theo tells me.

I nod. "I have. Just haven't met the right men to take me on."

I watch my words settle across them, and the air inside the car churns with their spinning thoughts. There. I've set the challenge. I'm not expecting anything in return, but damn, it would be so satisfying if they would be game. Still, I fight not to get my hopes up. I've been with guys before who say they get it, but ultimately, they really don't.

Aside from wanting to be fucked nine ways from Sunday, plus wanting to be emotionally stimulated by multiple minds, as well as supported and not judged, sometimes I also just like to be alone. I need time to be one with myself to take stock, center myself, and live off my own hard work and merits. And finding one person—let alone multiple people—who really understand that, has proven to be impossible.

Oh, well. A girl can dream.

* * *

I dreamed. A lot.

It's one of my things. If I'm not driving but am stuck in a moving vehicle for more than fifteen minutes, I just drop right off to sleep. It's probably not the most useful talent in the case of an abduction, so it's good that I'm half okay with what's happening.

Well, maybe more than half, I admit, as I nuzzle against a muscular chest and feel a hand slightly tighten on my waist. Air is huffed into my face and I smile towards it. I slowly open my eyes and find dark brown orbs staring back at me, surrounded by multicolored fur and a long strand of drool hanging off one of Puddles's jowls. Not exactly the good morning I was hoping for, or should I say good afternoon, or maybe evening?

I sit up, now very aware that I have no idea what time it is or where exactly I am. The sun is still out, which makes me think it's late afternoon, and the sky is gloomy and looks about as grumpy as Madix usually does. I realize that Brant is now in the backseat acting as my pillow, and Theo is in the front. I'm not sure when they switched places or why, but it doesn't really matter. There's a weird scratching noise coming from somewhere, but it doesn't last long enough for me to hone in on where it's coming from.

"There it is again. Do you think it's coming from the roof?" Theo asks as he pulls back the tan colored shade that normally blocks the moon roof. He peers up through the glass, trying to figure out if there's anything up there to see. When nothing obvious presents itself, he closes the shade. I turn to look at the pet carrier in the back, thinking maybe the rats got out, but they're cuddled together, taking a nap of their own. That's when I know what's making the noise.

"It's Coon!" I announce, and then try to roll down the window to invite her in, but of course, the child lock is still on. What do they think I'm going to do? Shove myself face-first out of the window of a moving vehicle? I'm pissed, not brain dead.

"What? How the hell would she be outside? We've been driving for hours, and she didn't come with us. I couldn't find her when I grabbed the rats," Brant objects.

"I saw her sneak in," I offer with a shrug. "You think I really would've let you leave without her?"

I would've lost my shit on them if I hadn't seen her in the back. Good thing Brant had the wherewithal to grab the rats, because if Coon didn't have her babies, there would've been a problem. Coon loves those damn things, and she's the only pet I was really worried about leaving behind, but I knew she'd follow without a problem. She can get just about anywhere. She's always been a little adrenaline junkie. She loves to climb to impossible heights, and then try to scare the piss out of me by doing some crazy ninja moves and falling in my lap when I least expect it. It wouldn't surprise me if she snuck out the back window while I slept so that she could go full Teen Wolf, hanging-ten on the roof of the car.

"You guys want to give me access to the window, or am I still deemed too much of a flight risk?"

No one answers me, but Madix flips a switch on the armrest of his door and when I try the window again, it rolls down. Looks like me taking a nap instead of trying to make a break for it has lulled them into a sense of security and trust. I'll see what I can do later to change that. They may complain, but I can tell that they like that I'm making them work for it, cute little alpha dudes that they are. I gotta keep them on their toes.

Cool mountain air whooshes past my face like it's eager to caress me with its fresh, chilly touch. The air is laced with moisture, and from the looks of the trees and mountain grass on my side, it looks like it rained again while I was sleeping. I put my hand out the window and lay it flat on the roof of the SUV, tapping the tips of my fingers against the metal.

I lean out the window as far as I can go without falling so that I can try to get to her. "Coon, sweet girl...come here, and I'll help you inside," I call out as I continue to pat the roof of the car.

I feel Brant's hands grip my waist. "Remi," he rebukes. "Get back in here."

He yanks me back onto the seat and buckles me in. "Hey!" I slap his hands away, but he doesn't budge or let me unbuckle. "Coon might be up there!"

"I'm not letting you fall out of the damn car," Brant retorts.

I ignore him and lean out the window, but I can't go far with the seatbelt now digging into my lap and shoulder. "Cocoon! Get back in here!"

"The damn opossum is not on the roof. There's no way," Madix argues, but he has no idea who he's dealing with. Coon lives for these types of shenanigans.

There's no answering noise or scratch marks indicating that she's making her way towards me and my now open window, but I have a feeling she's up there.

"Come back in here right now!" I tell her again, the rushing wind carrying my sing-song order away.

I open my mouth to tell Madix to pull over, but before I can, I hear, "Oh, shit!" erupt from Madix's mouth as he presses down on the breaks.

He doesn't slam the car to a stop, but he presses down hard enough on the pedal that we all jerk forward a little, which is fine if you have a seatbelt on, but Puddles doesn't, and Coon sure as hell doesn't. My blood goes cold when I hear the sound of Coon sliding forward on the roof, her claws scraping against the metal as she tries to stop her trajectory.

"Shit!" I curse, at the same time that Brant grabs Puddles so that she doesn't go flying forward.

Next thing I know, Coon's brown and white little body is sliding down the windshield. I don't know how she keeps herself from flying off, but relief floods me when she stops, spread-eagle on the pane of glass. Madix was already trying to slow down, but when Coon slides down into his line of sight, he slams on the brakes even harder. The guys all swear as they're shoved forward, and Brant's steel arms stay locked around Puddles as he tries to wrestle the middle seat belt to get it around her.

"Stop braking you idiot! You're going to send her flying!" I shout, reaching up to punch Madix in the arm. That's about when everyone in the car realizes that we're not stopping. Madix's alarmed, "Fuck...fuck...fuck!" fills the car, and I battle the panic and adrenaline that slams into me as the car goes sliding.

"I can't stop, and I can't fucking see with this thing on the windshield!" Madix shouts.

The big SUV starts veering to the left, but we're still sliding forward, and now Coon has her claws gripped around the windshield wipers, and I hear it start to snap as her tail flails around.

"Turn into the slide, turn into the slide!" I say frantically.

Madix turns the steering wheel to the right to try and straighten out the hydroplaning car, but he overcorrects and it sends us spinning in the opposite direction. Various versions of *oh shit* and *fuck* are shouted out and punctuated by my, "Hang on baby!" and a silent prayer that somehow Coon won't get thrown off.

The pleas and curses are replaced by yelps, as the front of the car tilts forward, and I'm suddenly convinced we're going over a cliff. My life nearly flashes before my eyes as my mouth starts spouting off everything I've hidden under my tongue. "Oh God, this is it! I love you, Daddy, I'm sorry I'm a stubborn asshole! And I *was* the one who duct-taped Braden Dodds to the flag pole and rubbed bacon grease all over him!" I confess. "He liked it though, which is why he'd never tell you who did it! Fuck, I can't believe I'm going to die before I hit my orgasm quota!"

I brace my hands against the back of Madix's seat, readying myself as much as I can for the inevitable freefall, while Madix has his head poking out through his rolled down window as he attempts to to not kill us all. When Coon shifts and the windshield wiper moves more, I catch a glimpse through the windshield, but instead of seeing sky or rocks, I just see trees. We're not careening off a cliff, but about to smash into a wall of timber.

Shit.

"Coon, save yourself! Jump to safety!" I scream, before the the front of the Explorer is clipped by an Aspen, putting us into a spin. We get serenaded by the sound of metal crumbling and glass breaking as the SUV slams into several trees on the passenger side and then bounces off to repeat the hits on the driver's side of the car. Coon is holding onto the wiper one second, and gone the next, giving us a clear view as we pinball down the hill. I scream, the guys shout, and then our way too fast-moving car hits one last tree head on, before finally coming to a stop.

We all slam forward and then back again as the car violently halts. I have Brant's arm clasped in a death grip, and he's still clutching onto Puddles, all three of us mashed together on the seat. We all breathe, staring wildly, as we hear the tick of the damaged engine and steam starts spilling out of the hood.

Madix is the first to speak as he clears his throat. "Everyone okay?" he asks, looking at all of us and taking stock. We all nod and sound off our *yeses.* "We should uh, probably get out."

"You should probably not fucking wreck the car next time," Theo snaps.

"You think this is on me? Her fucking pet made it impossible to see," Madix defends, but I can see the redness around his neck and ears. Poor alpha male is probably not used to fucking up like this, and I'm pretty sure he's embarrassed.

"Thanks for buckling me," I tell Brant. "Good foresight on that one."

He gives me a nod, and then the shock dissipates enough for my eyes to widen in panic. "Shit! Coon!"

Madix swallows. "Stay here. I'll go check."

He unbuckles his seatbelt and moves to open the car door. It's smashed in quite a bit, so he has to muscle it with his shoulder several times before he can get it to budge. I manage to unhook my tight grip from Brant's biceps enough to let go.

"You alright?" he asks.

I feel Theo's attention on me as well, both of their eyes running over me, and I nod. "Yeah. You guys?"

They both nod, and I pat Puddles's head, making sure she's okay as well. She gives my palm a slurp.

I look out of the cracked windows, but I can't see Madix anywhere, and my stomach clenches. "I need to see Coon," I say, feeling tears well up into my eyes. If she's hurt...

"Remi, wait," Brant implores, but I don't.

I scramble to the front seat where Madix left the door ajar, and go outside on shaky legs. I look around, trying to spot Madix or Coon on the ground. "Coon!" I call.

"Remington."

I whirl around on my heels and find Madix walking forward with Coon in his arms. My hand flies to my mouth at her prone form...right before her head pops up, and she clicks her tongue at me.

I drop my hand to my chest and let out a relieved breath. "Thank goodness," I say, rushing forward.

Before picking her up, I run my eyes over her. "Is she okay?"

Madix nods, looking a little impressed. "I checked her over. Didn't feel any broken bones or anything, and she seems to be moving around just fine. She was about a hundred yards back, walking around. Resilient little rodent."

"Marsupial," I correct automatically.

A hint of a smile passes over his face as he hands over my opossum into my arms. "Marsupial," he amends.

I cradle her in my arms, and she nips at my fingers. "She wants to see her babies," I tell him, and I feel Theo and Brant coming up behind us. Theo has the rat cage in hand, and the damn things are still sleeping. Coon wriggles until I let her down alongside the cage, and Theo opens it so she can get inside. She cuddles up to the rats immediately.

Puddles is sticking close to Brant, her brindle body right up against his leg. "Aww, you okay, honey?" I ask, kneeling down to rub her head.

"She pissed on me," Brant announces, and sure enough, there's a little wet spot on the knee of his pants. He looks at Puddles, apology bleeding out of his gaze for what she just went through, and it's touching how much she means to him and him to her.

"There's nothing wrong with having a weak bladder," I reassure Puddles, and Theo gives an amused snort. I give him the eye. "Don't make her self-conscious."

He smirks and buries his hands into his pockets. "Apologies."

Madix sighs, drawing our attention, and we all follow his line of sight at the wrecked and ruined car that is still puffing with steam. "That's not gonna run again," he announces.

All four of us seem to realize the implication of his words at once.

"How many miles are we from Endstone?" I ask.

"We're just over two-thirds of the way there," Theo replies.

I blink, because I know that Endstone is exactly 519.3 miles from my cabin. "Shit," I curse. "That leaves us with, what, maybe a hundred and sixty miles to go—give or take maybe fifteen?"

"Yep," Theo chirps back, as he pats Madix on the back. "Well, let's unpack the car and carry what we can. We'll have to ditch the rest. Looks like we're walking the rest of the way."

The guys grumble and groan, but a slow smile spreads across my face. When Madix sees, he's caught off guard, and starts eyeing me warily. "Why are you smiling? It's going to take us probably a week to walk down this mountain and get to Endstone."

"Because, this," I throw my arms out, motioning to the wilderness around me, "is what I do! I have exactly four favorite hobbies." I lift up my fingers and tick them off one by one. "Fishing, hunting, and camping," I say, my smile confident and excited.

"That's only three things. You said you had *four* favorite hobbies," Madix retorts.

"Well, fucking is right up there too, but I don't think you boys are ready for this jelly." I raise my eyebrows at him in challenge and then turn to practically skip my way toward the car to join Theo.

"Perfect. Just what we need on this mission from hell, a jazzed up Girl Scout," Madix grumbles at my back.

I snort. "Do I look like a cookie-toting Girl Scout? Hell no. My dad knew I'd be useless at that. No, I was a patched-up Boy Scout, mothersucker," I toss over my shoulder. "Camping is my jam, and I'm about to show you big bad Rangers a thing or two."

13

MADIX

W e have exactly one tent, three sleeping bags, some canned food, a box of MRE's, flint, a pot, canisters of gasoline, ammo, dog food, a tarp, rope, the clothes that we packed, and the letter we forgot that Sheriff April gave us to give to Remi. She glared at it for a minute, like somehow it was going to bite her if she touched it, but eventually, she just snatched it out of Brant's hands and shoved it into the back pocket of her cutoffs. We're at a higher elevation now, and the air is cooling more and more as the sun dips further towards the horizon, so her cutoff shorts are definitely not weather appropriate, but hell if I'm going to suggest she change. Her legs look too damn good, even if they are attached to a whole lotta crazy.

"Okay, we're not going to be able to carry all of this, so let's prioritize what we need," I announce.

"Food, water, the tent and sleeping bags, ammo, the tarp, and the rope should come in handy. We can cut back on the clothes we bring to make room for the heavier stuff like the food and dog food," Theo suggests.

"We honestly don't need the food," Remi chimes in, and we all turn to look at her. It's clear by the expressions that the other guys are giving her that they think her suggestion is just as ludicrous as I do. "I can hunt," she insists. "I'm guaranteed to get squirrels and some rabbits, but there's always fish if there's a stream nearby and even bigger game if we're lucky, like elk or deer. There's no point carrying all the heavy cans of food or those nasty MRE's when I can get us fresh meat and maybe even some veggies every night. Just sayin," Remi concludes.

I stare at her for a couple of seconds before dumping my pack of clothes in the back of the totaled SUV and start filling the now empty bag with cans of food. Remi rolls her eyes at me and shakes her head.

"No offense, but I'll take..." I turn the can I'm currently holding in my hand to read the label. "Bean and bacon soup over *squirrel* any day."

"Suit yourself," she replies, her tone light and nonchalant. "But you don't know what you're missing with fresh meat."

She reaches for the duffle that Theo finishes packing for her and opens it to start investigating the contents. The guys begin to empty their bags and fill them with the items that seem like the biggest priority. I divide the pack of water bottles between the four of us and grab the few empty bottles rolling around the back that we can fill up.

Remi unbuttons her shorts and then proceeds to slide them down her long, smooth legs. Without preamble, she bends over, giving me a nice view of her ass, and stays that way as she unties her shoes. All three of us are stuck frozen, watching the view and appreciating the black panties that cover her luscious ass cheeks.

Once she gets her boots off, Remi snags a pair of black leggings and pulls them on. When she stands back up, she looks over and catches the three of us gawking at her. A sweet smile sweeps across her lips, and then she turns back to what she's doing and pulls on a pair of olive-green cargo pants.

"Good thing I was mostly packed," she tells me pointedly. "If I didn't have my favorite pants with me, we would've had a problem. I take these on all my favorite adventures," she says as she buttons the fly.

I watch as she attaches a leg holster to her belt loop and pulls out a Glock. She checks the weapon over, gives a satisfied humph, and then secures the gun to her thigh holster. Then she digs into her duffel, finds a rifle, and slings that over her shoulder. The whole look suits her. When she glances up and catches me still watching her, I quickly look away.

The guys and I layer up with clothing for the impending cold that we can all feel creeping quickly into the air, and Brant puts a long sleeve shirt on Puddles to try and keep her nice and toasty. Her fur coat is her best line of defense, but I never say anything when it comes to Brant and the way he dotes on Pud.

The guys and I carefully pick through our bags, packing only the essentials, and I make sure we have plenty of water and food that isn't too heavy to carry. I keep just one more pair of pants, two more socks, two shirts. The rest of the clothes, I ditch. I make sure everyone has water, and Brant carries extra for Puddles. It'll be heavy, but we have to make sure we have plenty of water in case we don't find a source. If it rains, we can always use the containers to catch the rainwater, but we can't count on it.

Theo makes sure we all have a pair of rubber gloves and masks, just in case, and I pack the first aid kit in my bag, along with some extra ammo. When we're all packed, Remi hoists her bag over her shoulder, and I frown when I see that it's half empty. "You can carry more than that, can't you?"

"Don't need to," she says with a shrug. "I told you, I'll set traps and hunt wild game. It's what I've done the entire time I've been up on the mountain. I have extra clothes, ammo, and water. That's all I need. I don't need to be weighed down with cans of food," she tells me with a willful expression.

"If you don't manage to catch anything, then that means you'll have to dip into the reserves that we packed, which is fine, but four packs of food are better than three. You should grab at least a few things."

She straightens her shoulders and lifts her chin to a stubborn tilt. I cross my arms and widen my stance. We stare each other down, and I don't know what I want to do more; shake her until she gets some sense and listens to me, or grab her by the ass and fuck her against the nearest tree. Why does she get my blood pumping so goddamn hard?

"If you need help carrying your unnecessarily heavy bag, I'm happy to come to your rescue. You just say the word. But I'm not going to make things harder on myself by lugging around shit we don't need."

"Stop being so stubborn," I snap.

"Stop being so bossy," she volleys back.

Theo looks between us and rolls his eyes as he grabs the cage where the opossum and rats are still sleeping soundly inside. "Can you two not argue right now? Madix, let her do her thing. Remi, you know it turns him on when you get all challenging and shit. Stop teasing the poor guy."

I blink in surprise and cut my glare to a grinning Theo. "Shut the fuck up."

He holds up his hands and starts walking, while Brant ignores the entire thing and studies a watch/compass and the map that Sheriff April provided us with. "Alright, let's get going. We're losing daylight."

Remi looks over Brant's shoulder for a minute. "There's a stream a bit north from here," she announces, and falls into step with Theo as we all start to move out. "I think we can hit it before dark, and we can camp there and refill our water reserves. There should be plenty of game trails down that way, too."

"We should follow the road," I insist.

"But my way will be faster," she argues.

I huff out a sound of annoyance as I take up the rear behind Remi. It's not so that I can watch her ass as she walks. Nope. Definitely not.

"Like the view, Mady?" Remi says over her shoulder, catching me. I quickly wrench my eyes up. Dammit.

I clear my throat and force myself to walk in front of her. "We're taking the road."

"I've camped all over this mountain," she appeals at my back. "Just trust me."

I snort. "You visit wild bears, let rats live in your house, and you run *toward* lightning with large metal objects. I'm not sure you should be the one that we follow blindly. We're taking the road."

She mutters something that I don't catch, but whatever it is, it makes Theo toss his head back and laugh. "Fuck, this is gonna be great. You guys are either gonna end up fighting or fucking. Or maybe both," he muses.

"It'll be both," Brant announces beside me, and I shoot him a glare. He shrugs at me. "It will."

Puddles walks between us, and I reach down and give her a pat. At least she's one female that can't argue with me. She looks funny in the shirt that Brant put on her, but she looks happy as can be as she trots along, sniffing everything as we go. Brant looks more at ease, too. I would think that getting into a collision, having to ditch over half our supplies, and being forced to walk the rest of the way would have freaked him out, but if anything, he looks less stressed. Then again, us moving to Endstone did wonders for him too. I think he just does better with a simpler life nowadays, and there's no simpler way of living than camping and living off the land.

"Tell you guys what, you take the road, and I'll meet you at Endstone. I'm sure you'll get there a few days after me," Remi announces as we walk up the hill toward the road.

"Absolutely not," I snap. "We're not splitting up. I can't believe you would even suggest it."

I look over at her, ready to lecture her about all the reasons why that is a terrible idea, but my words die in my throat when I see the mischievous tilt of her mouth. I narrow my eyes at her. "You're just fucking with me, aren't you?"

"Yep," she says, popping the P at the end.

I sigh in frustration. "Can you stop doing that? You're driving me fucking crazy."

She grins at me and leans in. "I know. Why do you think I like doing it so much? I love to see you get all worked up, soldier." She salutes me, and my dick jumps behind my zipper. The fucking idiot.

* * *

"Are you fucking kidding me?" Theo whines, as we walk around another bend in the road that's a switch back. "We're taking forever winding back and forth, zig-zagging our happy asses down this road, when we could walk straight down through the trees in half the time!"

Fuck, he's right, but I'll be damned if I'm going to admit it, especially when Remi has that smart-ass grin on her face. I run my eyes over her features, and she pretends not to notice, which is good, because I can't seem to stop myself from watching her. She's like a puzzle I'm trying to put together, but I'm not trying to figure her out, I'm trying to figure out why I'm drawn to her in the first place. It's not lack of sex, which might be Brant's or Theo's excuse. I get plenty of that when and where I want to, but there's something else about this chick that I can't put my finger on.

I could live without her digs and attempts to fuck with me, and I vowed to myself in the car to just ignore her and not engage in her fuckery. But then I find myself wanting her to notice me, wanting her to crave *my* attention. It doesn't make any fucking sense. We approach another tight corner that is, yet again, another switch back, and I've officially had enough. At this rate, it will take us a month to get back to Endstone.

Fuck it!

I step off the cleared dirt at the side of the road and move towards the trees that provide a straight path down. I turn to Remi. "I don't want to hear a word," I warn her, not sure what I'll do if an *I told you so* snakes out of her mouth.

Why am I being so stubborn? Who gives a shit if Crazy was right about this? Even a broken watch will get the time right two times a day. Remington mimes zipping her lips and throwing away the key, but her smirk says everything.

I grab the map from Brant and point at the campsite that's supposed to be at the bottom of this dirt road. "We should still be able to get here before night fall."

Remington leans in to take a look and nods. "Yep. We would've been there already if you'd listened to me before," she puts in very unhelpfully.

I raise my finger to her. "I told you—not a word."

"My bad," she says with a shrug. "Come on, GI Joes. Remington April will lead the way," she says as she takes point with far too much pep in her step for my liking. Her opossum is riding on her shoulders, resting against her backpack, and both rats are hanging on top of her back, cuddling into her fur. The fact that I'm not even phased by this says so much about my life right now.

Remington ditches the road and leads us with the watch in hand, and we all follow. My fingers itch to snatch the map and watch and lead the way, but I know that wouldn't go over very well, so all I can do is hope she really does know what the fuck she's talking about and won't get us lost. Then again, I'm the one that wrecked the car in the first place, so part of this situation is my fault. Mine, and that damn rodent she insists is a pet.

As if it knows I'm thinking nefarious thoughts about it, the opossum picks its head up and looks over at me, and I swear, the fucking thing grins, showing off its sharp little dagger teeth. I shudder involuntarily and step further away from it.

"Dude. Coon is giving you crazy eyes," Theo says.

I feel slightly justified, glad to know I'm not just imagining it. But that knowledge doesn't really help, because I'm fairly certain the thing is envisioning jumping on me and clawing my face. It's looking at me like it knows I've been a dick to Remington, and she's now protecting her owner. Which is fucking crazy, because it's just a damn opossum that in no way has enough intelligence for that. I narrow my eyes at it and decide to step closer, refusing to cower. She sits up and hisses, and I immediately shift further away. Theo laughs at my quick footwork. Such an asshole.

I give Coon a wide berth for the next couple of hours, and the four of us settle into a relaxed camaraderie as we walk. I have to admit, if it was just three of us guys, I'd have taken the lead, and I'd be all business. I would have been worried, tense, and serious. But with Remington, she somehow has made this feel like a nice hike down the mountain as she points out game trails, collects edible plants, and gets excited every time she sees some animal scat that she recognizes. I've never seen anyone, let alone a girl, get so excited by shit.

It's way too easy to forget all about things like the Handshake Plague and death tolls when we have her here, so full of life and joy and excitement. I'm almost dreading getting back to Endstone—not that I'd ever admit it. Getting medically discharged from the Army was probably the hardest thing I've ever had to go through. It was harder than the injury and permanent damage to my ear; harder than any boot camp or ranger school, and harder than losing both of my parents when I was sixteen. I suddenly had no purpose or direction, and I've been floating around, not sure of anything, ever since.

For someone like me, who's always had a goal they were busting their ass for; something bigger and better always in their sights, having that taken away was crushing. So this task that Sheriff April gave us—and everything that his crazy ass daughter has put us through since we first laid eyes on her—has been a wakeup call in a way. I didn't realize how much I was just letting the tides of life carry me around until I met Remi, who has an uncanny ability to force me to swim and work hard again for something. I like living in Endstone and being with the guys. Hell, none of us would be as well off as we are without each other, but right now, I have purpose. I have a goal again that requires me to bust my ass to achieve it, and that keeps me on my toes, and I've needed that. Plus, it doesn't hurt that I feel this crazy attraction to her like I haven't felt with anyone for a long time.

The trees around us thin, and after a few more feet, we all step out into a clearing. There are designated campsites and a dirt road that connects them all, and I can hear the faint sound of moving water somewhere in the distance. Thankfully, there's no one around, and I once again tell myself that we are very far from the beaten path, and the likelihood that we'll run into anyone out here is pretty small. My reassurances fall a little flat though, after what happened at Remington's house. I thought we'd be safe and secluded out there, but that didn't last nearly as long as I thought it would.

Remington smiles at the view of the campsites. "We should choose something as close to the water as we can get. Let's drink our fill and make sure we're plenty hydrated, and then we can start boiling water from the stream and refilling water bottles. You boys can enjoy your *beans a la can*, and I'll go see what I can forage for myself," Remi announces, as she treks further back into the campground, and we all follow her like her newest collection of pets.

We settle on a good spot about twenty feet from the slow moving water, and Brant and I go find kindling and firewood, while Remi and Theo lay down the large tarp and start setting up our sleeping bags and the solitary tent. I watch them out of the corner of my eye, until the hunt for dry wood takes me further into the trees, and Remi and Theo are out of sight. Brant snickers, and I fire off a glare in his direction.

"What? You going to try and pretend that she's not everything you didn't know you wanted in one hot and incredibly weird little package?" he asks.

I give an incredulous snort and then raise my eyebrows in surprise at him. "Is that how you feel about her?" I ask, deflecting.

"Oh, so you *are* still swimming in denial," he retorts, rolling his eyes at me. "News flash, Mad, I'm pretty sure we're *all* looking at her like that. Like somehow she's the oxygen we're desperately trying to breathe in now that we know we've been missing it."

His words are eerily similar to my own thoughts not too long ago, and it unsettles me. Is it the mission that I needed, or is it her? Maybe it's both? I wave that thought away and pile more wood into the crook of my arm. "So, what, you and Theo are going to arm wrestle for her?" I tease, but Brant just shrugs, not a hint of humor in his face.

"Maybe it can be like what Remi talked about in the car," he says carefully, and I don't miss the way he shoots me a tentative look.

I laugh as I bend over to snag another broken branch from where it's leaning against a tree trunk. I look up, expecting Brant to be grinning or ready to laugh, but I'm surprised when I see that he's deadly serious.

"Wait a minute," I say, stacking the the branch on to the pile in my arms. "You're serious?"

"Why couldn't it work?" he replies quickly. "I didn't care when she was kissing you or Theo. I don't know why, but it just seemed...comfortable? You and Theo always fuck the dumbest girls. Girls you guys don't even really *like*. But it's different with her. We all like her, and she likes us, and maybe we could..." he rubs a hand over his face in frustration. "This isn't coming out right...I'm attracted to her. Fuck, we *all* are, but I don't think it would be that big of a deal for me if she was with you guys too. You and Theo are my family. I don't know where I would be without you, and it's plain to see that she'd be good for us. She's different, dude. And maybe that's what we need. Maybe *she's* what we've been needing. Ever since we got discharged, nothing's been...right." Brant shrugs. "I dunno, man. Isn't it at least worth talking about?"

When I don't answer, Brant sighs and moves off in the other direction, looking for more kindling. I stare after him for a minute, not sure what to think about what he just said. I'm not even sure why I feel like I need to solve the problem that is *Remi* right now. We've known her for a few days, and I don't understand this hurried feeling I have when it comes to her. Maybe it's an end of the world thing. Would I even be considering any of this if it weren't for the collapse of life as we know it? Would I even think the word *share* when it came to the woman I wanted?

My first thought is, no fucking way. There's *no* way that we could ever share the same girl. But if I admit to myself that I do want her, what then? Because Theo and Brant obviously want her too. Do I let her break us apart? Let the jealousy fester and destroy the bond that we have? Or do we all decide to stay away from her? I snort at that thought. I already know that wouldn't last long. Remi is...addicting. It would just be a matter of time before one of us got caught sneaking over to her place in town, and then we're right back to square one, except mistrust would've been planted and watered. Why the fuck would that be the better option? Like Brant said, I didn't completely hate seeing her with them. Maybe we *could* share.

But guys don't ever date the same chick. It feels against our nature. As I think that, the argument forms that Theo, Brant, and I aren't just any old guys. We're a unit. We've been through a lot of shit together, and we always have each other's backs. But even if I could somehow get on board with this, how long would it be before someone caught wind of it and then tried to shit on it? It's not like Endstone is a hotbed of open-mindedness and well-cultured people. I love the town and the residents, but it's still a small, sheltered town. Then again, why the fuck should I let society dictate anything about my life? What has society done for me? I'm just one among the many wounded soldiers thanked for my service and then practically forgotten in the next breath.

I stand in the middle of the woods, and really let Brant's words dig into my head. Society and knee-jerk reaction aside, what if it *did* work? Are the three of us actually capable of sharing? Do we *want* to be capable of sharing? And what about Remington? Would she honestly be up for something like that? I know she thinks she is, but the three of us...we have baggage. I am fully aware that I'm not an easy man to be with, but maybe that might actually be a reason why this could work.

Wasn't she saying shit about that? That sometimes she needs the asshole, and sometimes she needs the romantic? So maybe when my asshole is front and center, instead of her being beat up about it, the other guys can fill in until I rein things in, because let's face it, that's sure to happen. That's what always happens with chicks when I try to have more than just a hookup. Because I *am* an asshole, and they eventually get sick of it and bail. Not that I blame them. But maybe this could actually work, because Theo would be there to make her laugh, and Brant would be there to do all the fuzzy sweet shit, and we'd *all* be there to take care of each other exactly how we have been since the Rangers.

I think back to the kiss in the woods. I've been trying to avoid focusing too much on it, but I have to admit, when Remington kissed me, I was shocked as fuck, but when her little tongue snaked out and demanded some attention, I knew right then that I wanted to have more than just my tongue in her mouth.

My mind is spinning with the implications and the pros and cons of this kind of thing when I meander back into the clearing. Theo is setting an extra layer of rocks around the designated campsite fire pit, and Remington is gone, probably doing whatever scout bullshit she was so jazzed up about. I go through the motions of arranging the kindling and branches in a little wood teepee and getting a nice pile setup. Brant comes and goes, stacking more wood right beside the fire pit. I get the fire started in no time with the piece of flint, and then Brant gets Puddles settled with some food and water in retractable bowls he was smart enough to bring.

I don't notice that the other guys are watching me as I silently brood until Theo finally elbows me, snapping me out of my scattered thoughts. "Dude. What's up?"

I look over at them and realize that I've been stirring a can of beans for who knows how long, staring at the fire and not taking a bite. I look around to make sure we're still alone before I ask, "You guys are seriously considering dating her? Together?"

Brant and Theo exchange a look. They've always been more easygoing than me, and I wish I could be like that sometimes, too. But I have my doubts that they can actually be so chill about *this*.

Theo shrugs. "Why not? If she's up for it, and she's into us—which she pretty much spelled out for us in the car—then I'm willing to give it a go. She's hot as fuck, fun, and different. We could take *real* good care of her," he finishes with a cocky grin.

"But can she take care of us?" I ask seriously. Because come on, we're three virile guys. If we managed to keep our jealous and competitive natures at bay, could she honestly keep up with all of us?

"Don't you worry, soldier," I hear Remington say behind me, making me jump and spill beans down the side of my hand. "I can handle you three just fine."

I look over my shoulder, watching as she enters the campground. I clear my throat guiltily at being caught talking about her. When I notice her empty hands, I jump on it. "Did the hunting not work out for you, Scout?" I tease.

She rolls her eyes at me and then pulls a bag I hadn't noticed hanging from her thigh holster. She opens it, revealing a bunch of plants inside. "Found some wild onion, chickweed, and I even found some wild strawberries, which is crazy, because they aren't even in season yet," she says proudly.

I look into the bag she holds out and see the smallest fucking strawberries I've ever seen in my life. They're about the size of my fingernail, but she has a couple handfuls of them in the bag.

"You can't live off that," I tell her seriously. "Here," I thrust my can of beans at her. "It's warm. I stirred it."

"A lot," Theo says under his breath with a laugh.

I ignore him and watch Remington reach behind her and unclip something from the belt loop. "Thanks, but I'm good." She brings it around and it's a small gray and brown bird that's clearly dead. Remi sits down on the ground next to us and I stare at the small catch as she unties the string from its feet. "I set all my traps, so I should have more fresh meat by morning," she says confidently as she waves a dismissive hand at the can I'm still holding out to her.

I pull my hand in and watch her work as she pulls out a knife. Her moves are smooth and sure, and there's a grace to it that I find myself somewhat hypnotized by. That abruptly ends when out of nowhere, she snaps the bird's neck and in an impressive move, strips the skin and feathers off in one pull. She guts it and cleans it and before I know it, the bird is on a stick and she's holding it above the flames to cook. Remi is focused on her meal, and the rest of us are focused on her, the only noises around us from insects and the crackle of the fire as it consumes the logs.

"Are you seriously going to eat a malnourished wild bird, some weeds, and strawberry runts?" I ask, not sure how I feel about that. I know she said she can hunt and fend for herself, but this looks like a sad meal to me, and it sets my protective nature off. She really would be better off eating some of the canned food we were smart enough to haul.

"Trust me. This Mountain Quail, strawberries, and onions will taste a hell of alot better than your can of mush, but thanks for the offer."

I huff, doubting that statement, and she raises an eyebrow in challenge at me. "Don't knock it until you try it, Mady," she teases, and I get the impression that we're not just talking about her Bear Grylls's style meal anymore.

Remi pulls a few strawberries out of her bag and reaches out to deposit them in each of our palms. She does the same with a few onions and I stare at the puny haul in my hand. I don't really *want* to eat the weird weeds, but I do, because apparently I'm a sucker, and she looks so damn excited and proud of herself. I shove it in my mouth, prepared to swallow quickly, but surprisingly, the shit doesn't taste half bad. The strawberries, although small, taste better than any of that bland grocery store shit.

"Well?" she asks, but I'm too busy watching her lips close around a strawberry of her own. I'm suddenly thinking about what she must taste like right now as she chews the sweet fruit...and I'm hard again. Fucking hell.

"It was really good, actually," Brant tells her, clearly impressed by the *mad skills* she's been claiming she has.

"And it's healthy," she says with a nod. "There's nothing better than mother nature. She has everything we need."

"Yeah she does," Theo says under his breath, still staring at her mouth.

He's sure as shit not talking about nature.

14

REMI

"**G**o fucking fish," I say triumphantly, as I slap the pile of cards for Theo.

He laughs and shakes his head at me, but draws a card before Madix takes his turn. "Brant, you got any twos?" Madix asks.

Brant swears and hands two cards over, and I chuckle at his expense as Madix makes another book. Brant's eyes flash to me. "You think that's funny?"

I nod, unable to contain my grin. "Sure do. Your pile's looking a little...little," I finish with a laugh.

To my surprise, he leans in close to my ear, and my body instantly becomes very excited at the close proximity. His breath on my neck sends little pings of electricity from my chest, past my stomach, and lights up everything at the apex of my thighs." There's nothing little about my...pile," he tells me, his voice low and gravelly.

Before I can even attempt to reply, he pulls back and winks, and I'm *this close* to throwing the rest of my cards down and launching myself at him. I swear, ever since these boys showed up, my libido has been revved up and ready to go. I've sampled the tasting menu, and now I'm ready for the eleven course meal that is their hot, muscular bodies.

Just that thought sends my blood pumping hard throughout my whole body, and with what I overheard, I'm starting to think that maybe my fantasy isn't so out of reach. When I heard them talking about me on my way back to the campsite, I felt a little guilty at first, but then I just felt shocked as hell. I never thought that these three macho dudes would actually consider getting with me for more than a one night stand, but from the sounds of it, they were actually talking about more than just the hot sex I've been aiming for, and were trying to work out the logistics of an actual relationship. I've always been comfortable with my body and my sexuality; I go for what I want and move on if I don't get it. My views and proclivities are outside of the box, but that's never bothered me.

As far as living outside of the norm, well, I never saw much point in coloring inside the lines when I can draw my own damn picture. But I haven't found anyone willing to do that, not long-term at least, and I was coming to terms with the fact that I probably never would. I date casually, one-night stands and some threesomes here and there, but it gets old. Awesome sex is, well... awesome, but just sex starts to feel unfulfilling. Orgasms are great and a favorite part of my day, but like a mermaid once said, I want more. I want intimacy and orgasms, and I've discovered that is a very difficult combo to find.

But this? The three of them? It's a golden unicorn of a perfect scenario. It's a bit surreal sitting here with them around a campfire, playing Go Fish, while the world ends. I feel like a giddy kid on Christmas morning, but at the same time, I don't want to get my hopes up just to find out that my golden unicorn is really a donkey with a toilet paper roll tied to its head. If this actually turns into more than one night of hot sex, then I will have officially found the holy fucking grail. I run my gaze slowly over each of them and bite my cheek to keep the audible sounds of appreciation from sneaking out of my mouth.

There would be zero chance of me getting bored with these three. And it's not just because they're hot, but yeah, not gonna lie, that's a nice little perk. I mean, they've got muscles on muscles, with a side of muscles. There are so many strong and bendy things that would be possible with these three.

Plus, they're all so different yet complementary to each other, and the real golden unicorn prancing around this group, is that they're actually genuinely good guys. I suspected as much when I drew my gun on them on my porch and heard why they were there. But after watching them interact with each other and worry about the welfare of a complete stranger, their *good guy* status is officially confirmed.

"Remington," Madix says, drawing me out of my thoughts with his deep, husky voice. The sound of my name on his lips immediately sends goosebumps traveling over my skin.

He leans towards me, and I'm suddenly aware of the heat and closeness of Brant on my left, while Madix's movement on my right is setting up a delicious Remi sandwich.

God, I love sandwiches. Please let them be footlongs.

Madix's dark eyes smolder as he flicks his gaze over my body before meeting my eyes. *This is it,* I think to myself. The macho alpha is finally gonna give in to the intense sexual chemistry we have. Adrenaline courses through my body, and I clench my thighs in delectable anticipation.

"Yeah, soldier?" I reply, because I know it drives him wild. I see the way his eyes dilate every time I do it.

He raises a finger, and my lips part and my breath

hitches, waiting to see where he's going to touch me. He makes a straight line for my breasts, and I unconsciously jut my chest out because *hell yeah!* But right at the last second, his finger drops, and instead, he taps the top of the cards that I completely forgot I was even holding.

"You got any aces?" he asks with a smirk.

I blink several times, totally caught off-guard. "Huh?"

"You were the one that wanted to play Go Fish," he says, his lips tilting upward. Did he just do that on purpose? Did GI Asshole just read my building need like a book, and then *play me?* I take in the smirk on his face, and a resounding *yes* chimes in my head. This alpha dick knows *exactly* how much I'm dying to play with his .44 Magnum, and judging by the look on his face, teasing me and making my body respond to him is exactly what he's trying to do.

My eyes flick down to my cards and I groan. "You motherfucker."

He laughs, and it's the first time I've heard him do it. I swear, the noise makes my clit put on a skimpy dress and go clubbing, pulsing with the beat and begging to be grinded on. I puff out my cheeks and then blow out a breath as I pass him over all three of my aces, feeling both sexually frustrated and competitively frustrated, because now I'm losing, dammit.

Madix asks Theo for threes, and then sets the last remaining cards in his hands on the ground and declares himself the winner. Gah, he's even hot when he's smug.

We all groan in protest, and Brant starts to collect the cards and reshuffle them. Theo repositions himself on the log that Brant dragged over, but I can tell he's uncomfortable. I'm pretty sure it's his leg, since he keeps rubbing at his left thigh, and I want to ask if he's okay, but I don't want to be a prick and shove my nose in business that he clearly doesn't want to share, or embarrass him in any way.

Brant and Madix both give him a concerned once-over, but their lips stay sealed, and it's obvious that they're feeling exactly like I am. Once again, Theo's hand snakes down, and he rubs at his thigh. Fuck it. I was never one for pussy footing around anything.

"Is your leg bothering you?" I ask, and Theo's eyes shoot up to my face.

He looks at me for a minute, and then narrows his eyes at Madix and then Brant. I shake my head at his assumption. "They didn't tell me anything. I put two and two together when your tracks in the mud weren't the same depth, which meant the weight distribution was slightly different. And at home, Coon tried to give your leg a proper humping under the table, and you didn't feel it."

Theo chuckles nervously, shooting a glare at the pet carrier that's sitting on the other side of the fire. He rubs the back of his neck with his palm, and I can feel the debate going on inside of him. "Oh, what the hell," he announces, and then pulls up the leg of his pants. I watch as he presses a button on the side of the prosthetic, and it disconnects from a strap that looks like it's still attached to his leg. I've never seen a prosthetic before, and I'm curious about how it works, but I don't know if it will make him feel more awkward if I ask questions. My curiosity must be written all over my face, because Theo starts to explain things.

"This is the socket. It's where my residual limb or stump connects." He pulls off a white covering on his leg. "This is a sock that adds volume to my leg, so that the socket fits better. And this is a liner that has a strip glued to it that attaches to the socket and kind of keeps it all together so that it doesn't come off." Theo slides the liner down his leg, and it rolls off until it's inside out. He sets everything on the tarp, and I run my gaze over his injury. He has about four or five inches of leg below his knee, and a lot of scarring at the stump, as well as on his knee and the part of his thigh that I can see.

The sight sends a twinge of sympathy through me. I can't even imagine how difficult it would be to go through whatever caused his injury, and then have to recover from it. Theo catches my inspection, and his eyes run over my face, looking for something.

"Shrapnel shredded my leg. They couldn't save the bottom part."

"Does it still hurt?" I ask, holding his green eyed gaze.

"Sometimes it swells and shrinks, which affects the fit of the socket, and that can make things uncomfortable. I haven't been this active since my injury, so I'm sore, but I think I just need to rest and let my limb breathe, which I haven't been doing as much as I should lately."

"Why not?" I question.

Theo hesitates for a second and his eyes flit briefly to Brant and Madix. "I didn't want to draw attention to it."

I nod my head and then get up to move and plop down directly in front of him. "When my feet are sore, I like it when someone rubs them. Would that help at all?"

He leans away from me just slightly, and I can tell he's not sure what to do or say, so I stay quiet and give him time to process and decide what he wants to do. He looks to Madix, like he'll find direction there, but I don't take my eyes from Theo's to see what Madix silently communicates. Theo looks at me again, and for the second time, I get the impression that he's looking for something in my face— some kind of reaction, but I don't know if he finds it or not in my calm features.

"Umm, I guess...but you don't have to, if you don't want to," he adds quickly, and I can hear the uncertainty in his voice that's matched by the vulnerability I see in his face.

"Oh, you're not getting off scot-free. I fully expect the

foot rub to be reciprocated. I mean, don't be selfish," I tease him, placing my hands on his leg.

I push up his cargo pants and start on his thigh, which seems to surprise him for some reason, but it's what he's been rubbing at all night, so I figure it's as good a place as any to start. I massage the muscles slowly, and run my hands up and down in the direction they run. I have no idea what I'm doing, but I do have a body, and I know what feels good to me, so I just go with it.

I rub up and down his thigh, ignoring the tenting that starts in his pants when I move up higher. I roam over his knee and then gently rub at the bottom of his residual limb. I pay attention to his body, focusing on areas that make him flinch, and try to work out the soreness with a mixture of steady pressure and gentle motion.

Slowly, I feel him relax under my hands, and when I feel like I've done all I can, I move to his other leg, untie his boots, and then rub his foot, calf, and lower thigh. This seems to surprise him, too, but he doesn't say anything as I work. Oddly enough, no one does. Brant and Madix are quietly watching me, but the silence doesn't feel awkward or pressing. It feels relaxed and peaceful. I don't know how long I've been at it, but my hands are sore by the time I finish my awesome rub down. I lean back with a satisfied smile. When I look up again, I see Theo staring at me, an astonished look on his face.

"What?" I ask, tucking a strand of hair behind my ear.

He shakes his head like he's trying to clear it. "Nothing."

When I look back at the other guys, they're watching me with the same look of astonishment that's on Theo's face. The moment suddenly feels heavy with meaning, and I'm not sure what to make of it. Things feel entirely too serious right now, so I do what I do best and go for a laugh to lighten things up. I start to lift my foot up into Theo's lap so that I can claim that it's my turn, but a weird sound comes from the pet carrier, interrupting me. It's a very weird kind of chirping that I've never heard before, so I immediately crawl over to peek inside.

I gasp and my brows shoot up in surprise. I quickly cover my eyes and spin around with a squeak. Brant gives me a quizzical one, and he moves towards me.

"Don't look!" I warn him, my voice a higher pitch than it normally is. "I've read the situation *very* wrong. They're not her kids. They're her mates!" I blurt out.

The guys look at me, and I shake my head, peeking at them from between my fingers.

"I mean, I should feel proud of her, because, you go girl," I tell her, as she continues to get it on. "But I was *not* prepared for the orgy that is apparently taking place in there," I say, hiking a thumb over my shoulder to point at her. When another squeal sounds, I quickly hop to my feet and dart away from the cage.

I stand with my hand still over my eyes, and all three guys stare at me, as the four of us listen to three *very* male rats who have Coon making noises that I've never heard from her before. I didn't even think that interspecies sex was a thing. That's why I always assumed the bond was maternal —nothing else made any sense.

Madix is the first to laugh. He tips his head back and lets it out, the sound sinking deep within me like a sweet, welcome caress. His booming laughter sets off Theo and Brant next, and I drop my hand and blink wide-eyed, clearly still in shock by the new discovery, as they all laugh hysterically at my expense.

I watch them laughing at me with narrowed eyes, but their enjoyment is contagious, and the next thing I know, I'm holding my middle, laughing so hard that tears are falling onto my cheeks. It's so freeing to be laughing with them, and they must feel that too, because the mood shifts again, this time using our levity to morph into something more. Theo suddenly pulls me down on his lap, and the next thing I know, his lips crash against mine.

I don't hesitate to wrap my arms around his neck as he swallows the tapered-off ends of my laughter. Our mouths open at the same time, and then our tongues begin to flick against each other in a clash of passion. He's still hard from my earlier ministrations, and the feel of him underneath me makes me shift so I can straddle him. We never break the kiss, and his hands immediately move to grip my ass.

Before I lose my head too much, I pull away, my breath coming in short pants, and I turn to look at the other two. This moment right here will be the most important. If I don't treat them all right, this could break us before we even get started. I heard what they were saying. I heard the curiosity and the possible willingness to try this out. If I really want to give this a go, which I do, then I need to step up and lead them. I need to prove that this can actually work.

I lean back into Theo, kissing him again, learning his tongue and what elicits a moan out of him, like when I nip at his bottom lip and then flick my tongue out to stroke his top lip. I smile at him and then stand up. Theo grunts out his disapproval, but instead of getting off of him like he thinks I am, I simply turn around and sit back down.

My back is now pressed to his muscular chest and I grind my ass onto his erection, earning another delicious noise of approval from him. I let my hooded gaze settle on first Madix and then Brant, and they exchange a hesitant look.

"Trust me," I tell them quietly, my voice filled with heat.

As if to back me up, Theo grips my waist, and then he thrusts up, grinding himself between my straddling thighs. I tip my head back with a moan and close my eyes for a second to revel in the feel of him. Theo nips at my earlobe and then sucks at my neck, sending a strike of pleasure straight to my clit. I love feeling him take charge and moving against me. It's exactly the reassurance I need that he's into this and okay with my encouragement of the others. Brant leans forward like he's going to get up, but then he stops, unsure. I watch him, my gaze filled with invitation, and I hold out my hand to him.

Brant looks at it for a beat, but then he finally moves towards me. His hands reach out to cradle my face before fitting his lips perfectly against mine. I can practically taste the questions in his kiss, and we take our time passing back reassurances with our lips and tongues. Brant deepens the kiss, and I can feel him drinking me in slowly, savoring my taste.

My hand moves through his short dark-blond mohawk, and I tug lightly at the longer strands in the middle. He gives an appreciative groan, and what I'm doing seems to drive him a bit wild because he threads his hand through my hair, tugging with the same amount of force. A thrill shoots through me when he does it at the same time that Theo rocks into me, and the only thing missing is the brooding, dark-haired man who's still sitting on the other side of the fire.

I open my eyes, dazed from lust, and crook my finger at him. He doesn't respond. Instead, he settles back against the rock at his back, folding his arms over his chest. He looks like he's making his intentions clear that he's deciding to stay out of this, but instead of being dismayed, it spurs me on. He looks as rigid as always, but his eyes are fixed on what I'm doing with Theo and Brant, and that's at least something. Maybe a little show-and-tell is in order.

I lick at the seam of Brants lips, and then stand up and

walk a couple feet to the tent. I pull out the sleeping bags and start to unzip them until they can lay flat like a blanket, and then proceed to re-zip them together so that they're connected, creating one big bed.

I return my stare to Madix and lift an eyebrow in challenge. I don't miss the stiff bulge in his dark pants. While watching him, I reach down and slowly undo the button on my pants and then slide down the zipper. I shift my gaze from Madix to Brant and then to Theo. I push my pants down, hooking my thumbs in the leggings I'm also wearing, and shove everything over my hips, skim over my ass, and then let them fall around my ankles before kicking them and my shoes off.

"Fucking Christ," Theo curses, and a smirk slips over my face.

Brant groans as he looks at me. "Where the fuck did those come from? That was not the underwear you had on when you changed earlier at the car."

I glance down at the bright pink lace thong, and I turn slightly to give them a clear view of my ass. "What, these old things? I thought they set the tone much better than my previous bikini briefs. You like?" I model them from side-to-side giving them plenty of time to take in every angle.

"Shit, your ass is even better than I imagined," Theo admits, his eyes riveted to my lower half.

"So you've been imagining me?" I ask, my smirk morphing into a pleased grin.

"Of course we have," he says dismissively, like it's common knowledge.

"Good," I say with a nod. "Because I haven't been able to stop thinking about everything I want to do with your mouths, your hands, and your cocks."

All three men groan at that, and the sound fills me with such intense heat that I can't wait a moment longer. I grab the hem of my shirt and pull it up and over my head, dropping it to the ground.

"Help a brother out," Theo demands of Brant.

Brant helps him get up, anchoring Theo with an arm around his shoulder, and they both move over to where I am. Theo sits down on my sleeping bag bed, and I immediately drop so I can straddle his legs, while still facing Brant. I waste no time moving things along, pulling Brant toward me at the same time that I pop open his pants and push them down. He barely has time to react before I close my hand around his cock and then wrap my mouth around the head.

"*Fuck.*"

This comes from both Brant and Theo at the same time. I move my tongue around Brant's impressive length, while my ass grinds into Theo. He grabs two healthy handfuls of asscheeks, his hot hands squeezing slightly and keeping away the chill in the air.

"You're fucking gorgeous," Theo murmurs in my ear. He could be talking to me, or to my butt. Either way, I'm happy.

Brant is long, so I use one of my hands to curl around the base of his cock, while I work the rest of him up and down slowly with my mouth, taking my time the way I'm learning that he takes his time with me. I love getting to know what makes him pant, and I pay attention to every sound I earn so that I can log exactly what makes him moan. Brant threads his hands in my hair, but he doesn't move to guide me, he seems to just like the feel of my movement as I move up and down his long cock. I feel him start to tense, and I know he's getting close to coming, but I've got plans for exactly how I want him to come.

I pull my head back and release the head of his dick with a quiet pop, and then give it one last lick before turning around to Theo. "I hope you are enjoying the show, but there's a condom in my pant's pocket. Put it on. I want to sit on your cock while I play with Brant."

Theo's hold on my ass tightens almost painfully. "You have a dirty little mouth," he muses quietly. He salutes me with amusement, and reaches over for my pants.

"I sure do, soldier, and I hope you boys do too," I reply, before turning back around and running my tongue along the underside of Brant's very long, very hard cock. I take his head back in my mouth and give a satisfied hum as I look up at him. His hands tighten in my hair and his jaw clenches. "Jesus, Remi."

Theo must have gotten lost in the show again, because I'm not hearing the opening of a wrapper or feeling a lot of movement behind me. I impatiently jiggle my ass in front of him before arching my back. That seems to snap him out of his inaction, and his hands hook the strings of my underwear and promptly rip them off of me. It's hot as fuck, and I moan my approval as Theo uses his knee to widen the space between my thighs. His strong, calloused hands guide my hips down, and he positions me perfectly over the head of his cock.

I'm so turned on and wet that I don't need to follow the slow pace that Theo is setting. Instead, I sink down onto him hard, filling myself up. It feels so good that I'm forced to release Brant from my mouth so that I can toss my head back in pleasure. "Fuck, yes," I moan. "God, you feel good."

"Yeah?" he asks, thrusting up into me from his seated position and demanding another pleasure-filled moan from my lips. "You like that?"

My mind is a haze of pleasure, and I don't bother answering. Instead, I reach down and pull Theo's hands from my hips and move them up to my breasts. I move myself up his thick cock and then slide back down in delicious friction. Theo pinches my nipples through the fabric of my bra, before hurriedly unhooking it from my back and sliding it down my arms. I ride Theo slowly at first, working out which movements elicit groans from him. When I find a steady and very satisfying rhythm, my eyes find Madix again.

I keep my eyes locked on his as I slowly raise up from Theo, before slamming myself back down. I join Theo's hands on my breasts so I can pinch my own nipples, my breasts bouncing from the impact as I ride his cock. The firelight illuminates Madix's face enough for me to see him swallow hard, and when I slowly bend over again to take Brant into my mouth once more, I watch Madix undo his pants.

Fuck, that's sexy.

I lick the head of Brant's cock, and watch as Madix pushes his pants low against his thighs, and then he's fisting himself, watching as I take Theo and Brant inside of me at the same time. My stomach crackles with excitement and desire. I move faster and faster, and the guys move with me. All four of us are making carnal sounds that fill the woods, and it's so erotic that my orgasm takes me by surprise, crushing me with pleasure from the inside out.

"Fuck, yes. Ride out that orgasm as you ride my cock. Let me see how good we're making you feel," Theo demands, his hands coming around my hips to play with my clit. He flicks and pinches it, and the added sensations prolong my release.

"I'm gonna come, Remi," Brant warns, so I start working him harder, taking him all the way to the back of my throat as I reach down and grip his balls at the same time.

"Fuck, just like that, baby," he says, and he starts to fuck my mouth in hard thrusts.

I lose the rhythm of riding Theo, but he takes over completely and begins to slam into me, making me bounce on his dick, and it feels fucking *incredible.* My orgasm seems to roll into another one, until I'm a jellied, writhing, moaning mess that can do nothing but feel pleasure while they take control of my body.

Brant roars out his release and comes in my mouth, and I drink him down. Seconds later, Theo is jerking into me and pulling me away from Brant to hold me tightly against his muscular chest. Theo grinds into me shallowly a few more times, his groan buried against my neck as he tweaks my nipples again and nips at my shoulder.

I barely manage to gain enough wherewithal to open my eyes in time to find Madix, his hand moving up and down over his cock in hard, fast strokes, as he comes. When he sees me watching, his eyes take on a hungry, possessive look that shoots pleasure straight into me, and I tighten my core around Theo, making him groan again. We all let the last of our pleasure ride out, spent and panting. I feel so incredibly satisfied, and excited at how well our first time went. Even if Madix didn't actively participate, he still was a part of it.

Brant is the first one of us to move, and he pulls his pants up and tucks himself away. When he's situated, he reaches down for me and helps me up so that Theo can clean up. Brant runs his gaze over my face and traces his thumb across my bottom lip. "I'll grab your bag so you can get some clothes to sleep in," he tells me, and then he places a gentle kiss against my lips. The tenderness of it makes my heart sing.

I nod, watching him as he steps away and unzips the tent to search for my bag. I feel a tug on my hand, and look down to find Theo inviting me to sit down next to him. I do, and he immediately wraps a large arm around me, before grabbing my chin to turn my head and place a sweet kiss on my lips.

"That was fucking amazing," he tells me.

"It was," I agree, my eyes darting over to Madix again, who's still leaning against a rock on the other side of the fire. "Well?" I ask him, anxious to hear him say something. "Did you enjoy the show?" I ask with a smirk.

Heat banks in his eyes, and he tilts his head as he takes me in. "It was...enlightening," he answers vaguely, but there's a hint of something that wasn't there before.

"Think you'd like to be more hands-on next time?" I press.

He shrugs his shoulders. "Maybe," he answers, his tone and words nonchalant. But it's not a no, and that's sure as fuck a step in the right, golden-unicorn direction.

15

THEO

I wrap my arms around Remi's waist and feel her soft skin against mine. Madix insisted that we take turns keeping watch at night, and I traded out my boring staring contest with the dark wilderness to sleep beside Remi at about three this morning. I run my nose over the back of her neck and gently thrust my morning wood into the crack of her ass. I'm ready for some hot morning sex where I can pin her underneath me and fuck her so hard that her tits bounce, her eyes closing as she tightens around my cock and begs for more.

Fuck yes! I groan as push my hard-on against her again.

"What the fuck, man?" Brant bites out groggily.

My eyes fly open, and I scramble back when I realize that I wasn't just spooning my hot new obsession, but Brant. Puddles stands up and releases a massive doggy yawn inside the tent.

"Fuck, I thought you were Remi! Thought I might get lucky this morning."

Brant moves to stand, but is forced to crouch down because of the tent. He proceeds to cover his ass with his hands as he glares at me.

"Next time, open your eyes and double check who you're humping. Sexual assault is not the side I want with my eggs."

I smile and waggle my eyebrows at him. "What if I told you my dick tastes like bacon?"

Brant barks out a laugh and then kicks the bottom of the sleeping bag at me. "Shit, I was going to say I prefer sausage, but that comeback doesn't fucking work in this situation."

I laugh and reach for the liner and socks I need to put on before I can attach my prosthetic.

"You need help with anything?" Brant offers, but I wave him away.

"Nah, I got it. Thanks, though. What are the odds that Remi caught a wild pig and she's currently frying bacon over the fire right now?" I ask, the longing clear in my voice.

"I'm going to go with slim to none. With this virus and what's going on in the country, our bacon for breakfast days might be done for."

I groan. "Don't bog me down with shitty reality first thing in the morning. What kind of person shits all over a good bacon fantasy?"

"My bad. I'll make a note that you can't handle reality before morning coffee," Brant says, before his eyes widen. "Oh, shit. We probably won't have any of that for much longer, either!"

"You're a fucking sadist," I say, picking up a pair of pants to chuck at him.

He chuckles and ducks out of the tent, Puddles quick on his heels. I chuckle to myself, trying not to focus on the truth in his words. Instead, I enjoy seeing the playful side of Brant that hasn't been a prominent part of his personality since we got discharged. I know he's worked hard to face his issues head on, and with therapy and Puddles's help, he's come a long way. It's good to see these pieces of him again, despite what's going on around us. If I had to bet, I'd guess that Remi was another reason for his happy mood.

I roll the liner that attaches to my prosthetic over my stump, up past my knee, and feel to make sure the strap is in the right place. I decide to not put on the other sock, since I feel a little swollen from all the walking I did, and I won't need the extra volume that the sock normally provides.

I flash back to the night before, when Remi plopped down in front of me and asked to give me a rub down. I wasn't sure what to make of the offer. I kept looking for any sign that she was grossed out, or just offering because she felt sorry for me. But I didn't see any revulsion or pity, which surprised the fuck out of me. I mean, when I first saw the state of my leg *I* was freaked out by it. I just assume everyone else is too. Madix and Brant have caught glimpses here and there because we live together, but Remi is the first person I've ever really purposely shown it to.

I couldn't get over that she actually touched me there and didn't bombard me with a ton of questions about what happened. I really should know by now that Remi will never react how I think she will. Like when she effortlessly rode my cock while sucking Brant off and giving Madix a show. She was so confident and sure of herself, and it was damn sexy.

Fuck. I want to be inside her again. Maybe I can convince her that we need to get it out of our systems before we head out today. Otherwise, we might not be as productive, and we sure as hell still have a long way to go. I need to figure out how to make sex breaks every two hours a thing.

I adjust my boner and pull on a clean pair of pants and a shirt. I pull my boot on and exit the tent to find only Brant and Madix sitting around the dwindling fire.

"Where's our girl?" I ask, and Madix shoots me an unamused look. "Oh, come on, *Mady*. Don't be jealous because you benched yourself last night. I'm sure Remi will give you another shot if you beg hard enough."

"Don't you start with that Mady shit, too. I *will* kick your ass."

"Who's kissing whose ass?" Remi asks as she saunters into the clearing holding a couple dead rabbits by the ears.

She moves over closer to the fire and pulls a knife from a sheath inside the top of her boot. She bends over to deal with the rabbits, and all three of us tilt our heads. I run my eyes appreciatively over her nice ass. A flash of it bouncing up on my cock flashes through my head. *Yep. I definitely need to be inside her again before we leave.*

Madix hands me a can of what looks like some kind of bean soup, breaking through my stare. I tilt my head back and take a swig of the lukewarm concoction as I eye Remi's rabbits hungrily. She cleans them and gets them on sticks to cook like a pro. When I start smelling them cook, my mouth waters. I want meat. These beans are just not cutting it, and I could do without the magical-fruit-toots for the rest of this trip. Maybe if it looks like she has a little extra, I'll see if I can sweet talk her into sharing.

I swallow the rest of my unsatisfying breakfast and try not to be too much of a creeper as I watch Remi's every move. I catch Brant and Madix doing the same, and from the look of things, I'm not the only one wondering, *what happens now?* Do we talk about shit? Or do we just move on?

"You guys are going to make this awkward aren't you?" Remi sighs, glancing over at us. "Dammit, I had high hopes that we could just keep on keepin' on, but nope. You all have that look on your face."

"What look?" Brant asks.

"The, *I'm not sure how to talk to a girl after I stick my dick in her,* look." Remi shakes her head and rotates the skewered rabbits over the fire. "You commitment-phobes can slow your roll. There won't be any, *where is this going,* kind of questions from me, okay? I'm good with what happened. I'm super good with doing more of that, but I'm not expecting a ring or any kind of declarations. So all of you just take a deep breath and stop being weird, okay? It's freaking me out."

We're all quiet, contemplating what she just said, awkwardly shooting each other glances.

"Crap, I don't know how to stop being weird," Brant admits, making me chuckle.

He's right, I don't know either. One minute, I'm trying to figure out how I can fuck her again, and the next, I *am* wondering where we go from here. I do want to give her—and myself—a lot of orgasms. I find her interesting and fun to be around, but that might just be because of all the fucking I want to do. But maybe something long-term isn't so crazy. I mean, the guys seem open to it. Man, when did I get so needy and confused?

Fuck it. I'll leave the brooding to Madix. I shake off my thoughts and move to sit on the log next to Remi. I pull her onto my lap, and she gives a surprised squeal at my sudden repositioning of her body, but she doesn't say anything or try to move away. She just keeps cooking her rabbits, which are starting to smell *really* fucking good.

"Don't think I don't know what you're up to," she tells me with a knowing look.

I stare at her with confusion, because I didn't think I was up to anything. I was trying not to be awkward, and I wanted to touch her, so I just went with it.

Remi's smile turns into a smirk. "You think I didn't see you eying my breakfast," she gives an indignant huff. "After all the shit you three gave me about hunting and that you'd be fine eating canned food, you better think twice about trying to to butter me up now. This is my meat. And I love my meat," she says with a suggestive smirk.

"Hey," I object. "I'm pretty sure Madix was the only one giving you crap. Brant and I were quiet as church mice on that issue."

Remi flicks the tip of my nose and tsks at me. "Oh, yeah. You were quiet, alright, but you still stuffed your bags with canned food. Actions speak louder than words, GI Joe, and you, sir, ain't getting any of my rabbit!"

I give her an indignant look and then shoot one to Brant when he starts to chuckle. I adopt an innocent mein and run my nose over Remi's neck. "Don't be like that. I thought you were a fan of sharing," I tease with a wicked smile on my face to match the tone in my voice. "Let me eat some of your rabbit, baby."

Remi chuckles, but I don't miss the the goose bumps that rise on her skin or her hard nipples making themselves known through her shirt.

"Well, *baby*," she coos at me, and I swallow when she starts to slowly unbutton her black pants. "I wouldn't want to starve a growing boy, so I'll let you go right ahead and eat my *rabbit*. If you think you can handle it."

All thought of the meat she's cooking flies right out of my head. I hone in on Remi as she moves to lower her zipper. *Fuck yes*, I cheer to myself, as I instantly get hard at the thought of her wet pussy and the noises she would make with my head buried between her thighs. That would be the best breakfast ever.

"You two knock it off," Madix barks at us. "We don't have time for this shit. We need to get back as soon as possible where it's safe, and then you can go at it like *rabbits*," he says, his annoyance and anger practically throwing a cold bucket of water on me.

"Oh, come on, Mady. You can have a taste too, if you're hungry," Remi grins with a wink.

"I told you, don't fucking call me that. There's a time and a place for this, but now isn't the time," Madix growls at her.

"Dude, chill," Brant warns.

"I'll chill when we're safe in our beds again. Until then, maybe everyone needs to remember what the fuck we're doing out here. I'll pack up the tent. Everyone be ready to go in twenty minutes. We have a long-ass day ahead of us."

Madix stomps off toward the tent and angrily starts to break it down. I spend about two seconds wanting to call him a prick and telling him he needs to get laid, but truthfully, he's right. Just because we're not immediately being affected by what's happening in the bigger cities, doesn't mean we should lose sight of what's going on.

"I'll help with the sleeping bags," I mumble. "Brant, you scan the campsite. Make sure we don't leave anything we need behind."

Brant nods, and I move Remi off of my lap. I look at her, worried about what I might see in her face. I expect some type of pissed-off emotion to be radiating from her, but she just gives me a smile and returns her focus to cooking the rabbits. I lean in and steal a kiss, because apparently I'm needy like that now, and Remi obliges and nips at my lip as I pull away. I ignore the pulse beating in my cock, and focus on what needs to get done.

We get the entire camp broken down and packed up in less than ten minutes. We work silently and efficiently, just like always. I turn to ask Remi how much more time she needs to get ready, but she already has her pack on her shoulders, and she's kicking dirt on the fire to strangle it. It's out in no time, and she's off, nibbling on her rabbit kabobs and walking in the direction that Madix just announced we need to go in. At least he seems to be taking a more direct route back to town.

For a slim girl, Remi can sure as fuck pack it in. I spend the first hour thinking at some point she'd announce she was full and pass off a leg of meat or two. But nope, she devoured both bunnies and discarded the bones when she was done. Not even Puddles was spared a bite of Thumper.

I've spent the last hour coming up with a plan to convince Remi of my absolute devotion to her and her hunting abilities, and I feel confident that tonight I'll be dining on the spoils of her mad skills. Why I listened to Madix in the first place, I'll never know. I'm going to blame it on shock from the accident. I'm positive her rabbit meat was delicious, if her little *Mmm's* were any indication.

By late morning, Remi has once again become our unofficial leader. Madix keeps his death grip on the map, but Remi seems to know where she's going without it. Every now and then, Madix gives a grunt of frustration and double-checks where we are, certain that she's leading us in the wrong direction, but he's been wrong every time. It's making him turn into an even bigger asshole than usual.

Fun times.

"So, boys, how's Leonard Coleman's old house treating you?" Remi asks, as she pushes a low-hanging evergreen branch out of her way. "It took me a minute to connect who your uncle was, Theo, but I can put a face to a name now. He had that two story off of X and ¾ Road didn't he?"

Brant and I laugh. "Yep, that's the one. And why the hell do they have roads named after letters and weird ass measurements? Did you map the town's streets to read as O's and 18/19ths as part of your pranks?" I joke.

"I wish I could take credit for that, but nope. Endstone is just weird like that. Who knows why that town does anything that it does? Your guess is as good as mine," she announces, as she looks up at the sky for a couple of seconds before veering of to the right.

I try to hide my smile, knowing Madix is probably going to have that map open in less than a second, just to get pissed off again that she's right.

"My uncle's place was pretty dated, but we've been fixing it up," I tell her. "We updated the kitchen and the bathrooms, redid the flooring throughout the whole house, and we're in the process of replacing the roof. Once all that's done, we'll paint, and she'll be as good as new," I tell her proudly. "We've kicked ass on the house project, and it's almost unrecognizable on the inside now."

"That's cool, I'd love to see it," she tells us nonchalantly, and I don't miss the twitch that sneaks through Madix.

Apparently, neither does Remi, because she turns to him. "Before you go reading too much into that, I'm not inviting myself to move in, I'm just curious about the work you did. I have my own house up on P road that probably needs some TLC at this point."

"If you own a house in town, why don't you live there?" Madix asks, voicing the question that Brant and I are both thinking.

"It was passed down from my mom's side of the family. I never wanted to live in it. I knew at around fifteen that Endstone wasn't the place for me." Remi grows quiet, and I wait for her to elaborate, but she doesn't.

"What happened that made you want to leave?" I finally ask, at the same time Remi throws out, "So, where did you soldiers learn how to do all that manual labor and handyman shit?" We both pause and wait for the other to answer, and then both start speaking again at the same time. I crack up, and it's echoed by Remi's lyrical laugh.

"Ladies first," I finally manage, and Remi gives me a smart ass curtsey.

Before she can open her mouth to answer my question, a weird grunt and a rustling sound in the bushes off to our left make us all freeze. We listen intently, our eyes scanning our surroundings as we try to figure out what the hell that was. When another huff-like growl fills the air, I'm wondering if it's a bear.

At first, this thought makes me panic a little, and I look down the sights of my rifle, ready for the massive predator to show itself. But then I remember that Remi is like some weird ass bear whisperer, and think that maybe we'll manage not to get mauled today. She has a weird connection to animals in general. I mean, Brant is currently holding a pet carrier that has an opossum and a harem of rats for fuck's sake.

"Is that..." Brant whispers, but he gets cut off with Remi shushing him.

The next thing we know, the tall bushes rustle again, and then a huge rack of antlers appears. Okay, so it's *not* a bear. But what kind of mutant deer is this?

More of the animal comes into view, and Brant and Madix both tighten their hands on their rifles.

"Oh, shit," Remi exclaims, taking a step back when the moose comes into full view. It's not the response I expect from her at all. Not after seeing her smoking fish for a bear's breakfast and cuddling an opossum like it's a puppy.

Her blue eyes stay locked on the animal. And yeah, it's massive, but it's a shit ton better than a bear or some other kind of crazy predator.

I look from Remi's paling face back to the moose. "You hang out with huge-ass bears and opossums with razor teeth, but you're scared of a *moose?*" I ask with surprise.

"Moose are fucking crazy," she hisses under her breath.

Madix scoffs. "Pot meet Kettle."

She doesn't call him out on his jibe. Not only has the

blood drained from her face, but her eyes are stuck in a wide, fearful expression, and her body is tensed up like she's frozen in terror.

"Remi?" Brant coaxes her, like *she's* the wild animal in this scenario and needs to be calmed down.

When the moose opens its mouth and takes another bite of leaves, Remi starts singing *Stay Calm* by Griffinilla. She pushes her hands out for us to hold, but when we don't take them, she cuts off her song to say, "It can smell fear!"

"Then you should probably calm the fuck down because it's just a moose," Madix says dryly.

"I know what to do," she says, ignoring Madix completely. She takes a calming breath that doesn't seem to calm her at all, and then cups her hands around her mouth and....makes the weirdest fucking roaring noise I've ever heard. All of us flinch. Even the damn moose.

Madix reaches over and yanks her hands away from her mouth. "What the fuck was that?"

"Bear call," she says, perfectly seriously.

We gape at her. "Right. Because when you see a harmless moose, the first thing you should do is try to attract a wild fucking bear to help the situation," Madix deadpans.

She does the weird, obnoxious roar thing again, but when the moose still doesn't move and no *fucking bears* come to her rescue, Remi's fear seems to take over. "We're on our own! Run!"

Remi whirls around and starts sprinting in the other direction. Her pack slamming up and down against her back as she runs like her ass in on fire. We gape at her in shock, while the moose just continues to munch on another bite of leaves, looking like he doesn't have a care in the fucking world. We watch as Remi stumbles a little, catching herself on a tree before jumping back to her feet. "I'm okay!" she waves from behind her back. "Hurry, before it mauls us!"

Brant, Madix, and I look from the chewing moose and back over to Remi, who's managed to trip again in her haste, landing sprawled out on the forest floor, face-first. I...I don't even know what the fuck is happening right now.

Madix shakes his head. "Stop before you break your fucking ankle!" he hollers.

She looks behind her, seeing us still standing next to the moose, and she scrambles behind the nearest tree to peek out from behind it. "Get over here," she says, waving at us. "Hurry, before it attacks!"

I press my lips together tightly, but there's no stopping the laugh that erupts from my chest, and I hear Brant trying to swallow his own chuckle. I can't believe it. The badass gun-toting, trap setting, wilderness scout who chases lightning is scared of a fucking moose.

"Umm, Remi, baby? The moose isn't gonna attack," I tell her, unable to keep the smile from my face.

Of course, that is the exact moment when the moose decides to attack. Just my fucking luck.

It's as if Bullwinkle is suddenly tired of our shit, and it makes a loud grunt slash coughing noise and starts gunning for me. My eyes widen in panic, and I know there's no way that I am going to outrun Deer-zilla. A shot rings out, the bullet clipping a tree near the moose, and I see Madix and Brant drop to the ground. The moose veers to the left, pounding past me, its focus on some other target now. My heart tries to pound out of my chest, and I pant through the fear that's coursing through me.

"Shit, shit, shit," I curse, whipping my head in the direction of the guys to make sure they're okay. Brant and Madix are both starting to get up, but their eyes are focused behind me. I turn around to check on Remi, and my stomach drops as I watch the moose galloping towards her. "Run!" I shout at her.

Remi screams something and then she fires once more at the pissed off moose closing in on her. She misses again, and the animal keeps going for her, like it has a personal vendetta now.

"Stop fucking shooting!" Madix yells, but Remi has already turned around, taking off like a bat out of hell.

"Fuck! Go after her!" Brant demands, and we start sprinting in her direction.

I can't run as fast as they can with my prosthetic, so I fall behind, and all I can see is a streak of Remi's flapping blonde hair before she veers off, the moose doing some weird animal yell like it's letting her know it's never going to stop coming for her. Maybe it wasn't going to maul her before, but it sure as hell wants to now.

The moose is way faster than any of us, and I'm worried it's going to catch Remi from behind. She must be thinking the same thing, because at the next tree that she comes up on, she jumps, reaching the low-hanging branch, and hauls herself up. I feel like I'm watching a gymnast go for gold on the uneven bars.

Thank fuck the moose runs past her with an irritated snort, but it circles back and gouges off the bark of the tree that she's in with its antlers. Remi squeals and holds onto the branch for dear life when it does it again, and then puts its front hooves on the tree, like it wants to climb the fucker to get to Remi and teach her a lesson.

"Climb!" Madix roars at her.

Remi doesn't need him to tell her, because before the word is even fully screamed from his throat, she's already jumped to grab the next highest branch and has pulled herself up. As soon as she's secure on it, she cups her mouth and sends out another bear call—like that's fucking helping anything—and the moose opens its mouth and yells right back at her. I don't even know how shit like this is happening.

Just before we get to her, the moose just yells one last time at her before putting its feet down on the ground again. It slams its antlers against the trunk one last time and then with a huff, it turns and walks away. It shits on his way out, leaving a steaming pile of exactly what he thinks about our interruption of his grazing.

"What the fuck were you thinking?" Madix screams at her as we all rush forward, panting hard and looking up at her from where she's straddling the branch. "I knew you were fucking crazy, but that was stupid and reckless and completely uncalled for!" Madix accuses.

"It attacked!" she exclaims, her face flushed with anger.

He points an accusatory finger at her. "That moose wasn't dangerous until *you* spooked and irritated it! What the fuck were you thinking shooting at us?"

"It was running right for Theo, and moose are the most dangerous animals in the forest! Everyone knows that!" she argues, looking completely serious. "And if I was trying to shoot you, you'd be shot! I was trying to get the moose to run away. I didn't expect it to run towards the gun! Like I said, they're fucking crazy!"

"Then why the hell didn't you actually shoot the moose?" Madix challenges.

Remi snorts and gives Madix a scathing look. "Do you think I want all of its relatives coming after me for the rest of our hike back to Endstone? No fucking way, I'm not insane. Moose are like the mob when they have a vendetta. And I'll have you know, I'm an excellent shot," she adds tersely.

"You missed!"

"Yeah, but it was on *purpose*. See? Excellent," she retorts.

Madix shakes his head. "How the hell did we get tangled

up with *you* during the end of the fucking world?" he asks in exasperation. "You're a fucking fool, Remington April."

Oh shit. He just went there.

Brant, Puddles, and I take a step back, as if we're all just trying to keep from becoming collateral damage from the eruption that's about to happen. Even Coon and the rats back up inside the cage that Brant's still holding.

Remi jumps down from the tree, landing in front of Madix, and she takes a step toward him. Her blue eyes bright with anger, her temper rising up to meet his. "That's funny, because the only fool I see around here is *you*," she says, poking him in the chest. "You stomp around these woods like you own them, when you don't know shit, but you're just too much of a macho prick to admit it. What's the real problem here? You too much of a sexist pig to be shown up by a woman? Is that it? Not man enough to take what he wants or admit he's a lost little puppy who needs help some-times, *Mady?*"

Madix takes another step forward, crushing against her so that they're chest-to-chest. She lifts her chin defiantly, while Madix flexes his fists. They stare each other down, but the way they're looking at each other, I'm not sure if they're about to fight or fuck.

I'm going to go with C, all of the above.

16

MADIX

"I told you, don't fucking call me Mady," I growl at her, and Remi's eyes flash with challenge.

"What's wrong, *Mady?*" she enunciates the condescending nickname. "Afraid to get shown up by a crazy bitch?"

Is she serious? Oh, she's instigating the wrong motherfucking person. I plant my leg between hers to anchor myself and to make sure I don't give her an inch as I lean into her defiantly. Her breathing hitches ever so slightly as I bring my knee up, and I'm suddenly aware of the heat of her pussy through the material of my pants.

I kind of expect her to take a swing at me. Her eyes are filled with anger, her features radiating challenge, but there's more there, too. A spark of something that makes my own anger morph.

"I'm waiting for an answer," she demands, but her voice is breathy and low, and when I move my leg again, she barely suppresses a moan. *Fuck.* Why am I so turned on by that? I want to rip off her jeans and bury myself inside of her, but I also want to shake her, force her to stop doing crazy ass shit. If she dies because of her own stubbornness or stupidity, I'd never forgive myself. Why is she so damn exasperating?

"I don't have a problem with women. I have a problem with delusional, crazy people, who put us and themselves at risk."

She scoffs. "Go fuck yourself, Mady. Just because I do things differently, doesn't mean I'm crazy. You know less than that pile of shit over there about the world you landed yourself in." Remi says, motioning at the moose's parting gift to us.

I laugh humorlessly. "I'm not the one who can't accept what's going on out there. I'm not the one who's trying to ignore the end of the fucking world," I snap, my hand moving to clamp over her hip like it has a mind of its own.

She stands up on her tiptoes, but instead of pressing her lips to mine like I think she's going to do, she moves her mouth to my ear. Her breath caresses my neck, and it makes my cock harden even more. "The world, with you in it, can go fuck itself."

Her sassy mouth is my undoing. In one quick movement, I have her ass in my hands and her legs around my waist. I shove her against a big rock that's wedged between two tree trunks. Her pupils dilate, and I grind myself against her, making her entire body shudder.

"I don't think it's the world that needs fucking," I growl. "I think it's *you.*"

She reaches down and grips me through my pants, making me jolt against her. "Finally. Something we can agree on."

She squeezes, and I nearly blow my load right then and there. Slapping her hand away, I slip my fingers into her pocket where I know she stuffed condoms. I know this because I watched her get dressed this morning in the quiet of the sunrise, like some obsessed fan boy. I put the square packet between my teeth, holding the foil there while I undo my pants.

"Make it good," she taunts with a sneer, as she unbuttons her pants, too. "If you can."

I don't touch her clit. I don't check to see if she's wet. I just tear open the condom packet, roll it over my dick, and pin her with a forearm across her collarbone. In the next movement, I hoist her legs up and shove into her, bottoming out in one punishing thrust that makes her scream out my name.

"That's what I fucking thought," I tell her as I pull out almost all the way and then slam back in. I pause for a minute, reveling in the feel of her, but Remi narrows her lust filled gaze at me.

"Oh, don't tell me Mady is a two pump chump?" she taunts.

I growl at the insult and start fucking her roughly against the stone."Fuck you," I snap, as her hands curl around my shoulders.

"About fucking time," she snaps at me, and I shove my cock so hard up into her, that her eyes roll to the back of her head.

Her nails rake down my back, and even through my shirt, I know she's leaving scratch marks all over my already scarred skin. She wraps her legs around me, and I cradle her against me as I brutally thrust into her. She's wild, just like I knew she would be, and I don't ever want to stop. I don't ever want to lose this feeling of my cock pushing in and out of her, making her lose her mind the way she makes me lose mine.

"Faster," she demands, and just to be an asshole, I slow down.

She opens her mouth to tell me off, but I just lean in and bite her bottom lip hard enough to bring a sting of pain, before tilting my head and devouring her with a kiss. I want to ravage her. I want to feast on her until we're both filled. She nearly shot us, and then that moose went for her, and it fucking terrified me. I pictured her getting trampled to death, right there in front of me, and I fucking lost it. How the hell did she hook me so fast?

She pulls her head away to the side to break the kiss, but I'm still fucking her hard and slow, and I can tell she's getting frustrated. Good. I want to frustrate her. I want her to feel what she makes me feel.

"Madix," she growls in warning.

I chuckle darkly and continue my tortuous, slow pace. Her body is coiled so tight that she's shaking, just waiting for me to let her explode. "You're at *my* mercy right now, Remington," I say against her ear, moving a hand to grip her ass while my other one delves between us to finally tease at her neglected clit. "It's my cock in your greedy cunt, and you'll take exactly what I want to give. Don't pretend you don't fucking *love* it, I can feel you dripping all over me."

Remi moans in approval as I punctuate that statement with a deep thrust and then grind my hips against her. "Oh, you think I'm wet for you, Mady? Such a big ego. Maybe I just like Brant and Theo watching me fuck someone," she sasses back.

I suck her earlobe into my mouth and bite it, eliciting a half-yelp, half-moan. "I'm just someone, am I?" I rub slow circles around her clit and speed up my thrusts. "Whose name did you scream out when I entered this tight, wet pussy?" I slow my pace again, and Remi lets out a whine as I pull my teasing fingers from her clit and pinch a hard nipple instead. "Who's fucking you right now, Remi? Tell me, and I'll make you scream."

I swallow up her pleasure and moans with another kiss

and stamp my name all over her lips as I fuck her deliciously slow against the rock.

"You, Big Boy," she says. "You're fucking me." I open my mouth to demand my name from those wicked lips, but Remi starts laughing and I pause. "Sorry, that was just wrong. I'm officially scratching Big Boy off my sexy nicknames list. It's awkward and not at all a name you use when you want someone to fuck you harder." Remi grinds against me, trying to ride me faster, as she says the last part.

I'm lost in the sound of her laugh and how it lightens every heavy, overwhelming thing inside of me. I kiss her again, sucking on her bottom lip and teasing her with my tongue. "Who's fucking you, so nice and deep, Remi?" I ask against her lips, reaching for her clit again. My balls start to tighten, and I need her to fucking say my name so I can pound into her the way we both need and get lost in her body and our orgasms.

"You, Madix. You're fucking me. You're who I need," she says, making my cock lurch. "Oh God, right there," she pants as I press down on her clit and speed up. "Harder, Madix. Show me what you do to naughty little cunts."

With her dirty mouth to spur me on, I press her into the rock even more and fuck her as hard as she deserves. I put everything I have into each pounding thrust, and I feel her tightening around me. "That's right, Remington. Come all over my cock, while Brant and Theo watch how rough you like it."

"Yes," she chants, and I can feel how close to the edge of orgasm she is.

Hints of spasms grip at my punishing cock as I slam into her over and over again. "You wanted my attention, and now you have it. Is this what you wanted? To scream out my name as I punish this pussy?" I capture her moans with my mouth as she writhes. "Your pussy is ready to come all over my cock, isn't it?"

She moans again in response, but I'm not going to let her off that easy. "Isn't it?" I demand.

"Yes!"

"Good. I want you to milk me until I come," I tell her, my fingers circling her clit in rough, quick movements as I'm finally ready to give her everything she needs. "Make me come, Remington. Squeeze my cock dry and show me how much you've wanted me to fuck you like this since we first met."

She explodes. "Oh, fuck yes!" she screams and claws at my back.

Her pussy clamps down around me like a vise, and I thrust as deeply into her as I can, burying my fucking soul into her as my balls tighten, and I nearly black out I come so hard. I work her clit, coaxing another orgasm out of her and lose myself in the feel of our joined pleasure.

When I gain my wits enough to open my eyes again, I see Remington's forehead resting against my shoulder as she works to catch her breath. I have one hand gripping her ass, while the rock I've pinned her to supports the rest of her. I nip at her neck and watch her quiver against me, before I carefully lower her down to her feet. She's so jellied that she has to grip the boulder to keep herself steady.

I can't help the cocky grin that comes over my face, and she looks up at me and promptly rolls her eyes. "Yeah, fine. You fucked me silly. But don't go stroking your ego. I can make myself orgasm like that with my vibrator," she says as she steps into her pants and starts to button them.

I shake my head. "Liar," I say as I clean myself up.

She smirks, but steps forward, surprising me when she straightens my shirt for me, running her hands over the wrinkles that her fists made. "Do you feel better about my being right and you being wrong now?" she taunts me.

I fix Remi with an incredulous look. "And here I was thinking I'd fucked some sense into you. Clearly *that* didn't happen. Don't fucking shoot at me anymore." I demand, and just to be sure she doesn't, I grab for her rifle. Remi gives me a pointed look, but I'm unfazed. "You can have it back when you can be trusted with it."

She glares at that statement and steps into me, her nipples grazing the skin of my chest. "Fine, Asshole Joe, but two can play at that game." She grabs my hand and makes me cup her pussy. "You can have this back when you know how to respect it." With a smirk, she tosses my hand away and saunters off toward where Brant, Puddles, and Theo are lounging next to a tree.

The guys flash me knowing grins. "Glad to see you two working out your issues," Brant snarks.

"Yeah, we enjoyed the demonstration," Theo laughs like an asshole, but I don't miss that he adjusts himself as he gets all the way back on his feet.

"Let's get moving," Remi announces cheerily, giving Puddles some ear scratches and peeking into the carrier to check on Coon and her boys. "You want to double check that I'm headed in the right direction, or are you ready to accept that I'm capable of taking us where we need to go?" she asks me, that sassy mouth back in action already. I'll need to fuck that next.

With a sardonic smirk, I say, "Lead the way." I wave a hand in invitation for her to walk ahead of me and proceed to pull out the map just to piss her off.

She rolls her eyes, but doesn't say anything. "You're a walking shit show, Remington, but at least you have a nice ass to look at as you do your best to get us lost out here."

I can't help the smile the takes over my face as she holds

up her middle finger over her shoulder. Theo and Brant chuckle alongside me, and we continue to appreciate her from behind. I shake my head, amused and a little bewildered at how things have played out. I guess *we're* doing this. It'd be hard as fuck to turn back now, because if I'm being honest with myself, somehow, this unhinged little hellion *has* me, and judging by the looks on their faces, I know she has Brant and Theo, too.

I don't know if this makes us the fucking smartest and luckiest assholes in this dying world, or if we'll be the biggest fools Remington April has ever played. I guess we'll find out.

17

BRANT

I'm stuck again.

At first, everything is dark and peaceful. But the world shifts, and then I'm back in my gear and fatigues. The sun is fucking baking us alive now, but I know as soon as it goes down, it'll take all of the warmth with it, and that stark, desert coldness will sink into my bones. Theo and Madix are here, discussing the mission with our other squad members. We're in some rickety building, the wooden slats cracked and dilapidated from age and weather. It's an odd juxtaposition to have all of our expensive computers and military equipment inside the crumbling building. The ground is mostly hard-packed dirt, the floorboards rotted away years ago. Dirt surrounds us here. It gets fucking everywhere. I have to dump piles of it out of my boots every night when I take them off.

It's dark when the first explosion goes off. My brain doesn't register what's happening. One minute, I'm looking at coordinates, half-listening to Madix and Theo, and then the next, all I know is heat and weightlessness. The boom is so loud that my ears fail me. My body lands hard, and when I'm able to pick up my head again, I see the last of the rickety old building on the verge of collapse. Fire and smoke is everywhere. There's dirt caked on the inside of my mouth and nostrils, and I have to spit several times just to clear it enough to breathe. I'm about to call out to one of my squad members when the second explosion goes off.

One second, he's there, and the next... There's just burnt blood and pieces.

I can't move. I can't hear or speak. Panic wells up inside of me, and I force myself to get the fuck up, because I know if I don't, I'll die. Using every ounce of willpower I have, I roll over and get to my feet, but my eyes are burning, making my vision clouded, and it makes everything even more disorienting.

I squint, searching for my other squad members, but when I stumble forward, I just find another dead body. The panic wants to overtake me as I whirl around, desperate to find Theo and Madix. I start yelling their names, even though it's probably the stupidest thing I can do right now, since we're under attack.

I'm about to rush back into the building when I see a figure coming out of the smoke, tugging a body under the arms. I rush forward to Madix and help him pull Theo out of the building before the last wall falls on them. Blood is dripping out of Madix's ears, pieces of his shirt are burned to nothing, and it looks as if his shirt has melted into his skin. Madix is limping badly, but Theo... Theo's leg is just a mess of bone and blood, and he's unconscious. He has little wounds and cuts all over, and I look down at my arms and see they're in a similar state.

We pull Theo further and further away, trying to get to our convoy, and Madix keeps stopping to check for our other squad members, but we both know already—everyone else is dead. When we get into the vehicle, all I can think about is how that could have been our bodies scattered in pieces all over the fucking desert.

In a way, we did leave pieces of ourselves behind that day. Pieces that we can never get back.

I scream, feeling the dirt caked in my mouth again, smelling *blood and smoke. Hearing the god-awful sound of the explosion going off, before there was no sound at all. I just want it to end.*

The panic makes bile rise into my throat, and when I move to puke my guts out, I feel a cool hand covering my forehead and hear soft words speaking low in my ear.

My eyes snap open, and I look around wildly, but it's dark. When I feel a hand come up to touch my arm, I flinch, rearing back to shove the person away, but a strong fist catches my forearm. "Brant, it's okay. It's just us. You were asleep."

I have to blink several times to recognize Madix's voice, but it all comes together when a heavy, fur-covered body settles into my lap. The feel of Puddles pulls me out of my confusion, and I register that I'm in a tent. I recognize Remi's shadowed silhouette beside me, and my stomach plummets. "Fuck," I say, running my hands down my face. "I'm sorry. Did I hurt you?"

Her cool hand returns to my face. "You have nothing to be sorry for," she says quietly.

I drape my arms over my bent knees and shake my head. "I could've hurt you."

"We wouldn't have let that happen," Madix says.

Madix and Theo share a look, and then Theo clears his throat. "It's just about dawn. I'll go get some water boiling so we can get going."

Madix looks at Remi before following Theo out, leaving me and Remi alone. Puddles has moved to my left side, her wet nose pressed against my leg as she watches me. I let a shaky hand drop down to scratch her head. I feel embarrassed as fuck that Remi had to see me like this. "I bet you're re-thinking this whole thing with us now, huh?" I ask with a humorless laugh. "We're quite the catch. I swear, our baggage has baggage."

"Everyone's fucked up in one way or another," she says,

nudging me over so she can get under the sleeping bag with me. She's not close enough though, so I pull her into my lap and run my hand up her thigh. She's wearing thin leggings, and I think one of Theo's shirts with the sleeves rolled up at the wrists.

"You wanna talk about it?" she asks, moving her hand to the back of my jaw, where she lightly runs her fingers over it. I'm usually smooth there, but dark-blond scruff has collected over the past couple of days since I haven't had a chance to shave.

I blow out a breath as I start to rub circles over her thigh with my thumb. "We were the only three to survive the explosion." I pause, and for some reason, it's like I need a moment to swallow the reality of that statement even though I've lived and re-lived it for years. "We were just going over the final details of our recon assignment when it happened, and it wiped out the rest of our squad," I find myself telling her. "The night terrors and flashbacks started right away, and that was really fucking hard. I had a traumatic brain injury, but when I recovered, my eyesight was affected, and I had some balance issues for a while. Sometimes, I feel like I'll never escape, and sometimes I feel like I don't deserve to." Puddles leans into me more and I rub her neck and back.

Remi is quiet as she listens to me, and I'm grateful, because I don't think I could handle questions right now. "Theo's leg got fucked up. It could have been worse, but Madix got to him before the fire could and pulled him free."

"Jesus," Remi hisses under her breath.

"Madix blames himself. He was our squad leader. He had a lot of responsibility on his shoulders, but it wasn't his fault. We were in hostile territory. He did everything right, but he's never been able to let that guilt go. Hell, I don't know if any of us will really ever stop feeling guilty that we're here and they're not."

I see her nod slowly, like she's taking that information in. Her fingers dance from my scruffy, three-day-old beard to the back of my head, where she tugs at the strands of hair where my head and neck meet.

"I'm glad you guys have each other," she says quietly, and I nod, because I think that every day.

"What about you?" I ask, before I can stop myself.

She blinks at me, confused by the question. "What about me?"

"Do *we* have you?"

She tilts her head and studies me, and I wish I could snatch back my words and shove them down my stupid throat. Why am I even going there right now? We've had sex *once*. Nothing about our current circumstances is normal, and time isn't exactly on our side. According to Remi, we're only a couple days from Endstone now, and who knows what will happen in the future with this virus, with us, or anything for that matter.

"Do you *want* to have me?" she asks, like she's genuinely curious.

I could play things off and make a joke to lighten the intense tone I just set, but fuck it. I've dug the hole this deep already, so I might as well see if I can turn it into a nice sized swimming pool. One that I could use to drown myself in when Remi shuts me down at any moment. "Yeah, I do. I think you're exactly what we need."

We stare at each other, the shadows dancing across our faces, and she looks so fucking beautiful. I want to flip her on her back and give her so many orgasms that she has no choice but to admit that we're exactly what she needs too.

Finally, after what feels like a fucking eternity, she opens

205

her mouth to reply, but before she can put me out of my misery and say something, Madix suddenly flips open the tent flap. "We have a fucking problem. Get dressed, now," he says ominously, leaving before I can ask what the fuck is going on.

Remi and I immediately jump into action. I dig into my bag and yank on some pants and a shirt, quickly stuffing my feet into my boots. Remi is ready when I am, and we hurry out of the tent to find Madix and Theo with their guns ready, poised behind a couple of trees and eyes focused ahead. It's that weird time of morning, right before the sun comes up, so everything is bathed in tones of gray. Madix immediately puts up hand signals to fill me in on what's happening, and as I read them, my blood turns to ice and fear claws its way up my throat.

"What's going on?" Remi asks on a whisper.

"We've got people coming our way," I explain, and watch as she looks back in the direction that Madix and Brant are watching. I see the debate in her features, and I know in this moment that Remi still doesn't fully believe what we've been telling her. I just fucking hope that she's not about to learn the hard way by being exposed and getting sick.

"Get your gun," I tell her, my expression fierce and my tone crucial, so that she knows exactly how serious this is. "Do everything we tell you to. This isn't a joke, and we have no idea what they want. If they're sick..." my voice trails off as Puddles gives a low warning growl.

Madix and Brant suddenly back up towards us, and I wait for their instructions. Maybe we have enough time to pack up what we can and make a run for it. Evade and live, that's the goal, but one look at their faces shows me that's not an option.

"Five men approaching," Madix says as they come up

beside us. "Mid-twenties from what we can tell in this light. They have weapons—looking like hunting rifles. We didn't see them until just now, and we don't have time to pack up before they get here," he says, his face grim. "Each of us guards a point of the compass. Keep an eye out for anyone trying to surround us or come from behind."

I nod and call for south. Madix calls east, Theo chooses north, and Remi doesn't say anything at all, but turns to face west. I feel like we wait for an eternity in the gray mist of dawn, our backs facing each other as we keep in formation to watch. The morning air is cold, but my blood is running so hot that I feel a drip of sweat travel down the back of my neck. In the next moment, shadowy figures break through the trees into a wider clearing about twenty feet away.

As soon as the group steps from the treeline, we all have our weapons up except for Remi, who's holding hers half-heartedly with a wary look on her face.

"Don't come any closer," Madix barks out, and I see the group of guys freeze. They squint and turn in our direction, noticing us with our guns trained on them, and immediately hold their hands up. "We're armed, and we will fire if you try to come any closer," Madix says. "What do you want?"

The five guys look from one to another, and the shortest of the group clears his throat. "We're not here to cause any trouble. Our campsite got trashed by a moose. We saw your fire and wanted to ask if you had any supplies to spare, or medicine we could have."

At the mention of medicine, Madix tenses even more.

"Why do you need medicine?" he asks, his tone turning flat. It's not a warning sign unless you know him, but he's already going full Jiminy Cricket.

"Our friend twisted his ankle running from the moose, and another one of our friends is just...having some stomach problems." As soon the short guy finishes saying this, a couple other guys in their group share a look, and it sends alarm bells blaring inside of me. *Fuck.* They're sick, and any one of these guys could be contagious. I want to pull the neck of my shirt over my mouth and nose in an extra effort for protection, but I don't take my hands off my rifle or divert my focus.

"Turn back around," Madix says in that deadly empty voice of his.

The shorter man runs his gaze over all of us. "You guys military?" he asks.

None of us answer. He starts to say something else, but a lanky guy in his group talks over him. "Just help us out, and we'll be on our way," he demands, and then he starts looking over our things like he's making a mental tally of what he wants.

"I didn't hear a please with that request," Madix monotones, glaring at the lanky, entitled asshole.

"Fuck you," the guy retorts, and takes a step towards us. One of his buddies tries to grab his arm to pull him away, but the man just shrugs him off and points at Madix. "We know you got supplies, and you're gonna help us."

Shit. This is gonna go bad.

Brant and I tighten our grips on our guns, but Madix tips his head back slightly and laughs. It's not a nice sound. It's a dark, humorless laugh that is full of menace. And even though he looks like he's not giving these guys the time of day, he's watching them like a hawk. "That's big talk for a little guy like you," Madix says with condescension. "We aren't giving you shit. This is your last warning. Turn around and go back the way you came. You've all been exposed to your buddy's illness, and any one of you could be contagious. So I'm gonna tell you one last time. Leave. Now."

Two of the guys in the group look like they want no part

of this showdown, but the other three take another step forward. All friendly pretense is dropped as each of them raise their guns on us. I hear Remi curse under her breath and try to step forward to intervene, but Madix's hand shoots out and clamps her around the wrist. "Don't."

The tone of his voice must belie how fucked this situation is, because she actually backs down.

"Everyone just calm down," I say evenly. "No one wants to get shot."

"We won't be the ones with a bullet in us," Madix says darkly, and the twisted fucker actually sounds excited about this whole turn of events.

"Don't be a bunch of fucking dicks! Give us some supplies. First aid kit and some extra medicine if you have it. Food, too. Then we'll leave." I'm not sure if the guy is just an idiot, or if he's desperate, but I'm guessing it's a bit of both.

In answer, Madix fires.

Wet dirt flies up from the ground directly next to the lanky guy's right foot. I release a mumbled curse, because taking warning shots at people who also have their weapons pointed at you is a good way to get shot. What the fuck is he thinking? Thank fuck these idiots don't start pulling triggers in fear or retaliation. All five of the guys flinch, and two of them turn tail and run.

"Fucking crazy asshole!" the short man yells. "We just need some fucking help! He's puking his guts out, man! He's dehydrated, can't keep anything down. You want that on your conscience if he dies?"

Stupid motherfucker doesn't realize—Madix doesn't have a conscience right now.

"Everyone is fucking dying," Madix says evenly. "But you'll be going to ground first if you don't leave now. I gave you one warning shot. I won't give you another."

The guy stares Madix down hard. My heart is pounding, and my grip on my rifle is getting clammy. Remi is breathing hard beside me, and Theo's jaw twitches with tension. For a split second, I see the desperation on the other man's face, and my stomach plummets. This is what the world has become. We're already turning on each out of fear and desperation. Is this what the future holds for all of us, just more of these showdowns of take or get taken?

Madix is completely still, his legs spread with confidence, the guy in his sights. Finally, *finally,* the man lowers his gun and his two friends follow suit. With a sneer, he spits at the ground. "Fuck you. I hope you all get fucking sick out here and die."

Without another word, he stomps away back into the treeline, and the other two follow behind him.

None of us move or relax, just in case it's a trap. After a very long five minutes, when the group is long out of sight or hearing distance, Madix says, "Brant and Remington, pack up. Theo and I will keep watching."

Remi and I move and start packing up camp in record time. "That scenario was a bit intense," she mumbles.

I snort humorlessly. "You think?"

Thank goodness Madix didn't actually shoot one of those assholes. I'm even more surprised that one of their group didn't get trigger happy and shoot at us. That whole thing could've gone much, *much* worse. I want to get the fuck out of here before any of them decides to retaliate out of anger.

We head in the opposite direction that the other group went, but Madix doesn't lose the tension in his body or the way his eyes constantly scan the surroundings. The confrontation spooked all of us. Even hours later, Remi still hasn't lost the frown on her face, and she's been uncharacteristically quiet. None of us say a word as we continue to hike down the mountain, and it's not until late afternoon that Madix finally lets us stop for a break.

The reality of what's happening in the rest of the country—and probably the world at this point—just stood up and bitch-slapped all of us, and there is a renewed sense of urgency now to make it back to Endstone and to safety. We eat, drink, and get a move on, all without a word, and it isn't until about hour six on our feet that I just can't take it anymore.

I've been watching Remi and the others, wondering what's going on in their heads, but then deciding it's none of my business. I know they'll talk when they want to, but I hate the tense silence. I'm not an expert when it comes to Remi and her personality, but I doubt she's ever been this quiet in her life.

"I hate to be that guy who asks how much longer, but seriously, how much longer until we get to Endstone?" I ask.

I already know the answer, because we crashed when we were about a hundred and fifty miles from town, which means it'll probably take us about four or five days to get back. But I can't figure out what else to say to get anyone to talk. I figure the, *are we there yet,* tactic is better than the alternative conversation starter of, *so the world around us is dying, how does everyone feel about that?*

"We should get there before dinner tomorrow," Remi announces, and I want to high-five myself for getting her to talk.

"You doing okay?" I ask when she seems like she's about to fall back into the silence we've been wading through all day.

"I'm as good as can be expected," she deadpans, and for some reason, Madix gives an unamused huff.

"Something you want to get off your chest, Mady?" Remi challenges.

Here we go again.

"We've been telling you for days what was going on outside of your little hideaway home. Are you really that shocked by what happened this morning?" Madix grumbles. Remi doesn't answer right away, and that just seems to make him even more irritated. "Looks like you have no choice but to pull your head out of the sand," he adds, because he always has to poke the bear. Or in this case, the bear-whisperer.

"My head is about as far from the sand as it can be. So if you don't want the toe of my boot up your ass, you should shut the fuck up now," she says, sarcastically chipper.

Madix murmurs a retort. I can't make out what is, but Remi sure as fuck does, and she whirls on him.

"You don't know shit about me, where I come from, or what life has taught me. I'm not refusing to accept reality. I'm questioning your claims with good reason, like any *normal* person would. You can think I'm crazy all you want, but what would *really* be crazy is to blindly follow three strangers who show up out of nowhere and tell you the world is ending. *That's* fucking crazy!"

"So you can fuck us, but not trust us?" Madix retorts.

"News flash, Mady, sex and trust aren't synonymous."

Madix just shakes his head, but wisely doesn't say anything else, opting to brood instead.

Remi yanks out her hair tie, letting her blonde locks trail down her back as she runs her hands through the tangles a few times. "You're telling me that you're such a robot, that if you found out about some plague from a stranger, you'd just go with it, and it'd be back to business as usual?"

"No, we don't work that way either, but it was different for us," I explain before Madix can let any more of his asshole leak out. "We weren't in a city seeing things go down firsthand. The news reports were detailing what was happening, but we were safe in Endstone, and the risk of exposure was slim. You never think something like this is going to happen," I admit, shaking my head. "I mean, how many pandemic scares have we had in the last ten years? They all turn out to be nothing. Then this happens. I still can't believe it sometimes, but look what happened earlier. We're obviously not the only ones opting to go out to the wilderness, away from people. That was a really close call this morning. People are sick and dying, Remi." I hoist my backpack up, my eyes watching Puddles as she swerves between trees up ahead. Remi is quiet, and I honestly don't blame her for not believing us. Had I been in her shoes, I probably wouldn't either, but this is too dangerous of a situation to let her continue to live in denial. "When you hear about dystopian events like this, it's always some big bad war that tears civilization apart."

"Or a zombie apocalypse," Theo pipes in. "Although, if we're going to be dealing with that, I'll take the slow-walking ones as opposed to the *World War Z* kind. Those fuckers were fast and freaky," he adds. "We'd all be goners."

"Speak for yourself. I could Brad Pitt the shit out of fast zombies," Madix preens, and the guy actually puffs up his chest and does that gorilla walk that men do when their muscles are too big or they're acting like douches. I'm gonna plead the fifth as to which one of those is Madix right now.

I open my mouth to reply, but suddenly, I see a flash of blonde hair, and then Remi goes full on flying squirrel mode and tackles Madix to the ground. He lets out a pained *oomph* as she lands on top of him.

Madix stares up at her in shock. "What the fuck?" he asks between gritted teeth. He reaches for his balls, where it seems Remi's knee landed on during the fall.

Remi snorts from where she's straddling him. "Some

Brad Pitt you are," she announces, sounding vastly unimpressed.

She leans in close, and then bites his neck while making a weird fucking keening slash growling sound to mimic a zombie. Madix jerks away from her teeth, and she laughs and leans up. "You just got zombiefied," she says with triumph.

"You cheated," he scowls.

She shrugs unapologetically. "Zombies don't play by the rules, Mady."

He's still clutching his sore balls, and Remi reaches down and slaps his cupped hand before springing up and away from him. Mady groans in pain. "Fuck, woman." I reach for my own balls in solidarity at Remi's parting shot, and I look over at Theo, who's also wincing in sympathy.

She turns and starts walking again, but I catch the smirk on her face right before she passes me. I fall into step beside her. "If I didn't know any better, I'd say that you enjoyed arguing with him," I tell her.

She darts her eyes over to me. "Madix is hot-blooded," she says, quiet enough that only I can hear. "He likes to be riled up. He thrives on it, actually. He needs someone who can deal with him being an asshole, but also someone who will call him on his shit sometimes."

"And is that someone *you?*" I question.

To my surprise, she shrugs, like she's actually considered it. "A guy like Madix is always going to have his asshole moments. That's just who he is. He doesn't intimidate me, and when I think he needs a push, I'll push back. But when I think he needs to just be, I'll leave him to it."

"Sounds like you figured him out pretty quickly."

"I'm intuitive. I get people."

"People don't usually get us," I admit.

She looks over at me again as we continue to trek

through the woods, the quiet rumble of Theo and Madix's voice behind us. "People don't usually get me, either," she replies. "So I guess we have that in common."

She sounds incredibly sad all of a sudden, and the tone of her voice sends a punch straight to my gut. I want to ask her what she means. I want to ask her what has her sounding so alone. But before I can, she takes a deep breath, like she's shedding whatever memory had her so down. "Alright, Zombie Food," she says louder so that she can address all of us. "We can get to Endstone by lunchtime tomorrow *if* you can keep up with me," she teases. "I want to take a hot shower, sleep in a comfy bed, and have a hot four-some. Not necessarily in that order. I'm flexible. In more ways than one," she adds with a wink.

If she was trying to distract me and get me not to ask her questions about her previous statement and mood...then she's smart as shit, because it worked. I'm too distracted now that I'm thinking about her showing us exactly how flexible she can be, especially when she adds a pep to her step and starts to jog away from us, her ass and tits bouncing nicely with each step.

"Hold up, let's talk more about this flexible stuff," Madix says with a wicked grin forming on his face, *finally* snapped out of his bad mood.

"Yeah, Remi," Theo adds, quickening his step to fall in line with her. "I think we're gonna need a demonstration."

I've been worried that we've been pushing Theo too far with his leg, but my worry turns to amusement when he catches up to her and smacks her on the ass, earning a squeal of a giggle from her. Of course, because she's Remi, she reaches around and then smacks *him* on the ass in retaliation. He tips his head back and laughs, making Madix and I join in.

Theo turns back to look at us with the smile still on his

face, and it's nothing but sheer joy, free of all the pain and stress that's usually polluting him, and it tugs at my soul. This is one of those moments that I know I'll never forget, because right here and now, I realize what the three of us are, and it's something we haven't been for a really long time. Happy.

It's funny—with her, we finally feel alive. Too bad the world is dying.

18

REMI

When Endstone finally comes into view, I have a lot of mixed feelings. Relief, anticipation, uneasiness...and yeah, a little anger, too. I try to shove it all down as deep as I can as we look down from the top of the hill. We'll hit town limits as soon as we make our way to the bottom. We're all tired, but we're faring better than I thought we would be, and I'm looking forward to not living out of a backpack or sleeping in a tent anymore.

I'm also glad that the guys can stop eating those damned canned beans, because I can do without the ass acoustics. I swear, once one of them gets started, another joins in, like it's some damn competition to make it the loudest and grossest they possibly can. I don't get why dudes think it's so hilarious to let out a butt belch. Next time one of them does it, I'm going to give them a purple nurple, because that's how you gotta handle things with three dudes sometimes.

Puddles rubs up against me, and I run my hand down her spine, massaging as I go. She nudges me forward, and I smile down at her as I pat her head. "You sure I can't just stay on this hill for a little longer?" I ask her. She cocks her

217

head at me and gives me a look that makes me snicker. "Damn, Pud. No wonder you can keep those boys in line."

"She's talking to the dog," I hear Madix gripe to the others.

"Yeah, and you have a damn opossum on your back," Theo chirps back.

I grin at the look on Madix's face when he turns his head to glare at Coon who's perched across his shoulders. She's using the top of the backpack as a pillow, and her tail is dangling down his chest. "Damn thing latched onto me," Madix complains. "If I move her, she'll attack. Maybe not today, but I get the impression she holds grudges." He glares at a content and sleeping Coon. "I don't want to wake up in the middle of the night to find she's trying to remove my face, or anything else," he gripes. "Can you guys take the rats though? They keep trying to hump her, and it's freaking me out."

We all laugh and earn a murderous look from Madix. "I'm not touching her boyfriends. I'm with you on that whole grudge thing," Brant confesses, giving Madix and his shoulder companions a wide berth.

"Little fuckers need to learn that there's a time and a place, and that my back is neither of those things. Horny little bastards," Madix grumps.

Theo tosses me a rakish look. "I know the feeling."

I feel my body flush with heat—not from embarrassment, because I don't get embarrassed about sex. Just pure, unadulterated lust. Desire heats me up better than an open fire.

When I feel fingers thread through my own, I look over and find Brant beside me. "You okay?" he asks, and I love him a bit for that. People might think that he's not as present just because he tends to be quieter, but it's not true. Brant is just in his own head a lot. Sometimes that means he's being tortured with his memories, and sometimes that means he's just observing.

I give him a tentative smile. "Yep. I'm right as a woman."

He cocks a blond brow. "I think the saying is, *right as rain.*"

I scoff. "That's silly. Women are right *way* more often than rain. My saying is better."

He opens his mouth, but then promptly closes it again because...I'm right. I rest my case.

"Come on, woman," Brant teases, tugging me forward.

With him leading me, I take another step in the direction of a town I've never felt like I belonged in. There's tension all throughout my body, but I try to dispel it by watching Madix and Theo's asses as they walk. It's a nice view.

We travel down the rocky hill, and it's hard to miss that there's been a barrier wall of some sort erected around where Main Street leads to the heart of Endstone. It gives off serious Mad Max vibes. I shake my head and mentally concede to what these three have been telling me. It's definitely true that if any place is bound to survive a plague, it would be Endstone.

"Shit, they work fast," Brant observes.

"Wonder where they got all that sheet metal?" Madix asks, his eyebrows furrowed in thought.

I chuckle, but it sounds hollow. "They've probably been collecting it for years," I say. "This *is* Endstone we're talking about. They get off on hoarding supplies and swapping shit with their neighbors."

"True that," Theo agrees, and then the distinct smell of a silent but deadly bomb reaches me.

"Really?" I ask, exasperated. "Who did it?"

I am gonna purple nurple the hell out of them. I scrunch up my nose before pulling the collar of my shirt up to cover it. I glare at the guys, who are all feigning innocence while trying not to laugh. Predictably, they all point to Puddles at the same time.

I roll my eyes and drop Brant's hand so I can rub her head. "Men," I say to her. "Always blaming women for their shit." Puddles looks up at me and yawns, and I nod at her. "I know, it *is* exhausting!"

I break away from the group, giving them a pointed look so they know not to pass me. "I'll be leading the rest of the way. You guys stay downwind." I get three chuckles at my back, but Puddles wisely stays at my side.

Every step I take closer to Endstone feels like the beginning of the end. I haven't been here for years, or talked to my dad in that long either. My stomach churns with nerves at thought of the inevitable reunion. If I'm being honest with myself, I've been trying to figure out how to reconnect with my dad without having to reconnect with this town. I just never imagined it would ever be under circumstances like *this*. And yet, as crazy as it is, I'm glad I met these three life-sized GI Joes. I'm a big believer that sometimes, the universe gives you exactly what and who you need.

Puddles keeps to my side, and I work to convince my feet to keep walking towards the town instead of turning around and running from it like I want to. The memory of my dad, his eyes filling with tears as I threw another box into the backseat of my Cherokee before I drove away, tries to fight for my attention. I slam it back down and focus on my feet as they hit the dirt with each stride.

"Why so serious?" Theo asks me, doing a respectable impersonation of Heath Ledger's *Joker*. I laugh, and shake away the apprehension that's clawing at me. I turn to him, flashing a Joker-worthy grin across my face. He chuckles and pulls me in for a quick kiss.

"Stop mouth-fucking and let's go," Madix grumbles. "I'm tired, and want a shower as soon as possible."

"Oooh, in a hurry for some hot shower sex?" I tease. "I get that. I respect your needs. Last one there has to smell Theo's rotten-egg farts all night long."

"For the last time, that was Puddles!" he shouts at me as I sprint towards the last place on earth that I ever wanted to call home again. I laugh, letting the breeze that brushes past me carry some of my reservations away. I'm here now. There's no more hiding from this place. Besides, I now have three very muscled and sexy men to help me get over my issues and pass the time. If I have to face this place, I'm glad I have the three of them—and their cocks—to distract me.

We make good time, and before I know it, we're approaching the newly constructed metal barrier that blocks off the entrance to the town. Right before we leave the treeline, Madix pulls us up short.

"Hold," he says, in that soldier-bossy tone of his that makes me both bristle and get wet. I've never had a man as naturally dominating as he is, and I gotta say, it's sexy as hell.

We all stop and gather around each other, and Madix eyes us. It's hard to take him seriously with Coon still wrapped around his neck like a scarf, but I bite my lips to keep from smiling. "Okay, listen up. We've been gone for days. We don't know what we're walking into," Madix lays out. "For all we know, Endstone could have been overridden with the Handshake Plague by now. However, the fact that they've built a barrier is a good sign. It means they still have a reason to keep people out. I want you three to stay here while I check things out first."

Theo shakes his head. "No way, dude. You can't go alone."

"I'm not asking," Madix tells him. "If I'm not back in

221

thirty, I want you to turn around and make your way back to Remington's house."

"What? That's—"

My argument gets cut off from a voice over a megaphone.

"You four to the north! We have eyes on you. Come forward and state your business."

Madix curses and yanks Coon off his shoulders, making her hiss in protest. I reach out and take her, and Brant opens the carrier so I can put her, and the rats, inside. "Stay back," Madix orders us, but he's looking at me, as if he knows I'll be the one to not listen. Smart guy.

Madix turns and strides toward the wall, until someone yells, "Stop right there!"

While Brant is distracted, locking Coon and the rats into the carrier, and Theo is scanning Madix's back, I take the opportunity to sidestep around them and join Madix. The guys curse at my back and try to grab me, but I dart around a tree and over a bush before they can.

When I break through the treeline, Madix shoots me a glare over his shoulder, but I ignore it. I expect him to yell at me to go back, but he surprises me by instead holding his hand out. My blonde brows jump up, but I take his hand to stand next to him, and we both look up at the person standing at the top of the wall.

"Endstone is closed to outsiders," the guy says, holding up his rifle like he wants to make sure we don't miss exactly what he means by that.

When I squint and get a better look at him, I put my loose hand on my cocked hip. "Cletus Ray, I know that's you," I holler up at him. "Now get off your lazy, copper-lickin' ass and let us in!"

Cletus blanches and looks at me through the scope of his rifle, which is just about the stupidest thing he can do, because that means he's actively pointing his gun at me. In response to that threat, Madix drops my hand, whips up *his* gun and sets his sights on Cletus Ray. "You point that gun away from her, or I'll shoot out your kneecaps," Madix informs him in that scary, dead tone of his.

I huff out a breath. "Cletus Ray, you drop that gun right now, or I'll tell everyone about the time you tried to feel me up behind old Duke's dog house when you had the measles and a girlfriend. You married her, right? How is Lily doing?" I ask with a smirk.

Cletus very wisely points the muzzle of his weapon down, and I look over at Madix. "He's harmless," I say. "Cletus can't shoot a house five feet in front of him. He's definitely not going to be able to hit me, even if he did pull the trigger, which he won't."

Madix grumbles something aggressive and threatening under his breath which is just as sexy as his bossy soldier tone, but he lowers his gun. I turn back to the idiot that I went to school with. "I'm not waiting around all day, Cletus Ray," I tell him. "Open the damn gate so we can get in."

"Are—are you sick?" he calls back down nervously.

I cross my arms. "Do we look sick?"

He mutters something that I can't hear, and then itches his beer belly. "I'm not allowed to open the gate, Remi Francine. It's protocol."

I grit my teeth. "Fine. Then follow the damn protocol and get my daddy here to let us in."

"Yes, ma'am," he says, before quickly disappearing behind the metal monstrosity masquerading as a gate.

The guys all look at me in a mixture of surprise. "What?"

Brant chuckles and pushes his glasses up the bridge of his nose while taking out a bowl and filling it with water for Puddles to lap up while we wait. "Your accent is way more prominent now."

I inwardly groan, because he's right. It's like as soon as my feet touched down onto Endstone soil, the country girl in me comes out wearing plaid and chewing on a straw of wheat.

"I'm more interested to learn that your middle name is Francine," Theo says with way more excitement than I like.

"Don't even start on my name. Do you know how much I hated Remington Francine April growing up, when the rest of the world had classy, simple monikers like Charlotte or Elizabeth? How many girls do you know that are named after their father's favorite gun?"

Madix looks over at me, his dark eyes assessing like always. "You shouldn't hate your name. It suits you."

His words bring a surprised, but happy smile out of me. "You got a big ol' crush on me, Mady?"

He scoffs and walks past me to the metal wall so that he can lean up against it, but I don't miss the way the corner of his mouth tilts up.

"Sheriff April hopefully won't keep us waiting too long," Brant says, taking up position alongside Madix.

I shake my head at the use of "sheriff." My dad hasn't served in that roll for probably seven years now, but apparently, the title is like president. Once you're the president of the country, everyone just calls you that, regardless of how long you've been out of office. I take up the spot next to Madix and sit down, letting my back rest against the cool metal. The four of us wait for a good twenty minutes until we hear the squeal of brakes on the other side of the metal partition, and my stomach tightens.

Mumbled voices and the pounding of feet on metal rungs reach out to me, and my adrenaline spikes suddenly. I get to my feet, and we all back up from the wall so we have a better vantage point to see the people at the top. My heart beats wildly in my chest when a salt and pepper head comes into view, and then my dad is stepping out onto the parapet at the top of the gate.

My dad has more white in his hair and more worry lines in his face than the last time I saw him, but other than that, time has been kind to him. His denim-blue eyes immediately land on me, and when I catch the telltale quivering of his lip, I feel so much of my past anger and frustration suddenly feel like it just doesn't matter so much anymore. My throat gets tight, and I blink back my emotions as my dad and I take each other in for the first time in years.

"How's it going, Trouble?" he calls down to me, his voice heavy with emotion and yet somehow still casual, the way only my dad can pull off. I chuckle at the nickname he's always called me. The guys around me snicker and Madix mumbles, "Accurate."

"I'm good, Old Man," I answer back with a smile. "Who's winning the *best shot* battle this week, you or Zeke?"

"Do you even need to ask?" My dad tells me, and then promptly gives me *the look*.

"Of course she doesn't, she knows it's me!" I hear Zeke announce, right before he climbs into view next to my dad and slaps him on the back. He looks down at me, and I notice that he finally shaved his head like he always said he'd do if he lost any more hair. "You look good, sweetie," Zeke says, and I don't miss the hitch in his voice. "How's business treating you?"

"It's good," I call up. "I was just getting ready to head back to Alaska to lead my next wilderness tour before these fools showed up on my porch."

Man, I've missed Zeke and my dad. The truth of that slams into me, and I struggle with the fact that we've let this town drive a wedge between us that should have never been there. It was always Endstone that felt so suffocating and backwards. I had to leave. This place drove me nuts. But

225

when I told my dad that, he flew off the handle; he said that this town was his family. I could never get past that. *I* was his family, and his loyalty should have been to me first.

We argued, both of us saying things we probably shouldn't have, but I felt like he chose the town over me. He felt like I was abandoning him, and turning my nose up at my roots. In the end, we were both too stubborn to apologize. I left and refused to looked back, even sent letters to Zeke because I knew it would hurt my dad. I give a hollow chuckle and shake my head at myself. The ridiculous thing is, I left intent on becoming different and worldly, but I just ended up doing exactly what Endstone taught me to do.

Standing here, staring up at their faces, I realize how much I've missed having them in my life. It always felt like an impossible problem. This place was who they were, while I wanted nothing more than to separate from all of it. So I left, but now that I'm back, I wish I had found a different solution. One that didn't cut the people who love me—the people I love—out of my life. As if he can sense the struggle inside of me, Madix steps up and re-takes my hand.

I watch my dad run his eyes over our intertwined fingers, before sliding over to Theo and Brant, who are pressed close against my side and back. I can practically see the wheels in my dad's head start to turn. He's the master at playing it cool though, so he doesn't say or ask anything. He just continues his perusal of the guys and Puddles before nodding his head and quickly swiping underneath his eyes.

"Thank you boys for bringing her home. She's too stubborn to do it on her own."

The guys nod, and I just shrug. He's not wrong.

"Did you run into any trouble?"

Brant, Madix and Theo all turn to look at me, and I roll my eyes. Zeke and my dad's chuckles bounce over the wall, so I shoot them the middle finger, which only seems to make everyone laugh harder.

"Remington seems to be her very own brand of trouble," Madix answers.

"Hey!" I try to let go of his hand to smack him, but he just squeezes my fingers tighter, unwilling to let go.

"She is," my dad agrees. "But I figured if anyone could get her to come home, it would be you three. Seems I was right," he says, giving us a pointed look.

"Yep, we managed it. We aren't sick, although we did come across some who might have been exposed," Brant tells them. "But we've had no direct contact and no symptoms. We're all game for a hot shower, some food that doesn't come from a can, and some pillows."

Zeke nods. "We've got a quarantine house set up just a mile up on Grove street. It's got cots and clean sheets, but no hot water."

I grumble under my breath. Bathing in ice-cold water sounds about as enticing as stubbing a toe repeatedly.

"That's a big fat boo from me, Old Man," I tell him, and my dad's smile grows even bigger.

"Trouble, you're not even inside these doors yet, and you're already starting it." He shakes his head as he and Zeke share an amused look.

"You know how I am about hygiene and cleanliness. Showering in hot water is a necessity."

Madix snorts, and I shoot him a glare. I know his anal retentive sweet ass spent a whole day bringing my house up to his standards, but that doesn't mean it was dirty. It just means this big, beefy package of crazy has standards that are impossible to meet. This dude would think bleach is dirty, so he better not be judging me on my need for a nice hot shower.

227

"We have a mandatory quarantine in place, Trouble, and not even you can talk yourself out of that," my dad answers.

I smile up at my dad, and the phrase *challenge accepted* shines out of my toothy grin. My dad narrows his eyes at me. "These guys live on X and ¾ road," I remark. "That's off the beaten path and still secluded from town. Why don't we serve out our quarantine there? We can walk around the outskirts of town to get there, and in a week, you can come let us know we're free to mingle."

My suggestion gives them pause, and Zeke and my dad turn to each other, speaking low to each other, and I see my dad raise a two-way radio to his mouth and start speaking into it. I roll my eyes. "You know you don't actually have to ask permission. This town worships you and I know you're the one who conspired to get me here. I would've been just fine alone on my mountain," I remind him.

My dad looks down at me with a frown. "I don't want you dealing with life alone anymore, Trouble. If it takes a plague to get you home, then so be it."

"So dramatic," I mumble.

They go back to discussing my proposal, and Brant nudges me. "Nicely done. They might actually let us go home."

"Fuck, I hope so," Theo says, low enough so that my dad and Zeke can't hear him. "The thought of sleeping in my own bed tonight is about to make me come." Madix and Brant laugh and grunt out their agreement.

I hum in approval. "Just you wait, soldier. I'm going to have you coming so hard in that bed that you and your cock won't know what to do."

Theo grins, while Brant gives me an approving growl. "Oh, we'll see who gets fucked senseless. You forget that there's three of us and only one of you, beautiful."

I lick my lips and smile like a kid on her birthday. "There

228

are three of you and only one of me, isn't there?" I sigh dreamily. "This is about to be the most entertaining week ever. And I don't say that lightly, either. I once spent a week in Morocco with a suitcase full of sex toys, and a group of kinkers who had a fetish for plastic flamingos. You know, like the lawn ornaments? Anyway—"

Madix slaps a hand over my mouth. "We do *not* want to know. From here on out, our cocks are the only ones worth remembering. You got that?" he growls at me, and his demand and deep voice sink right between my thighs and send my clit pulsing with need. With his hand still over my mouth, I give him a salute.

"Well, shit, I was kind of hoping to hear what they did with the plastic flamingos," Theo mumbles, and I start to laugh into Madix's palm. Madix shoots Theo a glare, and a teasing smile spreads across Theo's face.

Oh yeah. It's going to be the most entertaining week for sure.

Zeke's voice interrupts us when he calls down. "Okay, Remi, we've pitched that to the mayor, and he's okayed it," he says, lowering the walkie-talkie. "You guys can use the old dried up river bed to get over there. Where's the car you borrowed?"

At that question, I blanch and dart a look to the guys. At this point, I'm so used to walking, that I completely forgot about the car. I can feel the others stiffen around me too, and not in the way you *want* three hot guys to be stiff around you.

Theo clears his throat. "Umm, sir. Well...it's a long story involving an opossum and a whole lotta crazy. Unfortunately, the car is totalled on the side of highway fifteen, about a hundred and fifty miles back, give or take a couple of miles," Theo tells him sheepishly.

Zeke runs a hand over his face in exasperation, and my

dad coughs to cover up the fact that he's laughing. "Remington, that car was only a couple months old. What the hell?" Zeke asks, his arms shooting out in exasperation.

"Why the hell do you think this is on me? I wasn't even driving!"

"It was totally her fault, sir," Madix calls up, throwing me under the bus, just like that. I go to yank my hand out from his but he clamps down on my palm trapping my fingers between his. Madix looks down at me, speaking just for my ears. "Come on, Remi, you could burn this whole place down, and they'd obviously find it adorable. Promise I'll make it worth your while if you take the blame. I mean, technically, it was your opossum that started this whole mess."

I shoot visual daggers at him and then proceed to do a mental kickboxing session with his balls. "How worth my while are we talking here?" I ask, and Madix smiles devilishly at me. My stomach flutters to life in response, but I keep my poker face on. "I want serious kinky fuckery," I tell him, and he narrows his eyes at me.

"How kinky are we talking here?" he counters. "I'm not doing ass shit, or anything involving flamingos."

I *tsk* at him and try to keep from smiling. "Oh come on, you might like ass play. I know I do." I watch Madix shift on his feet so he can try to adjust his hardening dick without my father noticing.

"You can suggest things, but I reserve the right to say no."

"Fine, but I reserve the right to try to convince you that *no* is a very limiting word, and in using it, you might be denying yourself pleasure, so you should keep an open mind."

"Fine," he agrees, and I pat him on the cheek and grin.

"We'll be happy to replace the car or try to tow it back into town and see if it can be fixed," Brant offers.

"Whose car was it?" I ask. I just assumed that it belonged to one of the guys.

"The Robisson's," Dad tells me, and I turn to hiss at Madix. "Oh, you *really* owe me for this one! The Robisson's hate me. Apparently, dyeing their precious poodle, Tank, bright pink was a step too far for them. They've wanted me to suffer ever since," I grumble. "Honestly, I think they were just mad because he *liked* being pink. I could tell. It put a pep in his step he did not have before," I say seriously. Madix just laughs, and it's such an aural orgasm to my ears that I almost forget why I'm irritated.

"Tell them I'll pay them for the damage, or for the car if it can't be fixed, and that I'm sorry," I say up to my dad. "Now can you please let us in?"

It's weird to be here, talking to my dad like I never left. We're both moving on from the fight that we had before I bailed, but I know we'll have to work stuff out. I'm just glad to get the short reprieve before we have to have *that* conversation.

"We'll bring Madix's truck down for all of you," my dad answers. "After the weeklong quarantine is up, we'll talk," he tells me, and I give him a nod of understanding. Even though the quarantine thing is frustrating, I'm glad I have an excuse to be holed up alone with the guys and get to know them even more.

We all nod in agreement, and Brant and Theo both shout "thank you" to the top of the gate.

My dad pauses, and his eyes well up. "Welcome home," he tells me, and the tear that streaks down his face is my undoing. I want to run and hug him, but I know it will have to wait. We need to talk first before we can have the full reunion we both want, and that's going to happen the second we are cleared from quarantine.

"Missed you, Daddy," I reply, and my voice cracks with the admission. He gives me a watery smile, and Zeke pats him on the back.

"We'll talk soon," he tells me affectionately, and I nod in agreement. I watch as he climbs back down from whatever they're standing on and disappears behind the huge metal gate. I exhale loudly, and wipe at the tears in my eyes as the words "Welcome home" echo around in my head.

19

THEO

When we finally pull up to our house, it feels like we've been gone forever, even though it's only been just shy of a week. It's weird how much has changed in that short amount of time, and I realize that's a bit of a running theme in my life. Things happen in the blink of an eye sometimes, and they can change things forever. I look to Brant and Madix, and realize the same can be said for all of us. I don't know too much about Remi, but I'm looking forward to finding out.

I wasn't sure what I expected when Sheriff April showed up at the top of the gate, but it wasn't the hostile exchange I suspected it might be. I figured he was the main reason behind why she hates this place, but after observing how much they clearly care for each other, it's obvious that it's bigger than that.

When Madix throws the truck into park, we climb out, all of us once again quiet and tired. The silence is comfortable, and I watch all of us as we look around and get reacquainted with our surroundings. This house has been our end-goal since we left, and it feels good, but it also feels somewhat anticlimactic to be back.

"I like the color choice," Remi says as she walks around the back to grab her things.

"Theo picked it. I thought it was too dark, but it turned out awesome," Brant tells her, and we all turn to the formerly mustard-yellow house that is now charcoal-gray with light-gray trim.

Puddles hops down, and Madix hands us the rest of the stuff from the back before slamming the tailgate shut. I lead the way into the house and chuckle at how nervous I suddenly feel. What the hell is my deal? I've seen Remi's house, *and* I've seen her naked. Hell, I've been inside of her for fuck's sake, so why do I suddenly feel like I'm about to meet a blind date or something?

I shake off my apprehension and unlock the front door. I don't bother untying my boots like Madix would normally demand. Knowing him, he'll probably spend all day tomorrow cleaning. Me? I plan on spending every second of tomorrow fucking Remi, and learning everything that makes her writhe and scream my name. If Madix would rather get his rocks off wiping out the already perfectly clean refrigerator, that's his loss.

The three of us stand in the entryway, watching as she takes it all in. If I had to guess, I'd say that Brant and Madix are just as nervous as I am at having her seeing our place for the first time.

Remi clutches her pet carrier in her hand and looks around. "Pffft. It figures that you three would have a gym for a living room. I would expect nothing less, given the circumferences of your biceps and ridiculous muscles on your bodies," Remi observes.

"You know you love it," I tease.

She smiles and doesn't argue that fact as she walks further in the room, trailing her fingers over our sparse furniture. "What I *really* love is that you put a couch in here too. I know where I'll be when you guys are going all meathead. Watching you work out will be better than watching TV," she says, tapping her lip in thought. "How do you guys feel about masturbating on the couch? Any hard and fast rules against that? Need me to put a towel down or something?" Remi looks purposefully at Madix, her face stone-cold serious, and Brant chokes on a laugh that gets stuck in his throat.

"Well, since none of us have ever sat on the couch and tugged one out, we have yet to establish any rules about it," Madix answers dryly. "I guess we could watch how you do it and then decide."

Remi seems unphased by the heavy sarcasm saturating every word out of his mouth as she continues to look around.

"Wow, you guys do really great work," she marvels as she runs a hand over the granite countertops. "I saw this place a long time ago, when I was just a kid. It was all shag carpeting and weird concrete countertops that had old rusty nails imbedded in it."

The guys and I nod. "Yeah, that was a bitch to remove," I tell her, remembering the demo. Brant goes to fill Puddles's water bowl and give her some food.

"Where's your bathroom?" Remi asks suddenly.

Brant points down the hall. "First door on your right."

Remi sets the carrier down and opens the door to it. Coon and the rats must be sleeping, because none of them come out to investigate. I watch Madix's jaw tick with irritation. I know the thought of these critters running around his pristine house is going to drive him crazy. It cracks me up, and I put a hand up to hide my smile.

Remi sets her bag down next to the pet carrier, and then crouches over it as she unzips the top. She digs around inside her pack until she pulls out a small case. She catches me watching her, and answers the question in my eyes before I can give it a voice. "Just some essentials I never leave home without," she announces, raising the bag in reference.

I nod and then track her as she moves down the hall. Fuck, I hope she's not on the rag. I mean, I'll still fuck the shit out of her, but I've been fantasizing about spending hours with my head between her thighs since I watched Madix fuck her against a rock, and I'd like to do that sooner rather than later.

I plop down on the couch, ignoring Madix's narrowed gaze. Yeah, I'm dirty and sitting on the furniture, and nope, I don't give a flying fuck about it.

As soon as we hear the bathroom door shut, Brant looks over at us. "Does this feel weird to any of you?" he asks quietly.

"What do you mean?" Madix replies, still frowning at me.

"I don't know, I feel like I'm just coming home from an extended tour. I'm not sure what to do with myself," he admits.

Madix strolls into the kitchen, and then returns with four cold beers. He hands one to each of us, setting the fourth on the coffee table, over a coaster. I take a long pull of the cold drink, groaning at how good it tastes. My stomach rumbles, and I mentally try to take stock of what food we have in the cupboards, because I doubt anything in the fridge will still be good. *Ooh yes,* I think we have chips and salsa. I'm fucking all over that after I get a shower.

"Dude, it's been a long week, and so much shit has gone down. I'm not surprised that's how you feel. It makes sense. I'm just happy to be back and to eat and sleep..." Madix trails off as he tips his head back and swallows half his beer in one go.

"Here's to not fucking dying," I call out, raising my beer to them.

It was a stupid toast we always used to do after every successful mission, and it feels appropriate as fuck right now, given what we've been through. Madix and Brant both chuckle and clink their bottles against mine. "To not fucking dying."

"Well, isn't this cute? Look at the three of you bonding and being all bro-y."

I look over at the sound of Remi's voice, ready to send off a smartass comment, but I end up choking on my beer instead because *holy fuck.*

Remi is standing there, butt-ass naked in all her glory, watching us like there's nothing unusual about her clothes' disappearing act.

"Ummm... not that I'm complaining about what's happening here, but where did your clothes go?" I ask.

Remi fixes me with a sweet smile, and then runs a solitary finger around her pink nipple, making it pebble. She then starts to trail that finger down her stomach slowly—fucking torturously slowly—until she hits the short, light brown hair at the top of her pussy. I swallow, watching hungrily as she presses her finger between her pussy lips and circles her clit.

"Well, the last two times I invited you three into the shower, I was left wet. Very, very wet, but all alone to deal with it." Remi brings up her other hand and pinches her nipple, as the finger between her legs circles her clit faster. I groan at the sight of her working herself, her pussy starting to glisten as she gets wetter. "So, let's try this again. I'm going to go take a shower, and you boys are more than welcome to join me," she says in that breathy way of hers that makes my balls swell and my cock jump against my zipper.

With that, she turns around, swaying back down the

hallway to the bathroom. I watch the muscles in her back and the sway of her ass. I blink in surprise and a jolt goes through me when I notice a sparkly blue gemstone sitting right in the middle of her round cheeks. *What the Fuck?*

"Is that a..." Madix starts to ask.

"Fuck yes, it's a butt plug," Brant announces, and then he pushes past Madix and practically sprints after Remi.

Oh, fuck no.

I scramble off the couch as I half-run, half-undress, to the bathroom. I feel Madix close on my heels, and I chuck my shirt at his face, laughing, in an effort to give myself more of a head start. We both get to the doorway at the same time, and shove at each other to get inside first. I win, by once again playing dirty, and trip him with my prosthetic leg, making him stumble into the wall and giving me free access to cross the threshold. I have to bite down on the victory roar I want to release, because...why the fuck would I roar? I have no idea. Sex makes us do weird things.

Brant is almost completely naked, and is bent over, pulling off his socks. I scrunch my nose up and look away. That is *not* the asshole I want to play with right now. I shove past him and pull open the glass door of the shower. We made the walk-in shower bigger than normal, because we're big guys and can use the room, but even so, there's no way we're all going to fit in here with her, and I'm not about to be boxed out. I move to take a step inside, but remember I still have my prosthetic on and that's a big no-no.

I pull the asshole move and stand in the doorway to the shower and start to remove my leg. Madix calls me a dirty cock block, and I smirk as I pop the socket off my stump, and take my time rolling the sock and liner off.

A wet palm runs down my back, and I'm reminded that a very wet, very horny, gorgeous woman is ready and waiting, so I pick up the pace. I throw everything as far away from the shower as possible, and then swivel around. I grab the handrails on the wall and use them to maneuver myself behind Remi.

Fuck, she's beautiful. She has her eyes closed and head tilted back under the spray, soaking her hair and sending water cascading down the rest of her incredible body. I keep one hand on the handrail and grab onto Remi's waist with my other. And I'm amazed to realize that I don't feel self conscious about my leg at all.

She opens her eyes and smiles at me, and the spark of desire in her eyes makes my cock twitch. Someone steps into the shower with us, but I don't look to see which one of the guys won. I'm too focused on the feel of Remi as I run my hand up her ribs and stroke under her breasts until my fingers brush against her hard nipple. Remi hums in approval as she lathers her hair with shampoo.

The tip of my cock presses into her soft stomach as I circle her nipple slowly with my finger. I reach behind me, feeling for the tiled seating bench and carefully lower myself to sit down, while Remi stays standing in front of me. Brant steps up behind her and his hands come down to cup her breasts, flicking her pink nipples.

Remi arches her back to both rinse her hair and press her breasts further into Brant's hands. When he starts kissing and sucking on her neck while still teasing her nipples, I reach down and grasp her knee and then draw her foot up, bracing it on the bench beside me. Her eyes are closed when I tilt my head down and lick up her slit. And she tastes fucking *good*.

Her head pops up, and her eyes open on a surprised moan. "Theo," she says huskily, making my cock harden even more.

"I fucking love to hear you moan my name," I tell her.

Her hands come around to thread through my hair, and

she shoves my face back against her pussy. "Less talking, more licking."

I chuckle against her. "Whatever our girl wants," I tell her, spreading her lips with my fingers and then going in straight for her clit. As soon as I latch on and suck, her head falls back against Brant's shoulder, and she mutters something.

I release the nub and look up at Brant with amusement. "What'd she say?"

Brant grins. "I think she said something about flamingos."

Laughing, I stretch my tongue out and lick up her folds, letting my hand circle her clit, and then start tongue fucking her, because I'll be damned if I'm shown up by a shitty lawn ornament.

Brant cups her jaw and turns her head, swallowing her moans with his kiss. The sound of their tongues and groaning, along with the taste of her sweet heat against my tongue, drives me insane with lust.

I wish I could pick her up and fuck her against the shower wall. Being down a leg definitely has its downfalls, but at least I have the perfect position in front of her cunt right now. I may not be able to lift her up and fuck her the way that I want to with my cock, but I can sure as hell safely fuck her with my mouth.

I shove my face into her patch of water darkened curls and suck Remi's clit into my mouth again, and she shouts and uses one of her hands to grab my head for balance, spreading even wider for me. I run my tongue up and down her entrance and feel her clench against my tongue. It feels so fucking good to turn her on.

I bring my fingers up to circle the plug in her ass, and my dick wants to be inside of her so badly that it starts leaking precum. I imagine all the things I want to do to her while my tongue and fingers continue working her over, and I watch her reach behind and grab Brant's cock to stroke him. My own dick jumps in response, clearly wanting to cut in line.

Like she knows I'm aching, she breaks off the kiss, still stroking Brant, and looks down at me. "I want to watch you stroke yourself while I stroke Brant," she says, and *holy fuck*, I almost blow my load right here and now, without even being touched.

I lean back, swiping my hand across my mouth from the shower water and her juices and settle my back against the cool tile. With my green eyes locked onto her, I fist myself while using my other hand to dip two fingers inside of her, letting my palm press against her clit. "Yes," she exclaims, her eyes watching my hand as I jerk myself off. Her hand mimics mine, and she begins to move faster and squeeze harder over Brant's dick, making him curse under his breath.

I look up to see Brant pinch Remi's nipples again, and she cries out as her orgasm overtakes her. I ram two fingers deep inside of her, and she screams in pleasure, encouraging everything that Brant and I are doing to her.

Remi's knees shake, but Brant wraps his arms around her waist to hold her up. She's right there at the peak, coming all over my hand, so to heighten her pleasure, I reach around and gently tug at the jewelled butt plug in her ass. Her orgasm intensifies as my fingers fuck her while my other hand thrusts the plug in and out of her ass.

"Fuck, yes!" she cries out.

She was already unsteady before, but when her orgasm finally crests, she goes totally limp. But before Brant can scoop her up, she's suddenly ripped from us both, and I hear her squeal as Brant shouts out an objection at the same time. My head whips up to find a half-wet Madix, carrying Remi out of the bathroom.

"What the fuck, man?" I shout after him.

"We can't all fit in there, and I'm done sitting back and watching," he announces. "Come fuck in my room. You guys don't get your dicks in her before me."

Brant, being the kickass dude that he is, reaches down and helps me to my feet. He supports me as we both hobble after Madix like a couple of rabid dogs, pissed that someone just took our favorite toy away.

Madix slaps Remi's ass and then flips her onto his bed. She doesn't look phased at all by the caveman antics. In fact, her grin grows wider. Madix goes to the side table next to the bed and pulls out a condom, and in response, she immediately spreads her legs for him. Her smile is challenging, and when Madix doesn't immediately press into her, she reaches down and pushes two fingers inside of herself like an impatient little minx.

I've never met anyone who is as sexually free and confident as Remi. I fucking *love* it. Watching her finger herself in challenge to Madix and his hesitation is so incredibly sexy.

Madix seems to snap out of it when a moan escapes her. He growls at her and grabs her wrist, forcing her to pull out of her pussy. He brings her fingers up to his mouth and sucks on them, his dark eyes roving over her wet, naked body. My cock jerks at the sight of him licking the orgasm that I gave her off of *her* fingers.

Brant guides me over to the side of the bed, and as soon as I hit the mattress, I immediately climb over towards Remi.

"So, Remington April, how does this work? How do we all get to fuck you at the same time?" Madix asks her.

Remi licks her lips and grins as she takes each of us in. "Well, Mady, we set up a steady rotation of pussy, ass, and mouth. You boys decide which you want and then take turns. That alright with all of you?"

Madix's answering grin is salacious as he leans over Remi and kisses her. She moans into his mouth as he rolls the condom on, and then he lines up with her pussy, and enters her with one hard thrust.

"Well, I guess that answers which one he wants," Brant snarks.

I laugh, and my cock twitches as Remi moans from Madix's thrusts, but then she reaches up and pinches Madix's nipple *hard*. He jerks back. "Fuck, Remington, that hurt! What the hell!" he scowls.

"Don't be greedy, I want all of you at the same time," she insists.

"Who's the greedy one now?" Madix mumbles, earning him a hard pinch to his other nipple. He growls at Remi again and then leans down and bites the top of her shoulder. She laughs and grinds against his cock, which is the opposite of how Madix was expecting her to react.

I look to Brant. "You want ass or mouth?" I ask, and he cracks up.

I look at him, confused by the random outburst of amusement.

He runs a hand over his face like he's trying to wipe away the grin. "Sorry, you just asked that so casually, like you're asking me what flavor of ice cream I want." I chuckle. "I like *all* the ice cream," he adds, and then moves toward the end of the bed.

It appears that Brant just chose *ass* for dessert. Remi pushes Madix and orders him to lay on his back. He looks like he's about to argue, but Remi shuts it down when she says, "Let me ride that cock, Mady. Then Brant can fuck me from behind, and Theo can fuck my mouth. Give me what I want, so I can give you all what you want."

Yep, she knows *exactly* how to handle him. Madix immediately closes his mouth and moves to lay on his back on the bed like a good little soldier.

Remi looks over her shoulder. "Brant, get the lube that I saw in Madix's drawer, would you? Slather it all over you and me, and then we're good to go," she instructs with a wink, and Brant moves to grab it.

Remi braces her hands on Madix's chest as she climbs on top of him, and she sinks slowly onto his cock. They both groan, and when she's lowered all the way over him, she opens her eyes and quirks a finger at me. I move toward her, happy to follow wherever she wants to lead me. She grabs the back of my head and pulls me into a deep, passionate kiss. She hums into my mouth when Madix grinds up into her.

"Fuck, you feel good," Madix declares, while Remi sucks on my tongue and wraps her hand around the head of my cock.

Brant returns with the bottle of lube in his hand, and pauses to take in the view of Remi riding Madix and jerking me off. The sight spurs him into action, and he squirts lube all over his dick. Remi leans forward when she feels his hand on her back, but she keeps fucking Madix. I don't know how he's keeping himself from coming. I'm almost ready to blow my load, and she hasn't even wrapped her plump lips around my cock yet.

"Mmmm," Remi moans and then looks over her shoulder at Brant. "Lube me up and then slowly remove the plug. Then I want you to push into me nice and slow, okay?"

Brant nods and squeezes lube all over Remi's ass. She stops fucking Madix so that Brant can do what she told him to. I watch as Brant's biceps flex slightly and then relax. It happens a couple more times, and I realize what he's doing when Remi groans appreciatively.

"You like that Remi?" he asks huskily. "You like when I play with your ass while you ride another cock?"

I look at Brant, shocked. I would have pegged Madix for the dirty talker, not him, but *fuck* if it's not getting Remi even more riled up.

"Mmmm, I'd love it even more if I were riding both your cocks," she tells him, and with that, Brant pulls the plug out completely.

He lines himself up, and starts to press slowly inside of her. Remi moans, and Madix moves his hands from her hips to start playing with her tits.

"You all feel so good," she tells us, her hand stroking down my length again.

All of us are lost to the sensations of Remi's body as she works each of us differently, but Madix stays still, careful to give her time so she can become acclimated to Brant.

When Brant is all the way inside of her, she turns to look at him over her shoulder. "You can fuck me now, soldier. I'm ready for you."

Brant pulls out and pushes back in, and all three of them groan in unison.

"Fuck, I can feel him fucking you," Madix bites out, his fingers digging into her hips again.

She leans down more so that her breasts hang heavy over his face, and he sucks a nipple into his mouth. "Now I want to fuck all three of you." On that note, Remi moves her head and opens her mouth around the head of my cock.

I grind my jaw at the feel of her hot, wet mouth around me. Madix and Brant start to guide her over their dicks, and after several movements, they get the hang of the perfect rhythm and start moving her together. Madix thrusts into her from below, Brant from above, and I fuck her mouth. She groans, and the vibrations from the sound shoots right to my balls.

Moans and mumbled encouragements fill the room, and it's all accompanied by the sounds of skin slapping against skin as we all fill her up and fuck her hard. Remi takes it all.

"Look at her, taking all of our cocks," Madix says in a low, raspy tone.

"Looks like she was right about being able to handle us," I say, right before she moves her mouth to suck on my balls, eliciting a grunt of pleasure from me. "She's *real* fucking good at this."

Remi pulls away from my balls with a *pop* and looks up at me with a sly smile. "Me? Are you sure you Joes haven't done this before?"

My laugh joins the other guys' chuckles, but it tapers off to another moan as Remi sucks my cock back into her mouth and swallows me deeply into her throat. I never thought the three of us would ever want to do this with the same woman at the same time, but it feels so fucking good that all I can think about is how I never want it to end. The three of us start fucking her harder and faster, and I can tell the moment she orgasms again when she cries out around my cock.

Madix shouts out with his orgasm next. Remi deepthroats me, and I can't hold back any longer. I come down her throat, and watch as Madix grinds his release into her. Brant keeps fucking Remi's ass, but he doesn't last much longer either before he declares that he's about to come. Remi reaches down and plays with her clit to draw out her own orgasm, just as Brant grunts into her with one final thrust and then lets his forehead rest against her shoulder.

The four of us are left panting, sweaty, and completely sated.

Fuck, that was hot. And now I'm exhausted.

Remi grunts. "You guys are heavy." She slips out from

between all of us, forcing Madix to shove Brant off and roll over.

When she's disentangled, she smacks Madix playfully on the ass and kneels at the foot of the bed, looking over at all of us. "You soldiers did really well," she says with a sexy little smirk. "Now move over so I can take a nap with you."

We all chuckle, but shift around until there's a Remi-sized spot on Madix's king bed. It's a tight fit for all of us, but surprisingly, we all fall asleep within minutes, which has everything to do with the blonde-haired vixen tucked comfortably between us.

20

BRANT

The week-long quarantine goes by surprisingly fast. The three of us basically fuck Remi as much as we can, in every way she wants, and shit, she is a thirsty one. The three of us would fuck her brains out, only to be woken up an hour or so after to do it again. And again. And again. We've had a fuck-ton of fun learning her body and what makes her squeal and moan and scream.

We've also learned a lot about each other and how to be respectful when sharing her, while also having fun with some friendly competition. It sounds crazy, but we've already fallen into a rhythm with each other. The thought of Remington leaving us alone leaves a bitter taste in my mouth. She fits with us, better than I ever imagined anyone could. She calls Madix out on his shit, she helps keep me present and happy, and even Theo seems comfortable in his own skin again; he hasn't been obsessively working out, either.

On day eight, the official end of our quarantine, I'm lured awake by the smell of bacon and something heavy and warm resting on my chest. I crack open an eye and see Remi standing at the foot of the bed wearing those cut off shorts that make her ass look phenomenal, and a tight t-shirt under Madix's cooking apron.

"You're only allowed to wear that if you're naked," Madix grumbles into his pillow.

Theo is stretched along the foot of the bed, and when he wakes up with Madix's feet in his face, he slaps them away with a groan.

"We don't have time for hanky panky this morning," Remi smiles. "It's time for you soldiers to get up. Come eat the breakfast I made and compliment me on how good of a cook I am," she says before turning and walking out of the bedroom with Puddles at her heels.

When I take my eyes off her ass, my gaze moves to the fluffy rodent curled up on top of me. "Coon," I complain. "Get off."

Coon peeks her head out from the scarf she's wrapped happily in and stretches, making her sharp nails dig into my skin. "Ouch! Fuck."

Coon pays my pain no attention as she slowly jumps down from the bed and follows Remi into the kitchen. Madix is already up and pulling on clothes. I get up next, passing Theo his prosthetic before yanking on some pants.

When we're all dressed, we head into the kitchen and find Remi already chowing down on some bacon as she sets a plate of sausage down for Puddles.

I frown. "That's not good for her."

Remi cocks a blonde brow. "Says who? That there is fresh meat. I made those sausages myself."

Madix's black brows furrow as he sits down next to her. "From what meat?"

She beams at him, but before she can open her mouth to answer, he cuts of her off. "I don't wanna know, do I?"

Remi leans over to peck a kiss on his cheek. "You don't want to know," she agrees cheerily.

Madix shakes his head but laughs and slaps her ass when she straightens up to grab some coffee. Remi fills all of our mugs and then sits down. Theo and I slide into the other chairs, and the four of us settle into easy conversation as we eat. We also make sure to give her at least three compliments on making breakfast. We made the mistake of not doing that after she made us pheasant one night, and she made us watch as she got herself off, and we weren't allowed to touch. We learned our lesson real fast after that.

When we're done with breakfast, Madix cleans up, while Remi perches on the counter, swinging her tanned legs back and forth and making me want to step between them and either wrap them around my face or my hips and take her right there. "While you sleepy heads were drooling into Madix's mattress, I got up to listen to the local news," she tells us, braiding her long hair over her shoulder. "Not only is it the end of our quarantine today, but the mayor called for a mandatory town meeting."

"When?" I ask, pulling on my boots.

Remi grabs Madix's wrist to look at his watch. "In about twenty minutes."

Cursing, we hurry to clean up as quickly as we can, even though Madix bitches and complains about us not doing it right the whole time. Who washes the dishes before putting them in the dishwasher? It makes no fucking sense.

We walk out of the door, and it feels a little weird not to be greeted by someone and be officially cleared from quarantine. I guess that's another perk to having the sheriff's daughter with us. We all pile into the truck to head toward the high school, but I'm worried. What if the mayor called a meeting to give us more bad news?

So far from what we've heard, there've been no cases of the Handshake Plague confirmed in town. Apparently, there was a scare while we were gone and some outsiders wanted to get into the town, but it sounds like it was handled and whoever it was took off. We've still not been able to get any radio stations aside from the local one, and the cell towers are still down, which makes news of what's happening outside impossible.

So now, we're all in this weird state of limbo. The guys and I have talked about what we'll do after our quarantine has been lifted. We are clearly the types that need jobs and purpose, but we can't all agree on what that should be. We've talked about coordinating a hunting team to make sure everyone in Endstone is fed, but we've yet to decide if we're all into that plan.

The parking lot is packed when we get to the high school. We pull into a space beside Nurse June and Dharla. Luckily, she's not naked this time, but she *is* holding a new can of soup in her hand and demanding that people pay up. June just leans against her car, smoking a cigarette, watching Dharla with an amused twinkle in her eye.

When Nurse June notices us getting out of the truck, she perks up. "Ah, there you boys are. I heard you were the heroes who finally managed to wrangle in Trouble and make her see sense," her kind eyes move to Remi. "How you doin,' sugar?"

Remi smiles and moves in to hug her. "I'm doing just fine, Junie May. How are you and Dharla? She keeping you on your toes?"

June laughs and drops her cigarette on the ground, crushing it beneath her shoe. "All ten of them, and my fingers, too," she jokes, before leaning back and studying Remi's face. "It's nice seein' you home. You look real good, Remington April. You remind me of your mama," she says, and I notice that they both get a glossy sheen over their eyes.

Remi kisses her on the cheek and looks over her shoulder. "Dharla's looking to get naked, Junie," she tells her.

June sighs and pulls out another cigarette to light up. "I'm gonna need another smoke first. Besides, it usually takes her a good five minutes to take her knickers off."

Remi laughs and reaches back to take my hand, threading her fingers through mine. Madix steps up and presses his hand against the small of her back, while Theo brings up the rear. A slow, wide smile spreads over June's face as she takes us in. "Oh, lordie, you handlin' all that?" June laughs delightedly.

"You know it, Junie," Remi says, with a wink.

June shakes her head, the laughter still escaping with the smoke from her lips. "No, sugar. Not you. I meant *them*." She gives us all a curious look. "You sure you three can manage her? She's more than a handful."

Theo smirks. "You're right. She's *three* handfuls. And we got it, don't you worry," he adds with a cocky wink.

June tips her head back and laughs in her croaky, smoker's tone, and it accompanies us as we start threading through the cars and people stuffed full in the parking lot.

"You *got it,* huh?" Remi teases.

Theo smacks her ass playfully. "Yup."

"Well, that went better than I thought it would," I observe. None of us really knew just what this small town would think about our *relationship* with Remi. This is our first trip out as a group, and even though it goes against all of my instincts, I'm trying to get on board with what Remi suggested we do.

"See, I told you, just to act like we normally do, minus the fucking, orgasms and nakedness. There are bigger freaks in this town than us, and not as many people will care as you think."

I chuckle and watch as Theo leans into Remi. "So you're finally admitting that you are, in fact, a freak," he taunts.

"I wave that flag loud and proud, soldier," she tells him

with a smirk. "And don't think that you aren't a freak too, or are you forgetting the other night with the vibrator, the raspberry jam, and the milk jug?" she asks.

Theo laughs and adopts a faraway, dreamy look. Kinky fucker.

"We should do that with honey next time. I think that extra sticky element will take things to a whole other level," he comments.

Remi nods her head thoughtfully. "That would be interesting. Let's stop by the grocery store after the meeting and stock up on necessities. Oh, and don't let me forget clothespins. I've got plans for those and Madix," she adds, beaming excitedly.

Madix sputters at the revelation and glares at her. "No," he growls, but Remi just pats his cheek as we approach the entrance to the gym.

"Whatever you say, sugar," she tells him sweetly.

"I'm serious, Remington."

"Of course, honey pot," she replies.

"Remi," Madix warns, and I can't help but crack up at the exchange. We all know he's going to do what she wants, and he's going to like it. We all like the things she does, but it's fucking hilarious watching him try to fight it.

They continue with this playful bickering back and forth as we follow a group of people into the gym. I blink back my surprise at the state of the inside. It's decorated with streamers everywhere, and there are hand-painted signs that say things like, "*We did it!*" and, "*Congrats, Enders on your endgame!*"

There's a stage set up on one side of the gym, directly across from where the bleachers are. It's packed, and just like last time, we head toward the white cinderblock wall on the side to stand and observe.

"What's with the decorations?" Theo asks.

Madix is still arguing with Remi about the clothespins, looking more and more distressed by the second, so they don't even hear us.

I shrug. "Maybe they had a basketball game or something and went all out in order to distract everyone from the virus. You know this place. They get hyped up about the weirdest things," I reply, and he gives me a snort of agreement.

When we first moved into town, they were celebrating something they called the *Two Tail Festival*. When I asked what it was, I was told that someone read an article about a town that had a festival for a chicken that got its head cut off, but managed to live for a couple years after that. *Mike the Headless Chicken Days*, it was called. Well, apparently, the mayor at the time decided Endstone needed its own peculiar set of celebrations, so when his niece found a lizard with two tails, the mayor pounced on it. I guess the lizard was named Uhtred, but that was way too hard to say, so the *Two Tails Festival* was born instead.

"It's called nipple play, Mady," I hear Remi telling him, and Theo and I have to swallow back a laugh when Madix instinctually raises his arm to protect the body part in question.

"I'll give you fucking *nipple play,*" he growls.

She just laughs and looks excited about that proposition. "I'm all for taking turns."

Restless chatter fills the gym, and there's sense of anticipation and energy that wasn't here at the last meeting we attended. I notice small groupings of more somber looking townspeople sitting amidst the crowd, and notice that each of them is wearing a black t-shirt with a white X on it. It looks ominous as fuck, and I suddenly wonder if people in town have become sick.

Worried, I turn to the others to ask if they noticed the

shirts too, but before I can, the townspeople suddenly burst into applause and cheers. I look up to find the mayor, the current sheriff, Zeke, and Sheriff April, all walking into the gym with big smiles on their faces.

My blond brows furrow, and I look over at Madix and Theo, but they seem just as confused as I do. Remi is just kneeling down beside Puddles, scratching my dog's belly and looking bored. We all watch the leaders of the town step up onto the stage and raise their hands in celebration while the townspeople eat it up and cheer even louder.

What the fuck am I missing here? Did the CDC get the virus contained? Are we celebrating because things aren't as bad as we thought? I fucking hope so. I look around the room again, trying to piece together what's going on. The mayor steps up to the podium and taps on the microphone.

"Alright, everyone, I'm here to announce the conclusion of our fifty-sixth annual End Of Days Scenario!"

The place explodes into applause again, so loud that it's like the fucking superbowl was just won inside our dinky gymnasium.

Madix winces from the noise level, but I'm too busy staring open-mouthed at the mayor as my brain races and then trips over itself.

Laughing, the mayor looks behind him to the others on the stage, who are also wearing smiles, and then holds up his hands to quiet everyone down. "I know you all are eager to get to the celebration cookout, so I'll announce this year's survivors and succumbers."

People whoop and groan simultaneously, and Mayor Jeffries grins and points to the groups wearing the black shirts with X's on them. "I'm sorry to say, you lot succumbed to the Handshake Plague. You had the lowest points of all, but the Bodean family got the worst of the worst." The crowd chuckles at their expense, and the Bodeans, a robust family of nine wearing matching holey overalls under their shirts and bare feet, wave everyone off and flash their middle fingers—even the five-year-old little girl.

"The Bodean family ran out of food on account of not rationing, their garden wasn't kept up, and instead of asking a neighbor all friendly-like, they tried to steal," the mayor says with a disappointed shake of his head. The crowd boos, and the matriarch, Mrs. Bodean, hocks a loogey onto the gym floor.

The mayor shakes his finger at them. "You know better than to turn on your fellow Enders," Mayor Jeffries rebukes. Mr. Bodean nods slowly, feeling obviously chastised. "Now, aside from that, you lost because your family then decided to try to scale the wall, thus leaving Endstone's safe borders and exposing yourselves. You were then overtaken by contaminated Plaguers," Mayor Jeffries points to the bleachers, showing a group of people wearing black shirts with a yellow biohazard symbol on it. "Thus, you succumbed." He picks up a large wooden gavel from the podium, slamming it down on the wood, and the crowd lets out a, "wah, wah."

"...What...What the fuck is happening right now?" Madix snaps, but I have no answers.

Theo is completely wide-eyed, and Remi is still petting the damn dog like nothing is happening.

At our expressions, she looks up at us from her spot on the gym floor and tilts her head. "What do you mean?"

I wave my arm around at this fucking mind-blowing scenario that's going on right now. "This! What the fuck is happening?"

She frowns and stands up, looking between the three of us. The crowd behind me starts clapping as the mayor begins to announce the *winners*. "This is Endstone, guys."

Madix scowls and his jaw tenses. "We fucking *know* it's Endstone. We live here."

"Exactly," she says, as her eyes run over each of our confused faces. "I mean, I didn't initially take you guys as the *militia* types, but I'm coming to terms with it, if that's what you're worried about."

"Wait," Madix cuts in. "What the fuck are you talking about?"

She shakes her head at us. "Oh, come on, guys! This party marks when you can officially drop the act. It's fine, I get it," Remi tells us, waving her hand dismissively.

Madix grabs her by the shoulders and leans down until his face is level with hers. "Remington Francine April. What. Are. You. Talking. About?"

Remi's eyebrows furrow until finally, her face takes on the same baffled expression that Theo, Madix and I are wearing. "Wait..." she looks between us, like she's just seeing us for the first time. "Are you telling me that this whole time, you didn't know that this entire town is a Doomsdayers Militia Group?" she asks in shock.

I blink.

Theo opens and closes his mouth.

And Madix...Madix just looks like his brain just malfunctioned. I'm pretty sure he's not even breathing.

"Wait..." I start, but my brain stalls at the implications that are running through my head. I rub my face with both of my hands and try to work through what this means. "Are you saying that the Handshake Plague *isn't real?*" I ask, completely bewildered. How the fuck is that even possible?

Remi nods, and I can tell she's trying *really* hard not to laugh at us, but it's proving to be difficult. "Oh my God, I can't believe you guys didn't know," she practically squeals with delight. "How is it possible that you didn't know?"

"Are you telling me that everything that happened in the past two weeks was some kind of sick fucking hoax?" Madix roars, his fists clenched at his sides and his face furious.

Before Remi can answer, we hear the mayor over the mic say, "And the grand prize winners with the most points accumulated this year are: Madix Ortega, Theo Coleman, and Brant Shaw!"

And then the crowd goes wild.

I turn toward the mayor at the sound of my name, my mouth still open in shock. He waves us over, a huge smile spread across his face, and I'm not sure what the fuck to do. A doomsdayer militia group? How the fuck did we miss that pivotal detail about this fucking town? Sheriff April gives us a quizzical look as the three of us are still standing here, totally gobsmacked.

Remi leans forward and shouts to us over the applause of the crowd. "You boys better get up there before the crowd turns on you for being ungrateful! The people of Endstone covet that first place prize. Trust me, you don't want to piss them off."

With that statement, I look around at the people in the gymnasium with a totally new perspective. All of these people are bat shit crazy, and the last thing we want is a crazy town to turn on us. Madix and Theo must come to that same conclusion, because they both take a step forward toward the still grinning mayor who has his hand outstretched, waiting for us to come up on the stage.

I fall into step with them, and the three of us swallow down our outrage as we make our way forward. We'll smile through whatever these insane people have to say, and then we'll get the fuck out of here. Logically, I realize that's the smartest thing to do, but the thought of suddenly having to leave what we built here sends a pang through my chest. Will Remi come with us? ...Is she in on all of this too?

I look over my shoulder at her, and she tries to hide her amusement behind the hand covering her mouth. Technically, we brought her here against her will. At least, that's how this all started. And then it hits me. This is the reason *why* she left. I thought when she kept saying she wanted out of Endstone, she just meant because it was a small town. I didn't realize it was because this place is a fucking insane end-of-times doomsdayers group. And we made her come back. *Fuck.*

We're still in shock as we climb the steps to the makeshift stage, and then everything is a whir of noise and flashing lights. Emma from the town newspaper points a camera at us, temporarily blinding us from the flash. "Front page!" she says gleefully.

People pat us on the back, the mayor's voice starts listing the way we've earned Ender points, but I'm so overwhelmed I can't process it all. Beside me, Madix has the fiercest glower I've ever seen, looking more like a cornered bear than anything, while Theo keeps shifting on his leg, like he's nervous from all the attention.

The mayor keeps going on about how we earned points for our "dedication to the seriousness of the doomsday scenario," as well as for our, "excellence in survival skills," and last but not least, our, "commitment to the Endstone community." Then we get an extra hundred fucking points because we managed to get Remington back home.

Some ladies wearing the biohazard shirts come forward, and before we know it, we're getting fucking sashed. Yep. *Sashed.* One minute, we're just standing there, gaping awkwardly at the insanity around us, and the next, the fake plague victims are putting sashes over our heads and handing us bouquets of flowers.

What. The Fuck.

I'm going to fucking kill someone.

Wait...I almost *did* fucking kill someone.

I almost shot those motherfuckers in the woods because I actually thought they were infected with a deadly virus, when really, the poor asshole who was sick probably just had food poisoning. If I had pulled the trigger...

I'm watching the mayor as he talks excitedly, but I'm not really seeing him or anyone else in here. I'm too busy running over everything the guys and I did since we were told about the fucking Handshake Plague. I thought it was real. I had no doubt in my mind, and why would I? They control the local radio station. They shut down the fucking cell towers so we couldn't get on the internet or make calls, and hell, we don't even get cable at our place.

The scene at the town square with the possible infected people, the first town meeting, the food rations...all of it was some creepy messed up role play. My eyes cut to Sheriff April, but he's too busy watching his daughter to notice me. I look down at the flowers being shoved in my arms, and then another round of applause sounds off before the guys turn and walk off the stage. I follow behind them numbly, my mind still whirling.

As soon as we get back to where Remi is standing, I snatch up her hand and pull her out through the side door. Theo and Brant follow behind us. The gym door slams shut behind us, and I toss the fucking bouquet of daisies to the ground and turn to her. I open my mouth to...I don't fucking know what I'm gonna say, because I'm too pissed, too shocked, and too overloaded with the insanity of this, to think straight. But before I can utter a single thing, Remington plants her hand over my mouth.

"Okay, I can see by the look on your face that you're ready to go all ragey on me," she says quickly. "But I didn't know that you didn't know! Scouts Honor," she promises, holding up three fingers. "So, I get that you're probably confused and pissed, but if you yell at me—*me*, who had nothing to do with this—then I will kick you in the balls," she promises, giving me a stern look.

We stare at each other for a moment, her light blue eyes flitting back and forth between my dark and angry brown ones. When she finds whatever it is she's looking for in my expression, she drops her hand from my mouth.

"I need you to fill in the blanks for me, Remi, because right now there are so many that I feel like I'm going to lose my mind. I mean, we almost *killed* people because of this fucking hoax..." I trail off, unable to voice how that would have broken all of us beyond repair. We've all been fighting tooth and nail just to get where we are today, and this fucking joke...this fake mission made me feel alive. I felt like I could get back to who I was. Anguish and relief wars inside of me, and I have no idea what to do with any of it. To think of all the shit we went through these past weeks...

Remi's face fills with empathy as she takes in the hurt that must be written on my face. "This town was founded a long time ago by people who didn't trust the government and were convinced that they needed to prepare and plan for the end of civilization as we know it. Every year, they do something like this. Pretend there's some catastrophic event, and then they work to survive it."

"So everyone in this town is part of this group?" Theo asks, and Remi nods. "So my uncle…" Theo trails off.

"Yeah, I thought you guys knew. I figured your uncle would have told you about this place, or even your parents would have clued you into what he was involved in." Theo shakes his head at Remi's words, and Brant bends down to pet Puddles, who's leaning heavily against his leg.

"So this is why you didn't want to come back?" Brant asks.

Remi blows out a breath. "Yep. I was raised here, and while I love the people in this town, it was driving me insane. I needed to get away from all the doomsday and prep talk. I just don't believe what they believe."

"What is it that you don't believe, Trouble?" a gravelly voice sounds behind us, and I turn to see Sheriff April and Zeke walk out of the door from the gym. He opens his arms wide—obviously expecting for Remi to step into them—and if this had been a week ago, she probably would have wrapped him up in a huge hug, but right now, she's glaring at him. Sheriff April seems confused by her hostility, and he lowers his hands in sad defeat.

"Dad, how could you do this to them?" she asks in an accusing tone, her arms motioning toward us. "It's one thing for you guys to play pretend and go to the elaborate lengths you do to play your weird doomsday games, but it is *beyond* messed up to pull people in who don't know that it's not real!"

Sheriff April immediately looks confused and turns to Zeke, like somehow he's going to have the answer. When

Zeke looks just as baffled, Sheriff turns back to Remi. "What are you talking about?"

Remi stares at her dad for a beat, and then it's like all of the anger drains out of her and is replaced with mirth. She covers her mouth with both her hands before completely losing it. We all stare at her as she breaks into hysterical peals of laughter. She bends over and holds onto her side as tears start to drip down her face and guffaws pour out of her throat. If I wasn't so pissed and feeling so lost, I'd probably crack up just from the sight of her, but my anger is too fresh and prominent.

I look to Brant and Theo, whose eyes are jumping from Remi to mine, clearly just as confused as I am about everything that's going on. I realize that we're all still wearing our sashes, and I rip mine away from my body in disgust. At the sound of the fabric tearing, Sheriff turns from his kid to me, and all of a sudden, realization fills his face and is quickly replaced by horror.

"You...you didn't know this was just an exercise?" he sputters.

Zeke's head snaps our way at Sheriff's words, looking equally appalled by that realization.

"No," I tell him, working to keep the rage out of my voice.

"But...how?" Zeke insists. "We're on a watchlist. I thought everyone knew about Endstone."

Remi wipes tears from her eyes and looks to Zeke. "Oh my God, that is not something to be proud of," she scolds him, but the pride in Zeke's eyes is not easily doused.

"No one fucking told us," I snap. "We haven't even lived here for three months yet. How were we supposed to just *know*?"

"It was in the contract you signed for your uncle's property." Sheriff announces, his eyes fixed on Theo. "It was part of his will; Zeke drafted it for him."

Theo's eyes widen with shock, and he starts shaking his head. "What?" he asks, panicked.

"Your uncle left you the property, but it was under the condition that you'd be part of our militia. Your uncle was a prominent figure around here, and he wanted you to carry on that legacy."

Brant and I turn to Theo and fix him with hard looks. "What the fuck, Theo? Don't you think that would have been pertinent information to give us *before* we all moved out here and unknowingly joined a doomsday militia?"

"*The* doomsday militia," Zeke adds proudly, rolling back on his heels. Remi, who's managed to get a hold of herself, slams her palm to her face and shakes her head at Zeke and his statement.

"I didn't fucking read anything," Theo shouts, his arms raised in defense as he takes a step back. Brant's mouth drops open and his stare grows incredulous.

"What do you mean you didn't read *anything*?" he barks at Theo.

He shrugs sheepishly. "It was a ton of paperwork. I just signed where the lawyer told me to. That was it."

I take a step towards Theo, enraged. "You made us join a cult because you didn't read the fucking paperwork?" I yell at him.

Theo blanches and Sheriff April raises his hand. "Not a cult, son. They're into all sorts of religious things, and that's not what Endstone is about. We believe in protection, preparation, and assembling against enemies both foreign and domestic. *That* is the Ender way."

Remi snorts, and her dad shoots her an unamused look. "Dad, stop trying to recruit them. Besides, from the sounds of things, they're already members," she teases.

Theo glares at her. "We are not."

"Yeah, I'm pretty sure you are," she counters, and points to his chest. "Your sash says so."

Theo looks down at the black and yellow biohazard "Handshake Plague Survivor" sash, and then promptly tears it off. "Who fucking gives sashes out for surviving a fake plague?" he grumbles.

"Normally, we don't, but Remi insisted you guys would really like them. We tried to get the crowns she insisted on too, but they didn't arrive in time," Sheriff April informs us.

The three of us pin our glares on her, and Remi has to swallow the bubble of laughter that tries to crawl out of her throat. She bites her lips and attempts to look contrite. "Sorry, I thought it would be funny to make you macho alphas get sashed and crowned."

I narrow my eyes at Remi. "Wait, when did you guys even talk? We've been in quarantine this whole time," I ask in confusion, which I'm starting to think is going to be a permanent state for me at this point due to this fucking insane town filled with insane people.

"Easy," Remi chirps proudly. "Flashlight out the window at night doing morse code. I also arranged for the Robisson's car to get towed back and repaired. We can go get the rest of our stuff from the mechanic any time."

I stare at her, completely at a loss for words. I put my hand up to my face and start rubbing at the headache forming behind my eyes. Of course she knows morse code. She was raised in a doomsday cult—militia—I correct myself, as if somehow Sheriff April is going to hear my thoughts and set me straight again.

"Crowns?" Theo pipes up, pulling me from my scattered thoughts.

Remi nods, her grin breaking through. "Yep, tiaras. The big beauty queen kind. I felt you G.I. Joes earned them after your stellar performance. Which I now know...wasn't a performance."

"Why didn't you say something about all of this?" Theo asks her.

She throws up her hands. "Like I said, I thought you knew! Enders take this stuff super seriously. They don't *ever* break character once they've been given one. Believe me, my whole childhood was spent trying to get people to do just that. I did try to get you guys to come clean with me. I asked logical questions about how you knew this was the end of the world, yada, yada, yada. I tried to trip you up, but you all had solid answers and arguments. What was I supposed to do? I thought you were in on the game."

I shake my head and run a frustrated hand through my hair before turning to Brant and Theo. "We need to talk," I announce, and they both nod their heads in agreement. Remi chews on her bottom lip at the expression on my face, but I can't look at her. She glances between us and then turns to her dad. "Let's umm...just give them a minute," she mutters.

The three of them walk back inside the gymnasium, leaving us alone. Brant takes off his glasses and squeezes the bridge of his nose while Theo whistles low. "Okay, well...I fucked up," he admits.

"Ya think?" I fire back.

Brant steps between us before we can get into a shouting match in the parking lot. "Let's just keep cool," he says, looking between us. "Whatever happened, already happened. Let's just be thankful that we didn't actually hurt anyone or get hurt ourselves."

I rub a hand down my face. "This is fucking insanity," I say, before whirling around to start stalking away.

"Where are you going?" Theo calls at my back.

I turn on my heel to face them again. "Where do you

think? I'm getting in my truck, I'm gonna go get my shit, and then I'm getting the fuck out of here."

Theo's face flashes with anger and hurt. "Just like that?"

I point towards the gymnasium, where we can hear more applause going on. "This place is like porn for apocalypse preppers. I'm not just gonna stick around and be in their twisted, paranoid fucking cult."

"Doomsday militia," Brant mumbles.

"Really?" I say dryly.

"Look, I know we just got the rug yanked out from under us. I know you're pissed. But no one purposely deceived us. This is just...how they live. They like to prepare for the end of the world. In the grand scheme of things, is that really so bad?"

"Did you drink from the fucking punch bowl?" I snap. "How can you be okay with this?"

He runs a frustrated hand over his scalp. "Fuck, I don't know, man. Endstone is fucked up, yeah, but...so is the rest of the world. So they like to prep. Is it really that bad once you start to think about it?" he challenges me. "It's like..." he looks around, trying to search for the words. "It's like the entire town just plays pretend for a few weeks every year. It's not the end of the world."

"Nice pun," Theo snorts.

Brant rolls his eyes. "I'm just saying, just take a minute and think. Try not to let your fucking anger rule you for once. Do you really want to give everything up? We've done so much better since moving to Endstone, and we all know it," he says, his eyes level with mine. "Don't fucking try to lie to yourself, Madix. Endstone has been good for us, despite its crazy townspeople, and even despite this."

I shake my head and stare at the ground, unable to believe what I'm hearing. "You're fucking crazy to even think about staying here."

"Why?" Brant challenges. "Just because it's outside of the social norm? Newsflash, Madix, we're all in a relationship with the same fucking girl. We're fucked in the head, with more damage from our time in the service than any of us want to admit. We're already outside of the norm. We wouldn't have come here in the first place if that weren't the case."

Shaking my head, I wave him off. "I'm out of here."

"You're just gonna walk away?" Brant calls at my back. "Leave us? Leave her?"

I scoff. "You're saying you just want to stay here in Looneyville?"

"I'm saying we should talk about our options and include Remi in those talks. You can't just walk away."

"Watch me."

Theo and Brant both call after me, but I ignore them as I stalk towards my truck. My temper is flaring so bright that all I can see is red. I hate being left in the dark, and I hate being caught off-guard. I'm so pissed that when I open the door to my truck and climb in, I don't even notice the woman sitting in the passenger seat until she speaks.

"Your pants are too tight," she says, making me jump in surprise.

With my hands gripping the steering wheel, I turn my head to look at her and sigh through my clenched teeth. "Dharla, get out of my truck."

She ignores my comment completely. "Men shouldn't be wearing pants that tight. It cuts off the circulation to your Peter Piper," she says matter-of-factly, as she continues to comb her gray hair with a plastic spork. "My Willy never wore pants that tight, and his little willy always worked. Right up until the day the bastard died," she tells me.

I rub my eyes, feeling the pulsing headache spread to my temples. She's still wearing her pink and yellow moo-moo dress, so at least there's that. "My Peter Piper is just fine," I tell her.

She reaches into the pocket of her dress and pulls out a bag of sugar snap peas and starts chowing down on them. "You boys must have more than fine willies, else that April girl wouldn't be sticking around with you. She's too smart to get blinded by the thing kept locked inside your too-tight pants. She's a good girl, you know. Doesn't toss her loyalty in the ring for many, but once she does, she'll stick by 'em," Dharla says seriously around a mouthful of pea stocks.

She holds up the bag to me in offering. "Fuck it," I say, and grab one before tossing it in my mouth. It's surprisingly better than I expected.

"You know, my Willy brought me here to Endstone when he retired. He loved this town. Won the annual scenario games two years in a row," she says.

"I'm sure you're very proud," I say dryly.

To my surprise, she cackles. "Me? Shit, no. I think this place is filled with crackpots," she says, and the fact that this is *Dharla* saying that only adds to the hilarity. "But..." she goes on. "It's harmless, and some people...they go feeling like they have no control of their lives, or even their deaths. Life hits them with one crazy curved dick after another, until they finally split. Endstone lets them feel like they can prepare for what life might throw at them," she says, her words eerily wise. "Plus, these people just really like playing pretend and winning shit," she says, before pulling out her dentures and picking off the pieces of snap pea that got stuck.

I wrinkle my nose as she puts her teeth back in and flicks green pieces onto the floor of my truck. Fucking fantastic. I'll have to get the whole interior detailed now.

"What's your point, Dharla?" I ask.

"My point is, your pants are too fucking small," she answers, glowering at me.

She shoves open the door and gets out, flashing me in the process. I slam my eyes closed. "Ugh! Dharla! Where's your fucking underwear?"

She cackles. "Left 'em for you. You'll have to find them," she says with a wink, before she starts walking away, singing her own cover song of *Ninety-nine Crooked Dicks in the Pant*s as she goes.

When she disappears from view, all of the tension rushes out of me with one long sigh. I press my forehead against the steering wheel and close my eyes, trying to let my brain catch up as my temper fizzles out.

When there's a tap on the driver's side window, I fully expect Dharla Fucking Cornburner to be standing there again, ready to accost me or some shit, but instead, Remington is standing there. We look at each other for a minute through the window, me not moving, and her not pushing me to.

But as soon as I open my door, Remi climbs in right on top of me, straddling my waist. My hands go to her hips and I yank her closer, so that her back doesn't dig into the steering wheel.

"What did you decide, soldier?" she asks me, her blue eyes running over my face.

It's amazing to me how much she gets me, even though we've only known each other for a short amount of time. She's not asking me how I'm doing, or pretending that everything is okay. She's just...putting the ball in my court.

"I...I don't know yet," I tell her honestly.

She nods like she completely understands, and threads her hands behind my neck. "I ran away from this place when I was fifteen," she suddenly says. "It was right after my mom died, and I was....well, angry at the world, but taking it out on my dad. It was right in the middle of Endstone's annual doom scenario. Bird flu," she says with a scoff. "I was so mad that I hitched a ride with a lumber truck out of town. My dad had to drive twelve hours out of Endstone to come pick me up at a gas station."

I shake my head at her. "That was dangerous."

"I know," she nods, her hands toying with the hair at the back of my neck. "That's why when I turned eighteen and we got into our huge fight, I was smarter. I got a job for this wilderness tour group in Alaska. I saved all my money, and when I left that time, I had no intention of coming back."

"Until us," I finish.

She nods again. "Until you."

"But you knew the plague was fake. Why'd you come back? If you'd have told us what was going on, I would have never forced you here."

She shrugs and moves her hands down to trail over my biceps. "I missed my dad. And the three of you intrigued me. I wanted to see where things would go," she says, her blue eyes fixed on my unsure gaze. "I want you to know, if you want to leave, there's no hard feelings. I understand, believe me. Endstone drives me crazy, so I get wanting to get the hell away from it."

I think about everything she said and let out a long breath, my thumbs tracing slow circles over her exposed skin where her shirt has ridden up. "Ten minutes ago, I would've agreed with you and driven off," I admit. "I have a quick temper, and my knee jerk reaction is usually to yell and then storm off."

Remi's fingers tense over my arms, and she drops her gaze away from mine. I can tell she's trying to stay quiet and impassive for my sake.

"But..." I continue. "Then Dharla Cornburner had to go

and make sense. And isn't that the fucking craziest shit you've ever heard?"

Remi's head pops up, and her blue eyes find mine again. "So that means…?"

I lift a hand up and grip the back of her neck, my thumb brushing against her jaw. "I'm pissed, but I don't want to storm off. Brant's right, and so is Dharla Fucking Cornburner." I shake my head and release a low chuckle. "Sometimes, the fools are the smartest ones in town."

Remi beams, but I swallow the grin right off her face when I crush my lips against hers and devour her. I kiss her long and hard, pouring all of my shock and frustration and want into the kiss, and it anchors me and frees me all at the same time.

I pull back and stare into fathomless ice-blue eyes. "So, to recap," I tease, nipping at Remi's jaw. "The world is not ending, and now we're stuck with a crazy chick, an even crazier town, and a pack of rodents for roommates."

Remi glares at me. "For the last time, Coon is a marsupial."

"Yeah, yeah, yeah. So you keep saying."

Remi's answering kiss is punishing, and just when I'm about to get lost in it, she pulls away. The truck doors open, and Theo, Brant, and Puddles, all pile in. Remi smiles at them and then back to me. "Let's go home. I have some scenarios of my own that I'd like us all to work through," she says, wagging her brows as she grinds against my lap. I give an approving growl.

"Oh, and by the way," she announces as she moves to the passenger seat and buckles up. "Remember when I said I wouldn't invite myself to move in with you? Well, I changed my mind. I'm totally moving in."

The guys chuckle from the back seat while I plant my hand onto her thigh and squeeze. "Yeah, you fucking are."

EPILOGUE

Remi
Three Weeks Later

S omeone pounds on the front door, and the booming sound is followed by what can only be described as furious honking.

"I've got it," I shout out, and move toward the front of the house. I smile, unable to help myself and walk calmly to the door, grabbing the folded papers I've been keeping on the coffee table for this exact reason.

I slip them into my back pocket, and I open the door to find Deputy Parks and Sheriff Dunn standing on the porch. They both tip their hats to me, and one seems to be waiting on the other to speak. Sheriff Dunn clears his throat. "Remington April, we would like a word with you, if that's alright?"

A large body presses into my back, and a hand grabs the door just above mine. "What's going on?" Theo asks.

I turn to him and give him a sweet smile. "I'm not sure, something about needing a word with me," I offer innocently.

Theo's eyes narrow playfully at me, and he fights to keep a smile from his face. "Oh, this oughta be good."

I step out of the house when the sheriff motions for me to follow him, and I hear Theo call for Madix and Brant. More honking assaults me as I follow the officers around the front of the house to the side. I work hard to keep a straight face at what greets me there, but it's so perfect I almost crack and start laughing. Car doors slam as Mr. and Mrs. Robisson stomp out of their newly fixed explorer and round on me.

"I demand that she's arrested for this vandalism, right this minute!"

Mrs. Robisson's shrill voice pushes me just over the edge, and an amused smile sneaks across my face.

"This is not funny, young lady. First our precious Tank and now this? The harassment ends now!" Mr. Robisson fumes, his cheeks wobbling with anger.

Theo, Madix, and Brant screech to a halt next to me, and all my efforts to keep a straight face go up in smoke when the three of them lose their shit and burst into laughter.

"No, you fucking didn't, Remi..." Madix huffs out before he bends over and gets lost to a fit of manly giggles.

"It's pink," is all Brant can manage, before he too can't form coherent words anymore. I cover my mouth as I chuckle, unable to help it, and the Robisson's both pin me with a murderous glare.

"Ms. April, did you paint the Robisson's Explorer hot pink?" Sheriff Dunn asks me, and I can tell he's trying to keep from laughing too.

"Yes, sir," I admit.

Deputy Parks shakes his head and fixes me with a stern look. "Remi that's vandalism, and we're going to have to take you in for that," he tells me as he reaches for what I'm assuming are handcuffs on his utility belt.

"They agreed to it," I announce, and everyone's eyes snap to mine.

"We did no such thing," Mrs. Robisson insists. "She has been harassing us with this foul color ever since she dyed our Tank's fur during her heathen April Fools' shenanigans."

I cut her off. "Psh, he liked it, and you know it. Real men wear pink, didn't you ever see those t-shirts?"

Mrs. Robisson ignores me and rounds on the sheriff. "I insist something be done about this immediately." She gestures from me to the bright pink SUV behind her. To be fair, the paint job looks amazing.

"Ms. April, what evidence do you have that the Robisson's agreed to paint their new car pink?" the Deputy monotones to me.

I pull the papers out of my back pocket and hand them to him. "It's on page three. Their signatures are on the bottom," I tell him, and he unfolds the papers and flips the pages.

After scanning it quickly, he nods and then looks to the Robissons. "It does state it here and these do look like your signatures at the bottom."

Mr. Robbison snatches the papers out of the deputy's hands and scours them. "These are the papers we had to sign for the repairs, but there is no way I would have agreed to paint my new car pink," he insists.

Sherif Dunn loops both of his thumbs into his belt. "Did you read it through, Frank?"

"Well, no, but I was told it was just an authorization for the repairs."

I nod my head in understanding and point my thumb in Theo's direction. "Theo can tell you all about the crazy things that can happen when you don't read the fine print," I tell them, and Theo gives me an unamused look. "To soon?" I ask sweetly.

Mr. Robisson loses it and starts tearing up the paper in his hands. He's making an odd squeal-growl noise that's actually a pretty good impersonation of a bear call. He throws the pieces of torn paper up in the air and glares at me, anger bleeding from his gaze. Madix, Brant, and Theo step in front of me, blocking me from his burning gaze. I love it when they go all macho.

I hear the sheriff sigh. "That is quite enough, Mr. Robisson. You will pick up every scrap of paper you just threw. We take littering very seriously around these parts. It's a thousand dollar fine for that," Sheriff Dunn says, and I have to cover my mouth again to keep from laughing.

I peek around Brant's shoulder to see the Robissons gaping at the sheriff, open-mouthed and furious. "My car looks like *that*, and I'm the one getting in trouble?"

I step around the wall of muscle surrounding me. "I already have an order for it to be painted back to whatever color you want. That was page four of the papers you just ripped up. April's Fools!" I try to joke. The Robissons don't laugh.

"Tough crowd," Theo chuckles.

Before the Robissons can stop glaring enough to reply, my dad pulls up next to the pink Explorer and climbs out of his old truck. He runs his eyes over the hot pink monstrosity and then fixes his stare on me.

I wave innocently. "What are you doing here? I thought lunch was tomorrow?" I ask, confused.

"I heard the call go out on the radio, so I thought I'd check things out."

"Dad, you need a life. Get a girlfriend, or boyfriend for that matter. Hell, get one of each. But stop sitting around and listening to the police radio," I exclaim.

He ignores me and looks to Sheriff Dunn. "Everything okay here?"

I roll my eyes.

"Just a misunderstanding, Sheriff." Even the *actual* active sheriff calls my dad sheriff. "The Robissons are going to pick up the paper they threw everywhere and then be on their way. Isn't that right Mr. and Mrs. Robisson?" Sheriff Dunn asks.

They both grumble under their breaths but nod, and start cleaning up, some of their fury ebbing out as soon as my dad showed up. He walks over to Madix, Brant, and Theo, and they all exchange handshakes and back slaps as they start talking shop about the range and business.

"You lot given anymore thought to joining the planning committee for next year's scenario?" he asks, and I growl in frustration at the question.

"We told you. We're not getting wrapped up in all of that. They're doing the bare minimum to meet the terms of the will and that's it."

"They could be assets, Remi. Think about how much better the scenarios could be with their guidance and experience."

"No, Dad."

Irritated, my dad turns away and takes in the guys one by one. "I know everything threw you boys for a loop, but it has to be said that I think you enjoyed yourselves, and everything worked out for the best."

I face palm. "Dad, no."

The slamming of car doors pulls me from the staring contest I'm currently having with my relentless father, and I look up to see the Robissons start their car and screech away. I think I catch a flash of an opossum tail through the back window, but they drive away so fast I can't be sure. Hopefully Coon doesn't give them too much of a hard time.

I grab Brant's hand and lace my fingers with his. "Well, gentleman, this has been fun, but we have a very big day of cleaning and then arguing about said cleaning, so if you'll excuse us." Sheriff Dunn and Deputy Parks tip their hats at me and then move toward their squad car.

"We still on for lunch tomorrow, Trouble?" my dad asks as he follows the officers.

"Yes, sir," I shout over my shoulder as I grab Madix with my other hand and pull them all back into the house. I make it one step through the doorway and then release the laughter I've been choking down this entire time. I picture the look on the Robissons' faces and I collapse on the couch into a giggling fit.

Theo starts chuckling with me, and I try to thank him for the idea, but I can't stop laughing long enough to create words. Madix nips at my neck and announces that he's going to go finish the laundry, because the dude seriously gets off on cleaning. I work to get a grip on myself, but when I think about how they tore up the paperwork to get the car repainted, I'm lost to the laughs again.

"You know you're hot as fuck when you're pissing people off right?" Theo teases, kissing the tip of my nose.

I pull back but I wrap my hand around the back of his neck and pull him toward my lips for more. He groans into my mouth when I use my tongue to play with his, and tickles my side. I squirm away from him and slap his hand away when he feints like he's coming for me again.

"You've already had over a dozen orgasms this morning and it's not even lunch time."

"What's your point?" I ask, confused by where he's going with this.

Brant laughs and plops down on the couch next to me, pulling me into his lap. "Are we going to have to start recruiting a fourth man to help us keep up with your daily orgasm quota?" he teases, while he runs his hand languidly down my side. The caress pulls goosebumps from my skin and wetness from my pussy.

"Not a chance in hell," Madix growls, appearing behind us, making me laugh. "Hey, I found this in the pocket of your shorts." He hands me a dirty piece of paper, and I unfold it to see my name written in my dad's handwriting.

"Oh, I forgot about this," I announce absently, as I run my finger under the sealed lip and tear the envelope open. I unfold the paper inside and stare at the words written there. I'm not sure how long I stay that way, before a slow smile takes over my face. I look up to find the guys staring at me.

"So, what does it say? Don't keep us hanging," Theo insists, so I hand him the letter.

He reads it and his eyebrows furrow in confusion before he shakes his head and gives an amused chuckle. Brant grabs for the letter next, and then Madix steals the paper from Brant's hands, just as Brant looks at me in shock.

"Did your dad...ship you with three guys?" he asks incredulously.

I laugh and lean over to kiss him. "Like I said, bigger freaks in this town than you, boys."

I look over to catch Madix reading the sentence over and over again. Finally, he holds it out to me, but when I go to reach for it, he grabs my hand and uses it as leverage to pull me up from the couch and over his shoulder. Madix slaps my ass hard and then palms it possessively.

"Fuck yes, you are," he says in answer to the letter, as he starts to carry me down the hallway to his room.

I bounce on his shoulder and read the one sentence that's written on the worn and dirty paper again.

"You'd be good for them."

Warmth fills me at all of the love that those five words

convey, and I vow to treasure the man who wrote those words and the men they were written about, forever.

"Who wants to play *pin the tail* on a naked Remi?" I throw out behind me, and I laugh when all three of them throw up a hand and shout, "I do."

"You guys are fools," I tease.

Brant chuckles. "Yeah, but we're *your* fools."

I beam. He's right about that. And to think, the world only had to fake end for us to get here. *Go figure.*

The End

RAVEN AND IVY'S TIPS TO SURVIVING THE HANDSHAKE PLAGUE

1. It's called the Handshake Plague, so, like...wash your hands, bro. And don't be giving out handshakes all willy nilly. That would just be dumb.

2. Tap into your inner voyeur. Watch so you don't drop dead. Touch only after you've quarantined the other party for at least a week. Oh, and stock up on toilet paper. That shit could be currency in the near future.

3. Are you an introvert? Do you try to avoid peopling as much as possible? Then you're in luck! With this plague, becoming a hermit is now socially acceptable. This is your time to shine you awesome recluse, you.

4. Have you been considering kidnapping hot guys for your amusement? Well, nothing gives you permission like the end of the world. Brush up on those trapping skills and build that harem you've always dreamed of. They'll totally get on board at some point. Just make sure you have enough sexy lingerie and canned beans on hand to seal the deal.

5. Is that potted plant in your living room wilting? Do you somehow manage to even kill fake plants? I sure hope not. Grocery stores are a thing of the past, so grab a marker and color that thumb green, baby. You gotta grow your own food now.

6. Heads up, Costco is probably going to become the new place to be. Weapons, food, and pretty much anything else you could need to survive the apocalypse is all there. So pick an aisle and stake a claim. You'll thank me later.

7. Need to get away from someone annoying? All you gotta do is a sneeze and cough a little. Trust me, it'll clear a room.

8. Stock up on board games. If you don't know what those are, google it quickly, before the internet goes down. Too late? Thank fuck you read as much as you do, because outside of the good times with your new harem, that's about all the entertainment you're going to get.

9. Hunting and foraging is the new 'it' hobby. Seriously. Everyone in Endstone is doing it. So lace up those hiking boots and get all nature-ey and shit. It's probably best if you leave the wild mushrooms behind though. There's enough crazy going on in this town already.

10. Communes are the new cul de sac. Those doomsday preppers everyone used to make fun of are now your best bet for survival. So cross your fingers that they'll let you hang with them. I mean, you're awesome, so I'm sure they'll be thrilled to have you, but maybe take a plate of brownies to sweeten up that first impression. No one says no to brownies, and if they do, that is not the cult you want to join.

Well, that's it! Follow these foolproof steps, and you should be all set to survive a plague. I mean, probably not a real one, so don't get too excited, but you're going to own the shit out of the fake ones!

We love you! Thank you so much for reading! Thank you to the squad of amazing people who help make these books possible. Thank you, awesome reader, for taking a chance on us and jumping into another world straight from the confines of our crazy brains. Here's to the next one!

Love,
    Raven and Ivy

ABOUT RAVEN KENNEDY

Raven Kennedy lives in California with her family. She is most known for her international bestselling Heart Hassle series. She writes in a range of genres, including dark romances, romantic comedies, contemporary, and fantasy. Whether she makes you laugh or cry, she hopes to connect with readers and create characters you can root for.

You can follow her on her (adult-only) Facebook Reader Group for insider information, games, giveaways, and more!

You can also sign up for RK's newsletter to stay up to date on new releases by clicking here.

Visit Raven Kennedy's website here.

facebook.com/ravenkennedybooks

instagram.com/ravenkennedybooks

bookbub.com/authors/raven-kennedy

amazon.com/author/ravenkennedy

ABOUT IVY ASHER

Ivy Asher is the international bestselling author of The Lost Sentinel series. She is addicted to chai, swearing, and laughing a lot—but not in a creepy, laughing alone kind of way. She loves the snow, books, and her family of two humans, and three fur-babies. She has worlds and characters just floating around in her head, and she's lucky enough to be surrounded by amazing people who support that kind of crazy.

You can stalk her on Instagram, her Facebook Reader Group, her Facebook page, Amazon, or BookBub.

Sign up for updates via her newsletter by clicking here.

Check out her website here.

That got a little bossy towards the end, but you know you liked it. ;)

facebook.com/ivy.asher.54

instagram.com/ivy.asher

amazon.com/author/ivyasher

bookbub.com/profile/ivy-asher

45412482R00174

Printed in Poland
by Amazon Fulfillment
Poland Sp. z o.o., Wrocław